THE DEATH OF PIE

Tamar Myers

This first world edition published 2014
in Great Britain and the USA by
SEVERN HOUSE PUBLISHERS LTD of
19 Cedar Road, Sutton, Surrey, England, SM2 5DA.
Trade paperback edition first published in Great Britain and the USA 2014
by SEVERN HOUSE PUBLISHERS LTD.

Myers, Tamar
The death of pie.
1. Yoder, Magdalena (Fictitious character)–Fiction.
2. Novelists–Death–Fiction. 3. Murder–Investigation–
Fiction. 4. Mennonites–Fiction. 5. Pennsylvania Dutch
County (Pa.)–Fiction. 6. Detective and mystery stories.
I. Title
813.6-dc23

ISBN-13: 978-0-7278-8381-0 (cased)
ISBN-13: 978-1-84751-512-4 (trade paper)

Typeset by Palimpsest Book Production Ltd.,
Falkirk, Stirlingshire, Scotland.

This book is dedicated to the love of my life, Jeffrey C. Myers.
I met him when I was just fifteen years old, and for me,
it was love at first sight. That was half a century ago!

ACKNOWLEDGMENTS

I would like to thank my three office assistants, to whom I am deeply indebted for their many hours of hard work. First, I would like to thank my office manager of eleven years, Miss Pagan Myers. Pagan is a basenji dog, whose chief tasks consist of guarding my second-story window whilst napping on her very own chair, all the while serenading me with her snores.

Next, I must give credit to my in-house copy-editor, Mr Kasha Myers, a ten-year-old Bengal cat, who can open doors with his paws, and has been taught to call me 'Ma-Ma.' Kasha's style of editing is to stroll across my keyboard, all the while whipping me in the face with his tail. When he is through making his changes, they are scarcely any clearer than the ones suggested by my actual publisher.

Last, but certainly not least, I am grateful for the en*purr*agement of Mr Dumpster Boy Myers, my faithful secretary of ten years. Dumpster Boy is an orange tabby who began life in a kitchen dumpster behind a restaurant, hence his name. He now weighs twenty pounds. Every morning he follows me up the stairs to my office, plops down just outside and purrs until lunchtime. At that hour he sees it as his duty to accompany me back down the stairs where – *poof* – suddenly he disappears, not to be seen or heard from again until after supper. His routine varies only on those days that Dumpster Boy decides that he needs to use the copy machine. Having learned where the 'start' button is located, Dumpster Boy will push this button and then hop on the machine to watch the paper emerge. Usually this thrill will not suffice, and he will try to 'help' the paper along with one of his giant orange paws. If I've been away, I can always tell if my secretary has been hard at work at the copy machine by the mountain of crumpled paper balls I find.

ONE

If it is true that only the good die young, I will live to a ripe old age. Indeed, I am a wicked woman. Well, perhaps I exaggerate just a wee bit, although in one way or another, I have broken nine of the Ten Commandments. Of course, none of this is anyone's business but my own. However, given that I do have a rather crucial point to prove, and that there is a certain method to my madness, I hereby go public with this list of all my worst sins.

For starters, I have never even seen an idol, much less had occasion to bow down to one. However, our idols can be things other than the images carved from stone or wood, things that are more important to us than God with the capital G. In my case, I got sucked into sin one Sunday morning as I lollygagged in my Jacuzzi bathtub, the one with the thirty-two jets, the one I have named Big Bertha. One moment I was soaking lazily, the next I was shouting Bertha's name at the top of my lungs and thrashing about like a great white shark. I was so ashamed, I tell you, that I never even made it to church that day.

My second huge sin is that I often use the Lord's name in vain. Why, just last week when somebody cut me off in traffic, nearly sending me up a telephone pole, I heard myself say 'jam and cheese!' Using someone's initials is the same thing as using that person's name.

Now, about honoring the Sabbath Day in order to keep it holy: I always thought that I did this until I acquired a Jewish husband and learned that the word 'Sabbath' is derived from the Hebrew word *Shabbat*, which refers to Saturday. It was the Emperor Constantine who declared, *ex cathedra,* that Sunday was suddenly our new Sabbath. Given that God trumps emperor – at least in the heavenly hierarchy – I had never once honored the actual Sabbath Day.

Some commandments are easier to follow than others; that said, it is virtually impossible for any American child to honor their parents by being obedient one hundred percent of the time. Children in the Bible had trouble obeying their folks as well, or else it wouldn't be necessary to address the topic of honoring one's parents in the Big Ten.

Don't get me wrong, I wasn't a rotten kid, and if I did mouth off, Mama wasn't above slapping my 'sassy trap,' as she called it. But when I got to be a teenager I learned that most parents really don't want to hassle their kids. They don't want a 'situation.' Therefore, if they forbid you to go to Joshua Stahly's barn dance, they probably have a good reason. But how was I to know that Joshua would somehow manage to sneak in a keg of beer, and that Marlene Deitlemeyer, who had all the morals of a basset hound in heat, would kick over a lantern in the hay loft, whilst having a roll in the same?

Alas, when my parents picked me up at the police station I was forced to tell them that I had *not* been drinking – so as not to disappoint them, of course – and it was because of the contents of Joshua's keg that I felt compelled to 'borrow' some gum from Marlene's purse while she was pulling up her stockings. Crash! Boom! Down went more commandments, the ones forbidding lying and stealing. But lest I be judged too harshly, surely one must take into consideration that I was only trying to honor my parents by preserving their image of me? And anyway, I still think that if they hadn't been quite so strict I wouldn't have had to lie or steal, and thus those commandments might still be intact. *Might.*

Don't think for a minute that I've glossed over the Fifth and Sixth Commandants. I shall begin with the Sixth Commandment, the one concerning adultery. Is my elderly cousin, Freni, correct when she claims that one can commit adultery with a Jacuzzi bathtub equipped with thirty-two jets? If so, then I must confess to having a torrid affair with Big Bertha. Oh, the shame of it all, for I am a happily married woman who finds herself torn between two lovers and feeling like a – well, a jerk. But then again, how can something so wrong feel so right? For now I comfort myself with the knowledge that this love affair (if indeed that's what this was) wasn't a dirty one. Not that it would have made a difference anyway; I am still an adulteress – if only an inadvertent one.

You see, I was once inadvertently married to a very handsome man named Aaron Miller. He was a smooth-talking bigamist with a wife stashed up in Iowa, and I was a country bumpkin who sincerely believed that the first marriage proposal to come my way would be my last.

The Ninth and Tenth Commandments are sort of one and the same. Here you will find a long list of things not to covet. A lot of that stuff, like menservants and maidservants, are hard to come by in our village of Hernia, Pennsylvania, but I will hereby fess up to coveting a good ass. For instance, my neighbor two farms down the road, Donald Hooley, has an exceptionally fine ass. No sooner did I set eyes on it than I begin to maneuver myself into a position to get my hands on it. I have always wanted a donkey – make that a pair of them – to pull me around in a wagon. Once, when I was a little girl, I saw a family of Amish children horsing around with a pair of asses and a wagon, and I immediately began to covet what they had. In fact, that is the first time I can remember ever really wanting something badly.

All right, that does leave the Fifth Commandment: 'Thou Shalt Not Kill.' I have saved it for last because it is the only one of the Big Ten that I have not committed – to my knowledge. I qualified that statement, but only because I can't be sure that one of my teachers wasn't driven mad by my presence in her classroom and subsequently did herself in. Ours is a small village, and although every other teacher can be accounted for, my kindergarten teacher, Miss Kuhnberger (who screamed, 'I can't take it anymore!' before moving to LA), has not been heard from since.

From the above I hope I have made it abundantly clear that I have never killed anyone in the literal sense. I have never shot, stabbed, struck or poisoned a human being. Sometimes I slap at mosquitoes, and I have set out cockroach bait. But allow me to reiterate, to make this point perfectly clear: I am not a killer. I am most definitely *not* a murderer. It was not me who murdered that despicable purveyor of pulp fiction, Ms Ramat Sreym.

Having said that, perhaps I should introduce myself. My full name is Magdalena Portulacca Yoder Rosen. Because I was married rather late in life and because my maiden name, Yoder, is ubiquitous in these parts, Yoder – Miss Yoder – is what I go by in my everyday dealings. Portulacca, in case you're wondering, is the name of a gorgeous flower that thrives in bright sunshine. This leads me to believe that my mother suffered from a rare flash of optimism.

I am five foot ten inches tall and skinny as a fence post. Each of my feet is as large as the state of Florida and, if I was ever truly destitute, I could hire my chest out as a billiards table. Fortunately, due to my God-given business acumen, the odds of rock-hard balls larger than my bosoms rolling hither, thither, and yon across my barren ribcage are entirely miniscule. I am, you see, a millionaire many times over.

My parents were simple Mennonite dairy farmers whose ancestors were Amish immigrants from Switzerland. Both the Amish and the Mennonites are religious sects – similar to Protestantism, but with some key defining differences. Chief amongst these is the fact that their members adhere to strict pacifism. Neither a Mennonite nor an Amish person will lift a hand against another human being – even to save the life of one's own child. There are many degrees of strictness, with some groups of Amish being the strictest, and some groups of Mennonite being the most liberal. For now, suffice it to say that the Amish are generally the ones you might see driving around in horse-drawn buggies, the men wearing straw hats, and beards with no moustaches, and the women decked out in their black travel bonnets and fetching black aprons worn modestly over their ankle-length dresses.

My, but I do get lost in my head! What I meant to tell you right off was that my beloved parents died early. Being liberal Mennonites, they were permitted to drive, but Pennsylvania where we live is a mountainous state with an exceedingly long tunnel. One fine spring day, when I was a mere lass of twenty, and my flat chest was palpitating with the sort of dreams that only the young – or stupid – dare entertain, my parents were squished like a bug in that tunnel when a truck carrying milk rear-ended their car, thrusting them forward into a semi-trailer loaded to the gills with state-of-the-art running shoes. Or was it the other way around? It doesn't matter – shoes, milk and parent parts were everywhere. It was unspeakably awful, and my younger sister, Susannah, literally did not speak for the next three years.

Now, I do not mean to say this unkindly – only with true Christian love – but Susannah, who was eighteen at the time, did more than just hold her tongue. She began dealing with her pain by driving into Bedford, the nearest city, and hanging out at its bars where she managed to convince evil men that she was of legal drinking age, and they indulged her. She soon descended into the world of— Hmm, how can I put this gently? The life of a harlot wearing scarlet, or perhaps a tart with a broken heart, or maybe even a floozy ever so boozy? I'm sure you get the picture. I have no doubt that our parents rolled over in their graves with such rapidity that they supplied our village of Hernia with enough electricity to see us into the twenty-second century.

This left me with no choice; I had to support both of us. Believe me, back in those days I would have much rather indulged myself by a day spent sitting on a lightly padded straight-backed chair, reading the Holy Scriptures, with the occasional break to refresh my energy by eating a slice of bread with jam. But pampering myself like that was not about to pay Papa's mortgage on the farm. Although our elderly Amish cousins, Mose and Freni, agreed to stay on to help with the farm work, it soon became apparent that I was not cut out for the life of a dairy farmer.

Fortunately our dear parents had the foresight to leave everything to me in their will, with the provision that I care for my sister in perpetuity, or as long as it took her to get on her feet financially – on her own. At that time I was to make some sort of just redistribution of property. At any rate, in the meantime, the farm was mine – *all* mine, to do with how I pleased. What pleased me was to turn my traditional farmhouse, with its authentic barn (and perhaps just two dairy cows) into a charming bed and breakfast. And since it was nestled in the western portion of the Allegheny Mountains in Pennsylvania, a state famous for its Pennsylvania 'Dutch' culture, I named it The PennDutch Inn. For the record, the Pennsylvania Dutch have nothing to do with Holland and windmills. The people referenced are descended from Swiss and German immigrants, and the 'Dutch' they speak is laced with English.

Unfortunately, bed and breakfast inns are a dime a dozen, so in order to succeed, my establishment had to have a particular twist. To put it frankly, the angle I chose was *abuse*. Hold your horses, please, because I know that sounds bad. But consider this: when one travels to a foreign country, one where men can be seen urinating in public, albeit against a wall, is that not a form of visual abuse? When one must bravely attempt to sleep upon a pallet of lumps, and a pillow of buckwheat or straw, instead of a proper pillow-top mattress and an eider down pillow like the Good Lord intended, is that not a form of abuse as well? Likewise, when a humble soul, such as myself, enters a shop and blurts out a cheery 'good morning, my dear sir, and where do you keep the laxatives?' and the proprietor turns up his nose, having taken deep offense just because I speak what is now considered to be the International Language, and I don't know any words of *that* man's language, which was once the lingua franca of the world, I ask you, isn't *that* abuse? So there you have it! People are prepared to pay outrageous sums of money for abuse just as long as they can view it as a cultural experience.

'*Voila!*' I shouted when this thought occurred to me. I devised a system called the ALPO plan, an anagram for a popular dog food in the United States – there being no connection, of course. My initials stand for Amish Lifestyle Plan Option. The Amish are mostly farmers, and as such very hard workers. By signing up for my system guests can pay up to three times the normal rate by performing chores. For an extra one hundred dollars they get to clean their own rooms; two hundred dollars more allows them the privilege of scrubbing toilets. Three hundred bucks gets one into the chicken house, along with the right to rake droppings onto the compost heap. Four hundred dollars buys guests the opportunity to muck out the cow barn, and then there is the once-a-year ten thousand dollar grand prize raffle (guests have to be present to win) which is draining and relining the cesspool.

To make a long, sweet story slightly shorter, I had a head for business, and was soon raking money in fist over tightly clenched fist. However, I say that tongue in cheek. I give God ten percent of everything I make, and twenty percent or so after that back to the community. With less than two thousand residents, the village of Hernia could not afford a police department, so I pay for a police officer's salary, as well as that of the mayor and the animal-control officer. Lest I get too much credit for my charity, I must hasten to point out that *I* am both mayor and dog-catcher.

Of course, I am much more than just a flat-chested, wealthy

woman, long of limb and somewhat hard on the eyes. I am a conservative Mennonite woman who chooses to wear her long, mousy brown tresses in braids that wrap around her head and are held in place by so many hairpins that I set off metal detectors wherever I go. Atop my metal mountain I carefully perch a freshly washed white organza prayer cap, although I hold it in place with yet another metal pin. This is because the New Testament instructs everyone to pray at all times, and that women should pray with their heads covered. I wear dresses that cover my knees (as well as my privates, of course) with elbow-length sleeves. I do not believe in wearing fancy-schmancy jewelry.

Now, it has been said that I am a stubborn, opinionated woman – even bossy at times. Rubbish! We Mennonites are a soft-spoken, gentle people, renowned for our humility. I, for one, am quite proud of my humility. But anyway, what is so wrong about a woman having an opinion? After all, we women are intuitive folk. Is it not true that a hunch from a woman is equal to two facts from a man?

One final, and confidential, bit of information that I will share about myself is that I suffer from a chronic and heartbreaking disease known by the acronym of STAB. The initials stand for sarcastic, tart, alliterative blather. I used to think that Lucifer was the reason I couldn't control all the alliterative words that flowed so effortlessly from my tongue. Believe me, I have prayed diligently about this matter. I have even worked with a speech therapist. The matter remains out of my control. I was on the verge of a deep depression until I consented to *one* session with a therapist, a very pleasant woman named Dr Luci Feragamo – a woman not of my faith. In that one session Dr Feragamo was able to convince me that alliteration is pleasant to the ear. She went on to say that only copy-editors and others like them – people who probably dance and stay away from fatty foods – find alliteration annoying. 'Just ignore them,' she said, and so I have.

Well, enough about me. Now I suppose I should properly introduce the corpse, that despicable purveyor of pulp fiction, Ramat Sreym. Her first name was pronounced Ram-it, to rhyme with a certain cuss word, and her last name was pronounced S-raym. She claimed to have been born in the nation-state of Sreymistan, but I can find no such place on the map, and Google is boggled as well. However, her accent was Midwest American – possibly one of the square states.

I will never speak ill of the dead unless, of course, it is necessary to do so in order to make a point or prove a case. I am afraid that I shall have to do both of those shortly, so here goes. Ramat was first and foremost a celebrity. My dear friend, and self-described literary critic, Doc Shafor, once quipped that Ramat Sreym might be able to write her name on the condition that she was allowed to plagiarize it. She was the sort of author who became famous overnight because her publisher bought space for her on the end caps of all the right bookstores. Again, this rather bitter sentiment came from Doc, who was a 'wannabe' writer and jumped to conclusions faster than a sports commentator. Personally, the only books that I read other than the Bible are autobiographies. As those are written by the subjects themselves, it stands to reason that, like the Good Book, every word in them is true.

But back to poor, misguided Ramat. By the time that I first met her, she had bought into the worst that American celebrity culture had to offer – hook, line and sinker. As a consequence (by her own admission), that meant fat-sucking, fat infusion, silicone implants, liposuction, toe removal, rib removal, dermabrasion and acid peels. The end result was a woman that even she couldn't recognize.

She had managed to become ageless, with perfect features and skin, yet at the same time curiously unattractive. For all I knew, Ramat was closer to being a century old than she was to being the fertile twenty-something she appeared to be from a distance. Let it be known that I have great reverence for the elderly, despite the fact that I have been scolded by many a crone (with just cause, no doubt). The cantankerous and hard-to-please are our national treasures and we must treat them that way: we must turn them over to the government for their safekeeping.

Still, a body has a right to complain – and vociferously – when an outsider like Ramat Sreym falls face down into my prize-winning apple pie, causing not only the death of said pie, but the premature end of *Hernia's 110th Annual Festival of Pies*.

TWO

'The clue was "it was a dark and stormy night,"' I said upon opening the door of the PennDutch Inn. 'The answer was "cliché."'

Our new Chief of Police scratched the back of his head with manicured fingers and attempted to wrinkle his unlined brow. He was our *only* police officer now that we'd been forced to downsize. Fresh out of the academy, and on the job for just two months, he was younger than my sturdy Christian underwear, but he was a very polite lad, which is all that really mattered to me. Honestly, it didn't bother me one whit that his given name was Toy Graham. *Toy!*

'Miss Yoder,' he said, clearly unable to make eye contact with someone as ancient as myself, 'would it be all right if I come in?'

I don't mind telling you that my cheeks burned with embarrassment. A Southern woman would have already fed him dinner, maybe even burped him in the time it had taken me to answer the door. In my defence, Toy Graham had not called ahead, and I was determined to get the answer to number fifteen across before I set down my crossword puzzle.

'By all means, come in,' I said, and with a grand sweeping motion showed him into my stuffy sitting room and bade him to sit on my notoriously uncomfortable furniture. 'Have a seat. There is no point in being picky because they are equally torturous on one's backside. By the way, would you care for a snack?'

'No, thank you, ma'am.'

'Are you sure? There are pies galore in the kitchen. As usual, Freni forgot that the contest rules allow only one pie from each category, and she baked multiples of everything, determined as she was to finally win this year. Before the contest even began, she sent Mose back here with the extras so that I could freeze them for her. Freni is Amish, you know, and they aren't permitted the use of electricity.'

'Ma'am, I realize that it was rude of me not to call first—'

'Indeed, it was.'

'Please accept my apology, ma'am.'

Just looking at Toy Graham is enough to fill my head with foolish thoughts. If I get too close to him, I have to concentrate on Mama's liver and prune soufflé to keep myself from self-combusting.

'Of course, dear,' I said, my eyes on his shoes. 'You have my partial attention.' Since folks never really listen to each other, it never mattered what I said.

'I asked if we could talk about Miss – uh – Miss—'

'OK, Chief, here's the deal. Ramat Sreym is an unusual name, a bit tricky for anyone to pronounce except for a native Sreymistani, so I suggest that henceforth we refer to her as either the "deceased," or simply "Ramat."'

He laughed with nervous relief. 'Yes ma'am. Anyway, she can't object now.'

'Oh, don't be so sure of that. That straight chair you're sitting on used to belong to my Granny Yoder. She's been dead for almost forty years and she still objects to just about everything that I do.'

The chief's boyish features lost a summer's worth of tan. 'What do you mean by "still" objects?'

'She's standing beside you right now looking like she's sucking on a lemon. I think she wants you to move.'

The poor lad shot up like a slice of toast. 'Ma'am, are you teasing me?'

'Well, I could say that I was toying with you, but you still haven't given me permission to use your given name.'

He breathed a sigh of relief. 'By all means, please, call me Toy.'

'Thank you, Toy. But sit over there – on that equally uncomfortable loveseat. I wasn't kidding about Granny Yoder. I know that a good Christian is not supposed to believe in ghosts – I prefer to call them Apparition Americans – but I can't help what I see. Right now I see that Granny Yoder has reclaimed her chair and that the five, three-inch hairs on the mole to the left of her nose are jiggling as she snorts in righteous indignation.'

While Granny snorted, Toy shivered. 'Oh, man,' he said, 'this is scary, ma'am – I mean, Miss Yoder – but at the same time, it's kind of cool. You should have a TV crew come in here and film a special. You know, where a priest tries to exorcise her. I saw a 3D movie about that. The special effects were awesome.'

Granny Yoder's ghost was not amused. 'Granny eschewed exercise of any kind,' I said, 'especially if it involved machinery. She claimed that treadmills were invented by the Devil – and that's with a capital D. As for 3D films, she believed them to be an unholy trinity. Now be a dear, and let us return to the more recently departed.'

'Yes, of course. As you know, the Coroner's Office believes that Ramat may have been poisoned—'

'*Excuse* me? I did *not* know this. All I know was that she was a guest judge at the festival last week and had been judging pies – *my* apple pie in particular – when she pitched face forward onto it and crushed it, along with my chances of winning a blue ribbon, I might add.'

Toy cocked his handsome head and scribbled furiously on an actual paper pad with the stub of a genuine wooden pencil. Just for that, I would allow the boy some latitude, no matter what he was writing. As if those weren't enough points in his favour, he appeared to be writing in cursive.

'Oh, yes, just between you and me' – he glanced over at Granny's chair – 'uh, and her, I'd say it's for sure that the method of murder was poison in a pie. I don't mind sharing this with you, Miss Yoder, because you are, after all, our mayor.'

'Well, clearly she wasn't stabbed or bludgeoned, given that she was standing right there surrounded by everyone and his shadow, and no one noticed a thing.'

'Miss Yoder,' Toy said, 'sarcasm is like a barbershop quartet – a little of it goes a long way.'

'In that case, please continue to share.'

'Strychnine,' he said.

'*What?* I didn't put strychnine in my pie. In fact, I didn't even bake my own pie— Oops! Well, if I had baked it, I wouldn't have put it in. And you know darn-tooting well that Cousin Freni didn't do it. That dear woman is seventy-eight years old and as close to a living saint as the Amish will admit to having.' Truth be told, the Amish will have naught to do with saints, and my elderly kinswoman can be as crabby as a seafood buffet.

'Miss Yoder,' Toy continued, 'I don't for a second suspect you of having anything to do with Ramat's death. To the contrary; I am here because I want you to help me solve it.'

'*Moi?*' I said coyly, and batted my colorless eyelashes.

Toy crossed his legs, his right ankle resting on left knee. Goodness gracious me! The boy wonder from Charlotte wasn't wearing any socks, but not only that, it appeared that he either waxed or shaved his legs. I kid you not; there are eggs in my refrigerator that are hairier than his calves. Imagine that: a police officer wearing a blue regulation uniform, supplied by our generous little community (i.e. me), but refusing to properly clad his feet. The lad either had gumption, suffered from a phobia or was too lazy to do his laundry. Time would tell.

'Yes, you,' he said. 'I have heard many good things about your sleuthing skills.'

'From whom?'

'Never you mind. Suffice it to say that even the County Sheriff over in Bedford will vouch for you.' Upon hearing that, Granny's ghost fluttered her shrivelled lips in disapproval.

'Will wonders never cease?'

He scribbled faster. 'Magdalena,' he said, 'you said something about it being a dark and stormy night. Was that supposed to mean something, or were you just trying to be funny, as I hear is usual?'

'I was referencing a crossword puzzle. You might have picked up on that had you been listening, but you are a man, and as every woman knows, the first five words in a conversation are wasted on a man.'

'What? Should I take umbrage at that remark?'

'Absolutely not, dear. In fact, you get extra points based on your vocabulary.' I paused to gesticulate. 'Stop that,' I said.

'I beg your pardon?'

'Not you, Toy. I'm talking to Granny's ghost.'

'Miss Yoder, if your grandmother's ghost bothers you so much, why don't you get rid of her? No kidding, it can be done.'

'Nonsense! Granny's ghost is part of the package deal that I offer my guests, just like her uncomfortable furniture. All of this furniture is in a late Victorian style called Eastlake, and it has never been reupholstered. That means that there are springs sticking up hither, thither and up one's yon. I've been told that sitting on a patch of prickly pear cactus makes more sense than trying to relax anywhere in this parlour.'

Toy rubbed his chin. 'Let's see: a ghost, no place to get comfortable – why would anyone want to stay at your inn?'

'But don't you see?' I cried. 'There is genius behind this madness. People like getting abused, just as long as they can pay through the nose and view it as a cultural experience. Why else would anyone travel to France? And this is the same reason why very expensive restaurants serve you microscopic portions, and why megastars make you wait two hours before they begin their sold-out concerts.'

The poor boy rubbed his hands through his hair and moaned. 'Gee, Miss Yoder, you sound so jaded.'

'Experienced, dear. Please bear with me, because this discussion is germane to your investigation. Coincidentally, it *was* a dark and stormy night when Ramat checked into the PennDutch, but she had made her reservations well in advance. This was about a year ago. Anyway, she was also quite willing to pay four hundred dollars extra per day for ALPO.'

'Isn't *Alpo* a brand of dog food?'

'In this case it stands for Amish Lifestyle Plan Option. By signing up for that brilliant idea of mine, she got to have the privilege of tidying up her room, setting and clearing the table at meals, washing the dishes, sweeping the porches and mucking out the cow barn. For a premium of just two hundred dollars my cousin Mose would help her try to milk Bessie, our most cooperative cow. However, we do ask all the guests to sign a disclaimer stating that they've been informed that Bessie has particularly sensitive teats and has kicked upon rare occasions.'

Who knew that the polite young police chief from Charlotte was given to fits of prolonged staring? 'M-Miss Yoder,' he finally stammered, 'you're really a piece of work. You do know that, don't you?'

'I shall take that as a compliment. Now, moving right along, not only did Ramat throw herself into her chores, and with a certain *joie de vive*, I might add, but she bought a genuine faux Amish get-up from my little gift shop in the lobby in which to perform these tasks.'

The stubby pencil hovered in midair above the tiny pad while

Toy cleared his throat. 'Forgive me, Miss Yoder, but how can something be both faux and genuine at the same time?'

I was impatient to get on with my fascinating tale, so I waved one of my shapely, yet humongous hands in a somewhat dismissive gesture. 'These garments are genuine in that they are sewn by real Amish women and they adhere to the image that the undiscerning tourist usually carries in her mind. But, you see, the undiscerning tourist generally prefers something a little – uh – sexier than what an Amish woman would wear. And with a zipper, instead of hooks and eyes.'

'The Amish can't wear zippers?'

I shook my head. 'Too modern.'

'Wow! Go on, please.'

'Now where was I?' I knew exactly where I was: I was in my parlour engaged in an important conversation, and major conversations must be conducted as if they were musical symphonies. 'The point of all this,' I said, waving my hands like a conductor, 'is that from a financial standpoint, Ramat Sreym was the perfect guest. Therefore, I didn't mind answering a few questions from her now and then.'

Toy made some unattractive noises with his larynx.

'Really, dear,' I said, 'must you? Young people today can be so vulgar.'

'Sorry,' Toy mumbled. 'I will try to contain myself.'

'Well, at first she'd ask only the occasional question. But you know me – or perhaps you don't. That is, I was born with a genetic disorder – one that I inherited from both parents – which is sometimes referred to as *Perilous garrulous*. This disease forces me to talk. Trust me; this condition has been my undoing on many occasions. Blab, blab, blab, my, my but how I carry on. So before I knew it, Ramat had all the dirt on Hernia that she needed to write that filthy, bestselling piece of trash. Of course, I hadn't the slightest idea that she was going to use the pearls that fell from my loose lips to sink my ship, or that of anyone else in this village. Like I said, I never read fiction. When that piece of trash shot to the top of the bestseller list, manipulated as it was by the publisher, our village's chief financial officer – that's my double first cousin once-removed, Sam Yoder – thought it might be a good idea to ask her to be a judge for our annual pie-eating contest. Of course, he didn't expect her to stay; even a rude negative response from her could be turned into good publicity for the festival by Sam. Can you imagine how gobsmacked we were when her publicity agent said that it was a fabulous idea? No doubt she had a sequel in mind: *Ramat and the Hicks of Hernia, Part II*. Something like that.'

Toy chuckled. 'Hernia! I still can't get over the name of this village.'

'Please, dear, show some respect. It was named in honor of my great, great, great-grandfather, Jacob Yoder, who got a hernia while building his log cabin up on Stucky Ridge. As you know, there's a picnic area up there now, as well as a cemetery. There's also a brass plaque at the exact spot where the unfortunate incident is supposed to have happened.'

Again Toy chuckled. 'Sorry. I couldn't help it. It's just that I love quirky things.'

'*Quirky?* Let me get this straight, *Toy. You* find *us* quirky?'

At least he had the decency to blush. 'Yes, ma'am, but in a good way.'

'Harrumph. Well, that is certainly more than I can say for Ramat. Do you know what she was going to originally call her tell-all book about life in Hernia?'

He nodded. '*Fifty Grades of Hay*.'

'Thank heavens she didn't; it would have made us all look like hayseeds – like the country bumpkins that we are!'

'So,' he said, 'instead, she titled her book *Butter Safe Than Sorry*.' Toy looked straight at Granny then, but of course he didn't see her, or else he would have jumped out of his non-regulation kidskin loafers. 'Miss Yoder, before we go any further, there is something I need to tell you. You're going to hear about it anyway, so you may as well hear it from me.'

'Stop right there,' I said, holding up my large, shapely hands. 'The fact that you're gay is none of my business. "Gay, schmay, have a nice day" – that's what I always say. Besides, Jesus never said one bad thing about you homosexuals, and he had tons to say about us divorcees. Although my divorce was purely fictional, given that it happened only in the pages of *Butter Safe Than Sorry*.'

First Toy reddened, then he turned even whiter than ricotta

cheese, and lastly he jumped to his feet. It is quite possible that he even leaped out of his loafers – well, maybe just a millimeter. My point is that I have never in all my forty-nine years seen someone that scared, and it had nothing to do with his sexuality.

'I see her! I see her! There she is!'

Indeed, he was pointing right at Granny Yoder whom, I might add, was a pacifist by conviction, but not adverse to stoning homosexuals if the Old Testament decreed it. Believe me, there were many others on Granny's stoning list, perhaps even including myself, and they were all drawn from the Bible. I think maybe it's because she didn't have a chance to get her rocks off at said sinners that Granny's spirit stayed behind when her heart stopped beating. It's just a theory, mind you; I can't find any literature to support this.

At any rate, this was the first time that anyone else had ever seen Granny since the day that she'd been laid, ever so carefully, into the ground, as per her sixteen pages of instructions. Needless to say, I was gobsmacked. I was not, however, speechless.

'Oh happy day!' I sang out in my strong, but perhaps slightly off-key soprano.

Granny cringed.

What mattered is that Toy found his tongue. 'M-Miss Yoder, h-how can you just sit there so calmly with her in the room?' He was, of course, standing. He was also back safely in his loafers.

'She can't hurt you, dear. She doesn't exist – not really.'

'Who am I to disagree with my elders?' he said disagreeably. 'But we're both looking at a ghost right now.'

'Then again, we are and we aren't.'

'Forgive me, Miss Yoder, but what you *are* is not making any sense.'

'This Apparition American – ghost as you called her – resembles my Granny Yoder, and would lead us to believe that this phenomena really does exist. Yet the majority of both Amish and Mennonites would reject such a belief, and if they were in this room with us, at this very moment, they would be unable to see my granny. So I ask you, what is the truth?'

Far be it for me to speak ill of the dead, but Granny Yoder was not the brightest candle in her candelabra while she was alive and, now that she was dead, her attention span was even much shorter. No doubt it was the word 'phenomena' that sent her flying from the room in a flurry of dust motes.

'You know, Miss Yoder,' Toy said, resuming his seat, 'I must have been hallucinating, or daydreaming or something, because I don't see anything weird anymore. Do you mind if we get back to business?'

'Indeed I do not!'

'Good, so moving right along, here is a list of suspects that I have drawn up based on my reading of *Butter Safe Than Sorry*. I thought it was an excellent novel, by the way. The mystery element kept me turning the pages so fast that they were smouldering. I thought, "Dang,"' I groaned inwardly at Toy's use of the offensive word, '"this would be a great book to take on a wilderness back-packing trip." You know, just in case no one remembered to bring matches! Hey, don't you think that what I just said would make a great book review?'

'I most certainly do not.'

'Now, this list I'm giving you concentrates on the folks living in Hernia and its environs, as these are the people who have suffered the most from all the negative publicity this book has received. I have omitted anyone from Bedford because they're not quite the itty-bitty ink spot on the map that we are. Besides, from what I hear, motels along the Pennsylvania Turnpike in either direction, as far away as Carlisle and Youngwood, have been jam-packed for the two months since the book has been out. How about you, Miss Yoder? I bet the PennDutch Inn has been booked solid, hasn't it?'

'Stuff and nonsense,' I said nonsensically. It was a phrase I'd read in an old English novel somewhere; I hadn't the slightest idea what it meant. Toy, apparently, didn't give a plump Turkish fig *what* it meant either.

'Good, like they say, a high tide floats all boats – well, something close to that. Unfortunately, your cousin-in-law, Dorothy Yoder, is on my list of suspects, as is your delightful mother-in-law, Mother Malaise of the Convent of the Sisters of Perpetual Apathy.'

'She's as delightful as a tick in one's underwear,' I said, without a shred of undeserved malice.

'Miss Yoder, do I detect a little bitterness there? I thought you Amish were supposed to be a kind, gentle people.'

I was careful to bite my tongue first before answering. I bit it hard. I have bitten it so many times over the years that there are permanent indentations into which various teeth now fit into rather neatly, and thus the pain is really minimal. As I bit, I counted to ten in English, Pennsylvania Dutch, Spanish, and French. One may rest assured, however, that my watery blue eyes remained focused on his face to let him know that he had stepped over the line. Finally, I cleared my throat, and hoped that whatever wattles I might have accrued over my forty-nine years were vibrating with authority.

'Young man, as I have explained to you at least a dozen times: I am *not* Amish, although my grandparents were. I am a Mennonite. I happen to be amongst the more liberal sort of my Old Order brethren. We Mennonites do not ride around in horse-drawn buggies. Having suitably rebuked you, allow me to remind you that I am indeed a kind and gentle person. Unless you have walked a mile in my size forty-four brogans with Sister Malaise as your mother-in-law, you are in no position to judge me.'

'Yes ma'am,' Toy said, for apparently I had managed to stare him into a state of semi-submission. He tried slumping in his straight-back chair as if he were a teenager with a strand of spaghetti for a spine. Much to my secret amusement, the chair refused to cooperate and Hernia's new Chief of Police slid off it and onto the floor.

I glanced over at Granny, who had reappeared. For the first time ever, her perpetually downturned mouth was a straight line! Arguably, one corner might even have qualified as 'slightly askew.'

'Moving right along,' I said, looking at the list Toy had given me, 'you have my best friend down as your number three suspect. Why is Agnes on your list?'

'Duh,' Toy said, having regressed even further in my book for using that loathsome word, 'Ramat made her out to be a total loser. It's no wonder she can't marry. I sure wouldn't date her.'

'Well, of course you wouldn't; you're—'

'Gay? Actually I'm not.'

'But you just said you were!'

'No, I didn't; I simply didn't deny it. My generation doesn't make a big thing of being gay like yours does. Now, what do you think of the last suspect on this list?'

'Doc Shafor? You have got to be kidding! He's an octogenarian, for crying out loud!'

'Octogenarian, huh? Never heard of it, Miss Yoder. But sadly, I'm beginning to think that a person's religion doesn't have much to do with whether or not he could commit murder.'

'It's *not* a religion you – you – Chief of Police!' All right, so I hissed like a goose sitting on her nest. At least I hissed with a soft 'c.' One should always be careful not to be tricked into hissing whilst reading sentences that lack hissing sounds.

Toy, who resembled a much younger version of Justin Bieber, shrugged. 'Whatever. Let's see, in my notes I've also got down that Doc Shafor is sort of an old guy. Is that true?'

'Yes, dear. As I said, he's an *octogenarian*. He and Columbus – the one who discovered America – were childhood playmates.' That was not a lie; it was an absurdity. Surely, even someone of Toy's mental capacity would never believe that Doc Shafor had been around in the 1400s.

'No way,' Toy said. He sounded truly impressed.

'Would I lie?' I said, still without fibbing. Meanwhile, Granny Yoder rolled her eyes.

'I've also got down that he's a skirt-chaser,' Toy said.

'A *what*?' I said.

'He likes the ladies,' Toy said.

'Oh, that,' I said. 'Yes, that's quite true. I remember hearing the names Nina, Pinta and Santa Maria.' Never mind that those were the names of Christopher Columbus's three ships, the ones he sailed on his maiden voyage to America. The fact remains that I did hear those names – back in grammar school.

Chief Toy's smooth, boyish hand skipped across his pad a few more times. 'One last question,' he said as he lifted his pencil, 'and I'll make myself scarce. Word has it that the doctor was one heck of a good cook, and that pie-making was one of his specialties. Can you confirm this?'

I thought about my dear friend, who was also my many times distant cousin. He was a lovable, lecherous old goat if ever there was one, who'd spent a lifetime treating goats. Doc was a veterinarian, not a medical doctor, but like some veterinarians are fond of saying, 'Veterinarians have to know everything an MD does, and more, because animals have all the corresponding parts that humans possess, but without the ability to describe what ails them.'

So Doc was certainly smart as a whip. He was also a widower, who missed his wife terribly, and I think that he transferred some of that grief to his female friends, where it was expressed as physical passion. Either that or Doc was just plain horny. But he was good company and always stuck loyally by his friends, just as close as lamprey eels stick to sharks.

I squared my scrawny shoulders and tossed my asymmetrical head. That last move nearly threw me off balance enough to dislodge me from my own less-than-comfortable perch. Trust me: even after much practice, a posture of defiance does not come easily to those of us who are aesthetically challenged.

Doc might have been an old goat, and I was becoming an old fool, but I knew exactly what Toy was after: my so-called 'expertise.' Ever since Hernia had a Chief of Police – or just a police officer – that person has approached me when the going got tough and asked me to get going for him or her. The reason is simple: I have both the mouth and the moolah. Moolah, by the way, is American slang for money, a term that entered into the lingo via the mouths of cinematic gangsters circa 1939. Why it is that a good Christian woman like me should know this word is really no one's business but my own, if you were to ask me. At any rate, I just knew that Toy was going to come up with an excuse that would saddle me with the job of grilling the village folk, making enemies out of my friends, and possibly even angering my husband. But what I absolutely refused to do was to rat on my friends. Magdalena may be many things, some even ending with an 'itch' – but she is *not* a snitch!

'Burn me at the stake,' I bellowed. 'Stretch me on the rack,' I rasped. 'Pull out my fingernails and call me Portulacca, but I will never turn on my friends. Never in a million years. Not for all the money in China!'

Chief Toy rose calmly. His soft features registered no emotion whatsoever, so I had no idea how he was reacting to my outburst. For all I knew, I'd gone completely bonkers and had never uttered a single word of it aloud.

'You may drive the cruiser car,' the chief said.

I jiggled my pinkies in my ears to make sure they were both working. '*Excuse* me?'

'Really, Miss Yoder, I'd rather not be seen in that old clunker. I bought a lightly used Mercedes sedan for my own use, and I'm having it painted and outfitted with the appropriate lights, sirens, GPS, communication systems and what have you.'

Even I can be speechless. If this condition persists, onlookers can sometimes become concerned. Such was the case that fine afternoon.

'Miss Yoder,' Toy said, after some time had elapsed, 'you are a handsome woman, but this is not one of your best looks.'

'How rude!' I cried.

'I've already installed the safest infant seat on the market,' my trim and tiny tempter said.

'Get behind me, Satan!'

'Since you don't have any official police training, you can't wear a uniform, but I don't see anything wrong with you wearing something that approximates a uniform.'

'Approximates?'

'I was thinking a longish navy skirt, a button-up navy shirt and one of our official navy police caps, but with the insignia removed. However, I've heard rumours that you may have the third largest head in America. Therefore it is possible that none of our caps will fit you.'

'That's OK, I'll cram my foolish noggin into that cap, you'll see! I'll get my head shrunk; I'll do whatever it takes, I promise!' Truthfully, I am a sucker for a uniform, but I still wasn't going to snitch on my friends, no matter *what* I turned up wearing!

There you have it; this then is the perfect example of the ability of power to go straight to one's – er – head. Suddenly, I wanted a uniform more than anything. Who knows, to obtain my goal of being a pseudo-law enforcement officer, I might have gone so far as to hike my hemline up to my knees and perform a sinful Irish jig, possibly even a Scottish reel or, heaven forbid, I might have gone so far as to gyre and gimble in the wabe.

Toy could see that I was tempted. 'How does that sound?'

'Like a dream,' I purred, and then ground the heel of one of my sensible black brogans into the toe of the other. Of course the act of trying to stifle my sinful nature only served to spark another question. 'What about shoes, dear? Do official shoes come with that getup?'

'Uh – yeah. Actually – no.'

'You're talking like a sausage, dear.'

The poor boy looked away. 'What I'm trying to say is that the very practical *things* that you have on now will do just fine.'

'That's OK; you may call them clodhoppers if you wish,' I said. 'And feel free to make gagging sounds if it helps.'

'Well, OK, thanks,' he said.

'Do you want me to wear white socks or navy?' I said.

'It doesn't matter, Miss Yoder. Wear whatever you like.'

'Well, it matters to *me*, dear. If I'm going to yield to temptation, then I'm going to sin *all* the way.'

'Then definitely wear white socks,' he said. 'White is a racier color than navy. By the way, did I tell you that even though you won't be authorized to pull anyone over to the side of the road with the cruiser car, as a private citizen, you are always permitted to make a Citizen's Arrest?'

'With handcuffs?' I said. Hope springs eternal, even in the flattest of breasts.

'Yes, ma'am,' Toy said, 'providing the accused cooperates and allows you to put the cuffs on him. Even if they don't cooperate, those handcuffs over there will look really cool hanging from the navy-blue belt of your navy-blue skirt.'

I could feel myself beaming like a lighthouse on the Isle of Wight. Over the past dozen years as Hernia's mayor, I have had the distinct displeasure of finding myself embroiled in every manor of mayhem, from mud-raking to murder. Throughout the years the Good Lord has blessed me financially to the point that I am by far Hernia's wealthiest citizen. Because we have fewer than 3,000 souls living within the greater community, we cannot afford to staff a full-time police department without help from the 'private sector.' When saying those last two words perhaps one should pause and think of me fondly – or at least pause. Sad to say, people are seldom grateful for what is truly free. Case in point: not once had I ever been offered the chance to drive the police car, which I'd paid for entirely with my own money.

Therefore, can you not see, that when the smooth-skinned Justin Bieber doppelgänger of yesteryear offered to loan me both car and cuffs, I had to consider the possibility that he really was Satan. And no, I am absolutely not making light of what was a serious situation. Consider this: the Devil – with a capital D – can assume many guises other than serpents. Take, for instance, Hitler, Pol Pot, Idi Amin and Robert Mugabe. Since the Bible states unequivocally that God is a He, I say thank heavens that Satan is a He as well. Otherwise, we women would be blamed for even more than we already have been, thanks to Eve and her desire to eat healthy. At any rate, it is the Devil's male gender that accounts for the fact that one doesn't find any women on my list of the Devil's most notorious aliases. Now, where was I? Oh, yes, until proven wrong, I was quite willing to believe that Toy from Charlotte was the Great Tempter.

On the other hand, it was possible that he was merely an unusually canny young male, entirely human in nature, having an invisible bag of tricks up his short white polyester sleeves. Whatever his shtick (a lovely Yiddish word, thanks to my dear Jewish husband), it behoved me to play along with Hernia's Chief of Police upon whose chest hung the shiny silver badge of officialdom. Either way, Devil or man-child, he had come to me seeking *my* help, and offering me an *enticing* bribe. Believe me, gift horses with perfect teeth don't come trotting into my stable just any old day.

Last, but not least, was the fact that two of Chief Toy's suspects, Agnes and Doc, were innocent. I would have been willing to bet the farm on that – literally – except that we Mennonites don't bet as a matter of religious conviction. As it just so happened, those two innocent people were my very best friends. Perhaps I could clear their names on my own, thus saving them the humiliating journey through Hernia's gossip mill. Although the truth was on my side, in this country we believe that justice is blind which, of course, makes as much sense as having a guide dog that is blind. Therefore it was I, Magdalena Portulacca Yoder Rosen, riding to the rescue – in a police cruiser, red lights swirling and sirens wailing.

'Flattery will get you everywhere,' I practically yelled. 'I accept your offer.'

From the corner of my right eye I saw Granny Yoder shake a bony finger at me, and then in another flurry of dust motes she vanished from my stuffy parlour.

THREE

'What was that all about?' my Dearly Beloved inquired delicately. To his credit, he'd been waiting patiently in the kitchen, along with our one-year-old son, Little Jacob, and Freni, my beloved kinswoman, who also happened to be our cook. I gave Gabriel points for patience, because I knew that he would have liked nothing better than to have stormed the parlour and thrown the 'little whippersnapper Toy' out on his ear.

'It was about the English woman, ya?' Freni said, hazarding a guess. To the Amish, anyone from the outside world is 'English.' The reason for this is because the Amish immigrated to America from Switzerland as a group in the early 1700s when England ruled the land. The Amish were an insular faith, keeping to themselves as much as they could. To them the outside world was English, and it remained so, even after the United States declared its independence in 1776. Hence, Hispanic Americans are considered English by the Amish, because they are not Amish, whereas an Englishwoman from England, who adopted the Amish faith, would no longer be English. Go figure. Thus the word English is used as a religious classification rather than a national one. To a woman like Freni, the expression 'English English' might well refer to a Roman Catholic from London.

'Yes,' I said. 'He needs my help in catching that horrible woman's killer.'

'Now, darling,' said the Babester (as I am wont to call my husband in the privacy of my mind), 'it isn't nice to speak ill of the dead. Or is that just a Jewish custom?'

'We Christians don't do it either,' I said, 'but because of all the unflattering things she said about your mother in that trashy novel of hers, your mother's name tops Chief Toy's list of murder suspects.'

At that the Babester bellowed like our prize-winning bull Lester did when our cow, Daisy, accidently kicked those particular blue ribbon features of his that made him a breeding champion. After that, Lester was forced into early retirement and Daisy had to be freshened at a neighbor's farm.

'My mother!' Gabe exclaimed. 'I can't believe you dragged my mother into this.'

'It wasn't me—' Quite possibly I would have carried on as loudly as Gabriel, had not I spied Freni's pitiful attempt to waggle her almost non-existent brows above a pair of rimless glasses. In this code, one perfected by eons of time, across countless cultures, she was trying to warn me about the perils of coming between a man and his mother. The dear woman knew that Gabriel and Mother Malaise shared a bond so tight that one glue company even used their photo on advertisements. While some men have to sever their mother's apron strings, Gabriel's mother trotted over from a pseudo-convent every evening to cut his meat for him. I use the word 'pseudo' because she made up her own religion, ordained herself as its head, and this so-called Convent of the Sisters of Perpetual Apathy is an old farmhouse that once belonged to my inadvertent first husband. Mother Malaise's misguided followers are a bunch of loonies in search of their tunes. Enough said – for now.

'Ach!' said Freni, recoiling as much as a woman can when she lacks any semblance of a neck. 'What you say is not fair to our skinny Magdalena. Your mama – this Mother Mayonnaise – she has plenty of meat on her bones, and she cannot be dragged by anyone.'

'It is all right, Freni,' I said. 'He didn't mean it literally.'

'Yah? Is that so?' Thankfully she didn't wait for an answer, but turned back to her stew pot, muttering all the time.

'Got to love her,' I said. 'She's my mother by a different womb.'

For the next few minutes Freni wisely stirred the stew while my Babester stewed. Meanwhile, the newest love of my life, the male whose apron strings I would *never* allow to be severed, clung to a stool across the kitchen and stared intently at me. In retrospect, I have no doubt that he was sending me a coded message as well, because without any warning he lunged forward and began lurching in my direction. This was only the third time that the little rug rat had ever attempted to walk on his own.

Needless to say, my arguably stunted heart threatened to burst with joy. Since nothing can compare to watching the fruit of one's womb perform amazing deeds, I actually felt a moment of solidarity with the erstwhile maligned Mother Mayonnaise – I mean, Malaise! Alas, my moment of charity lasted just as long as Little Jacob kept his balance. After five weaving steps he plopped on his rump, but instead of crying like I'd fully expected him to, he laughed and held up fat little arms. His little fists opened and closed as if to say, *Pick me up. Set me on my feet. I want to do it again!*

I am known for my quick, hawk-like reactions. I would go so far as to say that I am proud of my ability to respond quickly, and appropriately, in any given situation, but we Mennonites believe that pride is a grave sin. Instead, we have been raised to be proud of our humility. Some folks find this conundrum harder to live with than others do.

At any rate, my Dearly Beloved's swift actions were not quite as swift as those of yours truly – not by a long shot. The pouty look that his delicious, bow-shaped lips assumed was reminiscent of the time when my mother-in-law forgot to cut his Jell-O pudding for him, as well as his meat. Instinctively, if not from valuable experience, I knew that a man bested at a lunging sport – especially one played in the presence of another woman – was bound to be cranky and uncooperative for the rest of the day. The fact that the other woman was his mother's age, height, and build (inverted isosceles triangle) made no difference in a positive way.

'Oh, is my Jakey-wakey-snoogey-boogey looking for his Daddy-waddy?' I cooed as I scooped him up.

'Mags, stop it! We agreed on no baby talk.'

I breathed deeply of heaven's perfume – that is to say, a baby's head – and instantly defused the old grouch by depositing chubby Little Jacob into his father's strong, tanned arms. Suddenly, I felt totally at peace as well. In my book, there is nothing sexier than a father tenderly holding his child.

'Ach, you English *mitt der* funny names,' Freni said. She sounded almost disappointed that we'd stopped arguing. Admittedly, for someone like Freni who doesn't watch TV, from time to time the Babester and I do make for good entertainment.

'Not to worry, Freni,' I said. 'When he sees me decked out in my uniform, climbing into my black and white police car, he'll have kittens.'

I would like to think that Freni winked then. After all, it is hard to tell, given that the lenses in her glasses are a quarter of an inch thick. But if I were to be brutally honest with myself, I might admit that she looked just as shocked as my Dr Gabriel Rosen, the handsome cardiologist to whom I had promised to be faithful until death us did part. Fortunately, it was Gabe, the outsider from New York, who had insisted that we leave the word 'obey' out of our vows.

The Convent of the Sisters of Perpetual Apathy lay across Hertzler Road from the PennDutch Inn, about a quarter of a mile away. In the old days both properties were farms, operated by second cousins, third cousins, fourth cousins and fifth cousins, who also happened to be first cousins. The two men I'm referring to were my papa and Aaron Miller Sr, but trust me: their close blood ties were not unusual in our community, where family trees give way to thickets which can prove daunting to the casual genealogist. The reason for this is that the Amish marry exclusively within their community. As a result, even I, who am merely a Mennonite of Amish descent, am in fact my own cousin. Just hand me a sandwich and I constitute a family picnic.

Now where was I? Oh, yes, I was going across Hertzler Road (the Hertzlers are cousins as well) to what had once been a productive dairy farm. Then Aaron Sr died, Aaron Jr lied, and I cried. That said, after the marriage that wasn't, and I was branded forever as an inadvertent adulteress, the hunk without a heart sold the family inheritance to the mother of my current lover. There, I said it, if only in my mind! Yes, we are married, but the Babester and I are lovers just the same. *Lover* – what a sinfully sensuous word, something only an English would dare speak aloud. If Mama could hear me she'd spin so fast in her grave she'd generate enough electricity to supply all Hernia's needs into the middle of the twenty-second century.

I shouted it instead. 'Lover! Gabriel Rosen is my lover!'

This was my anthem, which I continued to shout as I drove from my front porch to the convent gates. This was my right for having survived adolescence as the tall, awkward girl with the horsey face who never stood a chance of having a boyfriend, if only because Mama thought that deodorant was too English. As a consequence my nickname throughout high school was Yoder with an Odour. I had to console myself with the fact that I was not hirsute, because Mama believed that females who shaved and used depilatories were in cahoots with the Devil. She was not alone in her beliefs. Poor Agganetha Freisen spent her teenage years with the moniker Shaggy Aggie.

Rest assured that by the time I reached the gates of the so-called convent, I was safely ensconced in *my* police cruiser, with the windows up, and the sirens wailing like a banshee on the Scottish moors. Perhaps Mama didn't hear me – based on my next electric bill – but the Mother Superior sure did. Mother Malaise, aka Ida Rosen, could *hear* a reference to her son *texted* from a bunker somewhere in wilds of North Korea. In short, my stout, ex-Jewish nemesis from Brooklyn, New York has *Gabe-dar*.

Call me remiss if I do not adequately describe the woman with the apron strings of steel. Rest assured that this is not judgment on my part, but merely a keen sense of observation. Although Ida is no relation to my much-adored cousin Freni, she shares her same top-heavy triangular figure. However, Ida's ankles are matchstick thin, and her feet the size of a new born baby's. It is above the triangle that the biggest differences are to be found: Ida has a neck. Granted, it is a stubby neck, but it is quite serviceable, allowing her oversized head to swivel a freakishly three hundred degrees by my calculations.

Yes, I have been known to exaggerate – just a tad – upon occasion, but Mother Malaise really did make one stop and consider the possibility that the woman might have owl blood coursing through her veins. Of course, it would have been a great sin on one or both of her parents' parts for interbreeding – well, it isn't my fault that my mind went there, *is* it? It was Mother Malaise who was to blame for wearing a dreary, greyish-brown habit with a wimple that sported two inexplicable tufts of fabric atop it like the ears of the Great Horned Owl. Like Freni, Mother Malaise required glasses, but hers were notable for their immense diameter rather than the thickness of their lenses.

So when my official police cruiser screeched to a halt in a spray of gravel and loose dirt, I was greeted by the visage of a Great

Horned Owl flapping its wings and hooting – albeit something other than 'who.' That is to say, my mother-in-law has a vocabulary guaranteed to make even the most hardened Baptist blush. After a good deal of wasted time, when it appeared that she'd run out of breath and had been reduced to a heaving habit beneath the giant rotating head, I jumped smartly from the car. The one thing that Toy had failed to outfit me with was a gun, mayhap rightly so; nonetheless, I patted my empty holster for dramatic effect.

'M-Magdalena,' Mother Malaise gasped when she could produce the necessary wind, 'this isn't Halloween, you know. You could get arrested for impersonating a police officer, and you certainly *will* get arrested for stealing a police car. In fact, I'm making the call right now.' She began fumbling within the yards and yards of coarse fabric that hung from her bodacious bosoms.

'Stuff and *nun*sense,' I said. 'I am, in fact, the de facto investigator in the murder of Ramat Sreym, the *nebbish* novelist who *plotzed* in a pie.'

Ida yanked her fat, fumbling fingers out of her habit and pointed one at me. Given the meatiness of said digits, it looked like all five were aimed in my direction.

'*Vhat?*' she rasped. 'I dun't understand a verd you are saying, Magdalena. Not a verd, but eet eez lies, all lies.'

I patted my empty holster again, and displayed a little attitude in the way I cocked my bony left hip. 'Hmm, if you ask me, this place is just begging for a few citations. When is the last time you've had your kitchen inspected? You have any illegals working here? How about you? Your accent sounds funny to me.'

My mother-in-law ripped off her wimple, and I could see that her face was the color of boiled rice. 'It vas only one rat,' she said. 'A small von – OK, so maybe not so small. Who knew dat dey make business like chocolate sprinkle? You know dis ting, Magdalena? So vhen Sister Distemper put dis sprinkle on zee cake zat I bring over for my Gabeleh's birzday—'

'Stop!' I shouted. 'That cake was delicious.'

Her oversized face regained some color as she nodded her head vigorously. 'Yah, like see cupcakes zat vee donated to zee school bake sale, no?'

'No!'

'Vaht you mean "no?" You dun't remember?'

'Of course, you ninny – I mean, you nunny. Can I please come in, so that I can get to the purpose of my visit?'

'Yah, sure. But first you tell me, did you see zat beautiful chocolate pie zat Sister Distemper enter in zee pie contest last veek? Such an artist, zat von!'

'Pie, schmie,' I said and swept past her. Then with all the authority bestowed upon me vis-à-vis the status of a pretend police woman, a counterfeit cop and an invertebrate investigator (I have been called spineless, mind you), I pushed through a pair of sagging wrought-iron gates and up the steps of the two-hundred-year-old wooden farmhouse.

There was no point in ringing the bell, as it had not been working for a dozen years. Knocking soon proved futile as well, so with Mother Superior, aka Mother Malaise, aka Ida Rosen, aka the Great Horned Owl, flapping at my rear, I merely opened the door and stepped into the empty main room. The farmhouse, otherwise known as the convent, had been added on to by the cult in a higgledy-piggledy fashion. Sister Disheartened, who had once been an architect, had eventually succeeded in connecting several outbuildings with the main house. It had been Mother Superior's desire to have a space where apathetic postulates could wander listlessly about, contemplate their *pupiks* (Yiddish for navels), and perhaps occasionally even pray. The end result was a large courtyard with a whitewashed tractor tyre as its center-piece. The tyre had originally been intended as a flower bed, but since no one had the energy or the inclination to plant real flowers, I'd taken it upon myself to stick some rather lovely silk flowers in it when I changed the old silk flowers from my parents' graves last spring and replaced them with new ones.

Mother Superior, aka Mother Malaise, aka Ida Rosen, aka the mother-in-law *not* from Heaven soon caught up with me, and since the weather was pleasant we sat outside in the courtyard on a pair of rickety wooden folding chairs. I had a perfect view of the white tyre, and I was pleased to see that the good sisters had also lacked the oomph to remove the price tag on the bouquet from Mama's grave. I usually remove Papa's price tag, but Mama was so tight when it came to money that she could pinch a penny so that not only could it scream, it could sing a Lady Gaga song

– in four-part harmony, no less. Once, when I was thirteen, and I *needed* fifty cents so I could buy you-know-what in an emergency situation from that dispenser in the girls' lavatory at school, she refused to let me have it; I had to sit on my book bag all the way home. So now I leave the tag on Mama's bouquet just to make her spin a couple of times. Besides, given all the electricity that she generates, I see it as a way to reduce my carbon footprint – maybe even that of my entire family.

At any rate, no sooner had my bony butt hit the seat of that rickety chair than Ida was all over me like butter on popcorn. 'Now vee talk,' she said.

'Yes, now you will talk. Ida, it is no secret that you found Ramat Sreym's depiction of you in her book to be insulting.'

The massive head recoiled. 'Vhat? Are you meshuggeneh? Zat voman vas a terrific vriter. Von of zee best, eef you ask me – like Tolstoy or Pushkin, mebbe.'

'Uh—'

'Vhat? You never hear of deez men?'

'Yes, I hear of deez men – I mean, *these* men. Look, Ida, you moved here from Brooklyn two years ago, but sometimes your Yiddish accent is worse than when you arrived. Then, on other days, you have hardly any accent. How can this be?'

My nemesis shrugged and smiled just enough to display her gold tooth. Why had I even bothered to ask? Ida Rosen might be old, but she was far from helpless. Like every female, everywhere, she had been born knowing how to manipulate her father. (Surely this is the reason why the word 'manipulate' begins with the word man.) However, Ida had progressed to become a master manipulator, bar none, and her fluctuating accent was just one of her many tools. Unfortunately the Babester was her most frequent victim.

'Nu, Magdalena, do you vant to discuss accents wiz me, or do you vant dat vee should put our kophs togedder and find zee man who killed zat vonderful voman, my dear friend, Ramat Sreym?'

'Your friend?' I gasped in disbelief. 'You didn't like her one little bit.' Gabe's mother was an all-too-frequent visitor at my establishment, and the two women often ran into each other—sometimes quite literally.

'I din't?'

'You din't! She constantly made fun of you. She described you as being shaped like a triangle standing on a point. She said that you had enormous bosoms and a humongous head. She had you speaking in an atrocious accent and mollycoddling your son. She even had you cutting his meat, for crying out loud!'

Ida beamed. 'Yah, eez all true.'

'Yes, but don't you see how emasculating that description of Gabriel is to him? Do you really want your son, a prominent, retired cardiologist, to be seen as a Mama's boy?'

'Eez nozzing wrong wiz dat. You vill see, Magdalena. Und anyvay, zees voman, she had zee hots for my Gabeleh, und she said zat eef you vood haf set him free, zen she vood haf converted und moved back to Brooklyn wif us.'

'Converted?'

'She vood haf become Jewish.' So saying, Ida crossed her paddle-like hands, on account of her bosom being so bountiful that her stubby arms couldn't reach any further.

'Why, that's the most ridiculous thing I ever heard. People aren't supposed to convert *away* from Christianity; if anything, Gabe should become a Christian!'

'What? And turn his back on four thousand years of Judaism?'

It was a good thing we were sitting, because my jaw dropped into my lap. Ida Rosen had suddenly lost *all* trace of her Eastern European accent. In fact, she sounded more Milwaukee than New York.

I slapped my jaw back into place. 'Golda Meir!' I cried. 'Have you reincarnated?'

'Vhat?'

'Don't "vhat" me, Ida. A second ago you sounded like a native-born Midwesterner. I've always suspected that there was something fishy about your accent. Now it's time to fess up; just who is the real Ida Rosen and where are you from?'

Ida jumped to her feet. This was not an easy maneuver, due to her monstrous bosoms and oversized head. Yes, I know, I could have let her land face down, but then I would have missed yet another opportunity to feel self-righteous. That said, I jumped spritely to my boat-sized feet and pulled her upright before her noggin could hit the pavement of the garden path, taking great care to stay out of the trajectory of that enormous bobbing head.

'S-s-spy?' she finally sputtered. 'Eez dat vaht you tink I am?'

'I didn't say that – well, not exactly.'

'Yah, but dat is vaht you deferred, no?'

'Hmm. Out of deference to you, I'll leave that one alone.'

'Riddles! Always mit zee riddles wiz you, Magdalena. You come here casting precisions on my friends und me, und den you start talking in deez riddles like some crazy voman. Nu, how can I be happy wiz my leetle Jacob, my bubbeleh, growing up wiz a meshuggeneh voman for his mama? Tell me, already, vaht vill happen to my poor grandson now dat his future stepmother eez dead?'

'*Oy gvalt*,' I growled, having picked up those Yiddish words a long time ago from this very *kvetching* grandmother herself. 'Look, dear, before I skedaddle, let me make myself perfectly clear: Little Jacob is the fruit of my looms, so to speak. I'm the one who endured the thirty-six hours of agonizing labor—'

'Eez dat so? From vaht I hear, you shoot him out on zee floor of a grocery store een feefteen minutes.'

'Maybe so, but they were fifteen minutes of agonizing pain. Although let's not forget the three agonizing minutes it took to get him in there in the first place.'

Am I ever glad that I don't believe in karma! How I would hate for it to turn around and bite me. I can only imagine the pain that a mother must feel to hear her daughter-in-law reference sex with her son. Oh, how cruel I had been to poor little Ida! This time I had definitely gone too far. I'd intentionally tried to pluck the oedipal strings that bound her to my husband, knowing full well that whatever I said on that score would crush her.

'Ach,' I said, settling back hard onto my rickety wooden chair. 'I went too far that time; sometimes the most unchristian things just slip out of my mouth.'

'Plez,' my mother-in-law said, smiling like a Cheshire cat, 'eez nahsing to vory about. Be-leaf me; I hear eet all before. My Gabeleh steel complains about his vedding night. Mama, he says—'

The worse thing about rickety wooden chairs is that they sometimes come with peeling plywood seats. The seat that I'd been directed to sit on was a virtual nest of splinters. Unfortunately I happened to be wearing a very inexpensive skirt, which was a cotton-poly blend with an open weave. The resulting combination was not unlike Velcro, so that when I leapt to my feet a second time, the chair seat broke loose from its moorings and came with me. Thus it was that as I strode angrily out of the courtyard and back through the main hall of the Convent of Perpetual Apathy, a roughly square piece of manmade wood flapped against my bottom, rudely spanking me with each step.

FOUR

Where does one go after being bested by the empress of platitudes, the nun of everything *nun*sensical, she who is the antithesis of apathy? Why, if one is Magdalena Portulacca Yoder Rosen, then one would drive straight into charming little Hernia then out again on Corkscrew Mountain Road. One would then drive another four miles on a bumpy gravel road with so many tight turns that it is sure to remind one of a horse's colon. Perhaps it is best just to trust me on that.

The point of the aforementioned travelogue is to demonstrate how great my affection was for Agnes Miller, who I was about to visit, and who, coincidentally, was also on Chief Toy's list. We had been best friends our entire lives, and after college our bond was strengthened by the shared knowledge that the two of us would inevitably remain lifelong spinsters. Then when the unbelievable happened and I married a bigamist, Agnes stuck by me, like a tigress to her cub. She never, ever judged me. Agnes never waivered in her faithfulness to me, not even when all of Hernia called me a Jezebel for marrying outside my faith.

The only negative thing I can say about Agnes really doesn't have as much to do with her as it does her septuagenarian uncles. Agnes belongs to a very liberal branch of the Mennonite Church, but these two loony uncles of hers became Presbyterians, then Unitarians, before quitting religion altogether. This, then, explains their total lack of shame and their unfettered delight in parading around in the altogether, which is 'American' for stark naked. It is bad enough to catch a glimpse of the brothers on a chilly day in, say, autumn or spring, but woe to the woman who finds herself staring face-to-face (actually down-in-front) with either of them on a warm September morning, as I was now.

We Americans are fanatics about equality. We even have it in our constitution that 'all men are created equal.' Although the Miller brothers were the only nude men I've ever seen standing side by side, if I were to extrapolate from this one example, I would have to conclude that the Good Lord did indeed play favourites. Either that, or God has a bizarre sense of humour. On this particular morning the brothers were standing in the middle of the road, shoulder-to-shoulder, facing oncoming traffic. Since I have a scientific bent (well, I did ace biology in high school) I thought it my duty to at least observe the situation in front of me carefully before tooting my horn. After a rather thorough study, and some photos on my cell phone, I concluded that a pony and a chipmunk were the two images that came to mind.

'I say there, Magdalena,' called the brother of equine proportions as he approached on the driver's side, 'you're supposed to try and pass.'

I shut my eyes tightly. 'I do, dear; believe it, or not, pass for sane. The two of you, however, might need to have your meds readjusted. I'll be sending those pictures on to your caseworker in Bedford. Does she know that the two of you are still running around like Adam before the Fall?'

That's when the poor brother with the rodent-sized equipment ran around to the passenger window and commenced banging on the glass. With my eyes closed, the pounding took me by surprise. I felt violated, and then suddenly very angry. Stupidly I lowered both front windows so that I could better confront the pair of senile old men.

'What the heck is going on?' I demanded. That particular 'h' word is almost as bad as I can swear, and I hardly ever trot it out.

'We're broke,' said the first brother.

'And bored,' said the other.

'Yeah. You see, we need spending money, and St. Agnes won't give us more until the first of next month, so Alvin here thought up a plan. We're pretending to be highway robbers. But the stupid plan isn't working.'

Alvin stuck his head and half of his naked, wrinkled torso through the window. Thank goodness Charles, the centaur, kept his distance.

'We were going to hit you up for twenty-five dollars to let you pass,' Alvin said, 'because you've always been nice to our little niece.'

'Plus, Alvin's always had a thing for you,' Charles said.

'Have not!' Alvin said.

'Not that it matters much,' Charles continued, 'because he hears voices, even when he's on his meds. Then again, I hear voices as well.'

'Do you ever hear voices, Magdalena?' Alvin asked.

'Hmm,' I said. 'Do you mean like God whispering in my heart? That kind of thing?'

'Could be. That's how mine started, what with God telling me how special I was, and that if I just had enough faith I could walk across the Monongahela River.'

'It didn't work,' Charles said.

'Yes,' I said, 'I remember. Alvin tried to walk across the river three times – twice when it was in flood stage. The rescue squad had to be called each time, and it ended up costing the state hundreds of dollars. Alvin, you could have at least tried walking across a pond, or maybe just your bathtub. Any place where the water isn't moving.'

'Duh,' Charles said.

'Hey,' I said. 'Play nice.'

'Sorry, bro,' Charles said. 'Hey, Magdalena, can we please hitch a ride back up the hill with you?'

Forsooth, I had to think about their request for a moment. They were, after all, buck naked, and I had just been handed the squad car. Didn't I have the right to enjoy it without all those sweaty man parts sticking to leather seats which I had yet the pleasure of sniffing? On the other hand, the brothers were officially elderly by social security standards (full eligibility begins at age sixty-six), and a steep hill lay between where we were and their house.

'Hop in, boys,' I said at last, 'but no talking, and positively no *shvitzing*.'

'What is *shvitzing*?' chatty Charles said.

'Stop,' I said, with mock sternness. 'I said no talking!' I said it dramatically enough to let them know how annoyed I was at both of them, and at myself for being so accommodating as I continued, '*Shvitzing* is Yiddish for sweating. I learned it from my mother-in-law.'

'A delightful woman,' Alvin said.

'Too late about the warning,' Charles said. 'Besides, it's not something that one can help.'

'*Oy vey!*' I cried and thumped the steering wheel.

The startled brothers jumped so, of course, when they landed they left new puddles of perspiration on my newly acquired leather seats.

In the old days, or so I've heard, a man threw a pair of horse shoes out the kitchen door and where the farthest one landed, that's where he built a cottage for his parents. This was called the Grossdawddy house. The Amish, who never collect social security money from the government, still maintain the practice of having the grandparents living on the farm. In the case of Agnes and her brothers, a separate cottage meant keeping the old coots out from under her feet, as well as not having to live with the guilt stemming from committing them to a nursing home. Like many of our inbred kin, and perhaps a good many of the English aristocracy, they are eccentric, not dangerous – except, perhaps, to upholstery.

Although Agnes is my age, she does not have to work. The reason is that her family made a small fortune inventing nail polish for horses, and horn polish for the beef cattle on the western plains. Named Happy Hoofers and Happy Hookers respectively, they became instant hits with dilettante and celebrity ranchers. Happy Hookers, which comes in neon yellow, fuchsia and chartreuse, all but eliminated the need for branding, even before the invention of the microchip. Free to do as she pleases, it pleases Agnes to sit on her sofa eating biscuits and watching television, for crying out loud.

Television! The Devil's mouthpiece, Mama called it, and she was right. Years ago there used to be one good show worth watching called *Greenacres*. It was about country living, and a pig, and a Hungarian immigrant with a charming accent – really good stuff. Today it is about fornication and violence, and violence while fornicating. Seriously, you wouldn't believe the TV programs that I've had to suffer through, and all of them on behalf of my church, Beechy Grove Mennonite. Some of our young people had been caught watching the tube in the homes of secular friends, and some poor adult had to volunteer to discover just how much worldly temptation they might have been exposed to.

At any rate, when Agnes opened her kitchen door that morning, her red, swollen eyes resembled a pair of Chinese lanterns. I gasped appropriately, although I wasn't shocked; Agnes is a world-class crier.

'What happened, dear?' I said. 'Were you using your night-vision goggles again looking for Martians? Isn't that risky, given that your uncles run around in the buff?'

Agnes sniffed and dabbed at the corner of each eye with a delicate flowered handkerchief. 'Really, my dear,' she said in a BBC accent, 'you haven't got a clue, have you?'

I prayed for strength enough to hold back my exasperation before sighing. It isn't my fault if some of my prayers go unanswered.

'Actually, I do have a clue. It's just that silly show of yours about a daunting abbey.'

My land of Goshen, you would have thought that the poor dear had kissed a hornets' nest, so red did her face become. Fortunately, Agnes can't be both English and angry at the same time, so she ditched the fake accent.

'*Downton Abbey* isn't just a silly show, Mags! That was a terribly insensitive remark to make at a time like this. No wait; you don't even know what I'm talking about, do you? Do *you*? And I bet that you wouldn't care if you did.'

'Well,' I said, 'I sort of feel like a sheep that has been asked a geometry question. Although in the spirit of full disclosure, I don't know very many sheep that have been asked such questions.'

My dearest friend did not seem to appreciate my effort to answer honestly in an amusing manner. More is the pity, if you ask me.

'Matthew is dead!' she shouted. 'D.E.A.D. – dead! He was killed when his car ran off the road and hit a tree. Now I'll never get married!'

'*Excuse* me?'

'Don't you see? Now I'll have to help Tom sort out the problems of the estate—'

I waved my gangly arms in front of her Chinese lantern eyes. 'It isn't real!' I shouted back. 'It's a *television show*. They are made-up people with invented lives.'

'That may be, Mags, but it is a real castle; I read that in the *TV Guide*. And it is still occupied by a real Lord and Lady.'

That did it; that hiked my hackles. We plain people, we who are proud of our humility, we who sailed to the shores of the Thirteen Colonies in 1738, book no truck with inherited rank.

'Aha!' I said, spotting an easy avenue in which to score. 'We're not supposed to call anyone 'Lord' except God or Jesus. If you don't believe it, then look it up in the *King James Bible*, which was written by the English themselves. Besides, the Our Father is also known as the Lord's Prayer, not the Earl's Prayer.'

My friend smiled. 'Now you're being silly. You know that the English didn't write the Bible; English wasn't even a language when the Bible was written.'

I returned her smile. 'Agnes, might I come in, dear? If you fix me a cup of tea and some ginger biscuits, I'll let you lay your hoary head upon my shoulder and have a proper cry.'

For the record, Agnes is one of those women who proudly claims her gray hair. It is her staunch belief that dyeing one's hair is the same thing as lying. That is, of course, unless the face that goes with the colored hair is as shrivelled as a prune. Agnes, however, is a 'fluffy' woman, with a full, round face. In her own words: 'Fat don't crack.'

It requires more to sustain that face than just ginger biscuits and tea. 'I have a broken heart, Mags,' Agnes said. 'It's either going to be lunch at the Sausage Barn or I'm taking to my bed with pumpkin pie and a can of whipped cream.'

'Then its lunch,' I said, 'but I'll have to call home first. Freni was making a big pot of stew but I'm sure that she'll understand.' I can always be coaxed to eat out in a restaurant, even if that means eating at the Sausage Barn, which is owned by my second-best friend/arch-nemesis, Wanda Hemphopple.

'Sure, Freni will understand,' said Agnes as she practically pushed me off the kitchen steps and made a beeline for my car. 'That woman always understands.'

But Agnes made it only halfway to the cruiser before she stopped dead in her tracks, causing a one-person pileup. Believe me, when one is as tall and spindly as a clothesline pole, with the musculature of a spaghetti strand (that is to say, none), it is possible to fold up rather easily on oneself.

'Aack!' I squawked.

'What the heck is that?' Agnes said.

'What does it look like, dear?' I said, rubbing my nose while at the same time trying to push it back to its original spot on my face.

'I can see that it is Hernia's one police cruiser,' Agnes snapped, 'but what on earth are you doing with it?'

'Ah, that,' I said. 'Well, you see, our illustrious author's death has now officially been ruled a murder, and—'

'Wait,' Agnes said, 'let me guess: Toy, the boy, feels that his status as an outsider will be a disadvantage for him in solving the case. You, on the other hand, have roots in this community that go back to the time when Moses gurgled in the bulrushes, not to mention that your size twelve gumshoes have gum all over their soles from prior cases that you've successfully cracked. Am I right, or what?'

I snorted irritably, despite my normally cheerful demeanour. 'You are irreverent, wrong, and right – in that order. I wear a size eleven shoe.'

Agnes was unapologetic. 'Ha, I'm mostly right! So now I'll guess something else: I'm on your list of suspects, aren't I?'

'How did you know?' I said. But it was a silly question.

'Hmm, let me see,' Agnes said as she slipped into the front passenger seat unbidden. 'The meanest writer in America publishes a book in which she makes a ton of cutting remarks about me being fat, my loser personality and my crazy naked uncles, then the book becomes a huge bestseller, and then she has the audacity to come back to the scene of the crime to strut her stuff under the guise of judging our pie festival. Who wouldn't kill her, if they were me? Oh, I know that you wouldn't, because you're close to perfect, but I'm not! And besides, since you showed up driving the cruiser, and offering to let me lay my "hoary" head upon your shoulder despite the fact you have, like, major touch issues – well, there you have it.'

'Harrumph,' I said. 'Now let me call Freni and tell her that we'll be going to the Sausage Barn for lunch.'

'No need to call her, Mags. Like I said, she won't mind.'

Who was Agnes trying to kid? Freni is about as fond of change as a cat is of swimming lessons. Nevertheless, I managed to reach Freni on my car phone.

'Ach! What am I supposed to do with enough stew for ten people?'

'What were you going to do with it anyway?' I said calmly. 'One less person won't make that big a difference.'

'Yah, maybe,' Freni said, 'but that Agnes Miller can eat enough for six people. I tell you what, Magdalena, you bring Agnes home with you for supper and that will fix our problem.'

'I heard that!' Agnes shrieked. For a woman who hovers around the half-century mark, Agnes can emit sounds almost as deafening, and every bit as annoying, as a five-year-old girl on a playground.

'Ach,' said Freni, 'it is the smoke alarm. I must go.'

'It's Agnes; you just tripped her offense alarm.'

'Now is not the time for riddles, Magdalena,' Freni said with surprising sternness. The woman who had practically raised me almost never raises her voice to Yours Truly.

'I'm speaking on the car phone, dear,' I said. 'Agnes heard you call her "fat."'

'But I did not call her fat; I inferred it.'

'That's right, Magdalena,' Agnes said. 'She only inferred it. You are the one who just now called me fat.'

'*Oy vey!*' I cried. 'I can't win for losing.'

'*Ach du Leiber!*' Freni said. 'You are driving me up the walls.'

'I believe that would be just one wall, dear,' I said.

'No,' Freni said, without missing a beat. 'Already it has been two walls, Magdalena, and it is not yet noon.'

'Surely you jest,' I said.

'Now it is three walls.'

'You go, girl,' said Agnes, speaking directly into the built-in microphone above my windshield visor.

'Agnes,' I hissed, 'stay out of this.' Incidentally, one must always hiss using an 'S' sound. Some fancy-schmancy novelists actually try to get away without following this rule.

I've always maintained that a healthy Amish woman, or a Mennonite woman of Amish descent, can induce just as much guilt in her charges as any Jewish or Catholic mother. Well, I was wrong on that score. The former are way, way better at it.

'Magdalena,' Freni said, suddenly sounding completely

resigned to her miserable lot as the downtrodden housekeeper, 'I work my fingers to the bone all morning making the stew, and what do I have to show for it?'

'Bony fingers,' I said helpfully.

'Yah, and they are crooked too with the authoritis.'

I have spent decades gently trying to correct Freni's pronunciation of certain words, but to no avail. An inflammation of published writers and painful swollen finger joints – perhaps in the grand scheme of things, there is no difference.

'Now I feel really guilty about not going with you back to the PennDutch,' Agnes whispered. Alas, Agnes whispers as softly as a flock of scrapping seagulls.

'*Gut!*' Freni said decisively. 'That one can come and eat for how many people that she likes.'

'But I *need* carbs, Mags,' Agnes begged. 'I'm a grieving woman; I *need* pancakes, not stew.'

'What?' Freni roared. 'Pancakes in the middle of the day? Whoever heard of such a thing?'

'Freni,' I said in my most motherly, intentionally soothing voice, 'lots of people eat pancakes and waffles in the middle of the day. This is a free country, after all.'

When Freni makes her 'disgusted' face, her thin, gray lips take on the shape of a well-weathered volcano as seen from above. A dozen or so fissures suddenly appear around the perimeter of the volcano's cone and a smattering of white hairs give the illusion of a dusting of snow. Of course, I couldn't see Mt. Frensuvius over my car phone, but I could picture it in my mind's eye, which routinely performs with HD clarity.

'It is a sin, if you ask me,' Freni said.

'*What* did you say?'

'You heard me; it is a sin that so many things must change all the time.'

'Well—'

'First Agnes wants her pancakes for lunch, then maybe one day for supper. Who knows, is it not possible that one day she wants only pancakes? Pancakes, pancakes, pancakes! Magdalena, I ask you, is this healthy? Is this what Gott wants us to put into our bodies? This kind of thinking is the way of the world, Magdalena. They even have a name for it: they call it Edenism.

These Edenists think that pleasure is a good thing! Imagine that! You must not be reduced by such thoughts, Magdalena.'

'Freni, dear,' I purred, 'I hardly think that eating pancakes three times a day will have much impact on reducing me.'

There followed a moment of silence in which I knew that I had gone too far in teasing my mentor and my friend. 'So now you mock me?' she finally said. 'Shame on you, Magdalena Portulacca Yoder Rosen. You are better than this.' Then she hung up the phone.

To be honest, the vehemence of Freni's response embarrassed me. Yes, I'd known Agnes my entire life. We'd been bathwater babies – literally shared the same washtub as infants – and gone to school together, laughed together, cried together, fought each other, lied to each other *and* once we even snuck off to a dance together, but I still hated being treated like a child in front of my best friend. I especially chafed at her last line. Those were words that I'd heard a million times growing up, and I had not been a troublesome child; merely ungainly and awkward, with atrocious handwriting.

As I sat there for a moment pondering my next move, I felt an annoying tear escape from my right eye and slip boldly down my cheek. No one, but no one, gets to see Magdalena cry in public these days. In another second I would have blotted that tear with a man-size handkerchief had not my spherical, sister-under-the-skin interrupted my thoughts.

'Mags,' Agnes said, 'I just felt a goose walk over my grave.'

'Why you?' I wailed. 'You're not the one who is at fault.'

No doubt there are still those who claim that people are incapable of wailing; only sirens can wail, these folks say, and then they toss heads and stick their noses in the air in such a manner that one would think that all of France agrees with them. Well, these people may be right about everything else in life, but they have never been near Magdalena when she is feeling guilty for having hurt an old woman's feelings. Nor have these dismissive people been around Magdalena's lungs when she realized that by conducting an investigation she will miss out on spending time with the little fella who, until recently, has spent more time inside her than out of her. So *wail* she did!

'Dang it!' Agnes said and clapped her shapely but plump hands right in my face to snap me out of my reveries. 'Does *everything* have to be about you, Mags?'

'*Whuh?*'

'Remember, you're not the one whose fiancé just got killed in a fatal motorcycle accident while racing back to the castle to fetch the family doctor.'

'I thought you said it was a car accident. And he wasn't your fiancé; he was an actor, for Pete's sake!'

'Just step on the gas, would you? I'm starving.'

Because I did as my friend bade, I was not saddled with the title of World's Worst Friend. What's more, because I held the pseudo-official, almost-legitimate, genuinely faux rank of Assistant Investigator and Honorary Dog-catcher, and was driving a car outfitted with all the bells and whistles, I was able to realize speeds heretofore unrecorded in Hernia.

Wanda Hemphopple was an English Englishwoman. That meant that she was neither Amish nor Mennonite, and her ancestors actually hailed from across The Pond. However, like just about everyone else in this valley, Wanda's ancestors made the trip over during the reign of King George III. During the interim, one of Wanda's English forbearers mated with one of the more unfortunate European races – quite possibly a Frenchman. The resulting mongrel was not tall and sturdy, and did not possess the classic rose-pink cheeks of the English. Au contraire, poor Wanda was a short, wiry woman with a beak for a nose. Neither was she blessed with an Englishwoman's sense of decorum. Oh no, Wanda Hemphopple was born with a burr under her saddle, sand up her bathing suit and a splinter under her thumbnail – in other words, in a perpetual state of grumpiness that I seemed to exacerbate. But other than the fact that I invariably drove her up the wall, I'd say that we were close friends. As a matter of fact, she was my second-best friend, after Agnes, of course.

A fellow businesswoman, Wanda was the sole owner and proprietor of the Sausage Barn, Hernia's nearest restaurant. This eatery is actually located in Bedford, up near the Pennsylvania Turnpike and just past the charismatic Protestant church with thirty-two words in its name.

This restaurant is a traditional American *diner* in that it began as the dining car of a train. Of course, much has been added, and today one would be pretty much hard-pressed to detect 'diner' from 'add-on' when viewing the inside. Originally, in the tradition of American diners it served a wide range of food, from breakfast to sandwiches, meat and potatoes, and was open twenty-four hours a day. But then gradually – and only the Good Lord knows exactly why – this diner became regionally famous for its breakfast sausage and pancakes. Americans, you see, have a perverse fondness for mixing savoury and sweet in the same meal.

Perhaps this perverse characteristic will help explain my relationship with Wanda. She was the fraternal twin sister I've always had but never wanted. We were always friends, but we began being best enemies in grade school, beginning with the day she dipped one of my braids into a pot of bright blue poster paint. I retaliated by mashing a wad of chewing gum into the base of her ponytail. To say that we developed a hair fetish might be going too far, but we were still pulling pranks in high school, when I might have stepped over the line a wee bit.

Wanda must have been about seventeen then, and she wore her long, hardly-ever-been-washed hair in a rather loose French twist that we, her classmates, all called her 'hot-dog bun.' Well, one day the Devil got into me and I slid a *real* hot dog, a one hundred percent meat wiener down into the space created by the twist. The fact that Wanda's hairdo managed to keep its shape must be credited to the great number of hairpins that she used, plus all the accumulated grime and oil which must have acted as a sort of cement. Nonetheless, the weight of a plump wiener composed of pig lips, jowls and usual by-products caused the 'bun' to sway this way and that, like the cradle in the nursery rhyme.

However, much to my relief, the bough did not break and the baby did not fall – if you get my drift. Thankfully, no one saw me do it, except for God and maybe Granny Yoder. The latter's malevolent, but unseen presence in our school cafeteria might explain the horrific taste of just about everything that was served, or at the very least why the milk in those little cartons was invariably spoiled, no matter what due date was stamped on them.

Now where was I? Oh, yes, because my crime went undetected,

and because the Hemphopple family were hygienically challenged, the presence of a wiener in Wanda's wobbly wonder was not immediately detected. In fact, it wasn't until a full week later, on a warm spring day in boring Mrs Lehman's boring American History class, that a stray cat jumped through an open window and headed straight for Wanda's hair. I've been told that it was like a scene straight out of a movie. If indeed this is the case, then I can see now why it is that so many people pollute their minds with cinema. I'm telling you: Wanda's battle to save her bun from the destructive forces of a hungry pussy was extremely thrilling to watch.

'*Brava!*' I'd cried, temporarily forgetting the depth of our schoolgirl antipathies.

Unfortunately, the pussy had prevailed, pulling open Wanda's pungent bun, thus releasing the rotten weenie, which had somehow managed to catapult over to boring Mrs Lehman's desk and land in the middle of her open copy of *American History for a New Generation*. In that moment Mrs Lehman ceased to be boring. Although Mrs Lehman was a faithful Mennonite who did not believe in dancing, she did a jig of sorts while bellowing like a bull that had just been made into a steer. She was obviously trying to flip whatever it was off of her book, but when that didn't work, she took the next logical step and chucked history out the window altogether.

'You!' she roared, then able to focus her attention on Wanda. 'March to the principal's office.'

Somehow, also in that moment, Wanda immediately knew that the origin of the fetid food was none other than Yours Truly. She arched her back, looking so much like a cat that the authentic feline in the room hissed, and leaped through the back window.

'You!' Wanda then screeched at me. 'It was *you* who put that thing in my hair.' She whirled and faced Mrs Lehman. 'Magdalena Yoder put a human finger in my French twist, and that's what landed on your book, Mrs Lehman!'

Upon hearing Wanda's imaginative assumption, Mrs Lehman, whose undercarriage had been designed by her Creator along the lines of the pygmy (but still rather sizable) forest elephant, had fainted dead away. It only was because the Good Lord had seen fit to give her the thick ankles of her Alpine peasant ancestors that she remained aloft long enough to make us think that she had fallen asleep whilst standing. Consequently, when Mrs Lehman had fallen, it was with a resounding, skull-fracturing thud. Poor Mrs Lehman was out of commission for the rest of the term. Meanwhile, we had to put up with a substitute teacher named Cynthia Kettles-Brooke – a hussy who wore red lipstick, and who hinted that she might actually believe in evolution.

Sadly, Wanda never forgave me for that unfortunate incident, but nonetheless we managed to forge a friendship of sorts. As it turned out, the Good Lord blessed both of us with entrepreneurial skills: I created a charming bed and breakfast and Wanda built her Sausage Barn. Truly, we have never thought of ourselves as business competitors. For one thing, the Sausage Barn does not offer accommodation, and the guests who stay at my inn almost always avail themselves of a second breakfast over at Wanda's, if only to get a decent cup of coffee.

A scrupulously honest Magdalena would admit that Wanda and I were competitors when it came to everything else. But I will not admit to this, because in my community of believers, *competition* is a sin. Many of us have been known to vie for the position of being the least competitive person in the church. However, there is nothing wrong with *out-performing* someone else with one's God-given talents. It is all in how one slices the onion, don't you think?

I am always ready and eager to out-perform, so when Agnes and I showed up in the squad car at the Sausage Barn late that morning, you can be sure that the siren was wailing and the red lights on the roof were flashing. The sight of us was certainly arresting. If only I had had the nerve to arrest someone as well. That would have shown Wanda!

Nonetheless, Wanda and thirty-eight customers came pouring out like killer bees from a toppled hive. Last to emerge was her shirtless and very hairy fry-cook. Within seconds, nineteen of those customers ran to their cars and drove away. One would think that I'd busted up a drug ring or a gambling parlour, not merely just showed off at a high-stakes, heart-attack-on-a-plate dining establishment.

Since the squad car was equipped with a bullhorn, I was tempted to use it for some clean, Christian fun. You know, like saying: 'Freeze! Immigration! Papers, everyone!' Harmless things like that.

Wanda also has a bullhorn; it's attached to her lips. 'What the heck is going on?' she bellowed. (Sadly, Wanda, who is a Methodist, used a stronger word than 'heck.')

Then she got a good look at me, resplendent in my faux but officially approved police attire, and puffed up like a bantam rooster on steroids. 'What did you do with that boy, Toy – I mean, the Chief of Police?'

I switched off the siren, but not the flashing lights. 'Excuse me?'

'You killed him, Magdalena, didn't you?' At that, as many as nine more of her customers fled the parking lot.

'She most certainly did not,' Agnes declared hotly. When my best friend attempts to cross her plump arms across her full bosom and straightens her back, she can be rather intimidating – or alluring – as the case may be.

Wanda lowered her hackles a wee bit. 'Yeah?' she said. 'Did she convince you of this before, or after, she killed that lovely Miss Syri – iri – oh, the heck with it, I mean that hog-awful writer who butchered almost everyone in this town, including *you*, Agnes.'

'*Me?*' Agnes said. Her arms fell to her sides and her lower lip trembled. 'I don't remember there being anything bad about *me* in the book. My uncles, yes, but – but— Oh . . .' The poor woman began to sob as her memory caught up, although being of Amish-Mennonite extraction they were restrained sobs, perhaps similar to those emitted by an English Englishwoman. 'BBC sobs,' we call them.

'Exactly,' Wanda said cruelly. 'Your butt. And other parts of your anatomy as well.'

'Enough already,' said the shirtless fry-cook. He stepped sideways toward Agnes and would have slipped a hirsute forearm around her heaving shoulders if it hadn't been for Wanda's incredibly swift reaction time.

'Back to work!' she barked at the man.

'Yes, ma'am,' he said and then, looking back at Agnes, he said, 'Well, I think you're beautiful. I've always liked a woman with meat on her bones.'

That's when I took another look at the hunk from Hoboken. All I'd known about him up until then was that his given name was Stanley, and that he was originally from New Jersey. *That*, and that he had a variable number of front teeth (he always had a full set on Tuesdays). Oh, yes, and that he also made the world's best pancakes.

'Mags, did you hear that?' Agnes said. She'd gotten her mojo back in a nanosecond. 'He likes a woman with curves!'

Harrumph, I thought. Yes, I was jealous. I would rather be a sphere than a stick, any day. A sphere can get around, but a stick tends to just lay there.

By then us three amigos were practically alone in the parking lot. It reminded me of our best of times, which were also our worst of times. Unlikely trio that we were, the three of us had survived some hair-raising times together, solving some of Hernia's most difficult mysteries. One of the cases had even involved Wanda's infamous hair, which had had to be uncoiled and lowered down into a sinkhole, as if it were a rope, in order to rescue a desperate maiden. Experiences like that bond one for life; we were like sisters, which meant that we were stuck in a relationship whether we liked each other or not.

'Well,' Wanda said at great length, 'you might as well come inside so that Agnes can eat.'

'What is that supposed to mean?' Agnes hissed, appropriately too.

'It means,' Wanda said, 'that you have scared off all my customers, and the only way for me to make up for it financially is for you to eat your fill.'

'How rude!' Agnes said as she headed for the restaurant door. She was walking as fast as I'd ever seen her go.

'Stop complaining,' Wanda said. 'I'll seat you in the booth nearest the kitchen pass-through so that you can make googly eyes at Stanley.'

'Tell him to put a shirt on,' I wailed inappropriately. 'I don't want hair in my pancakes.'

'Oh, stop your whining,' Wanda said. She clomped ahead of me back into her restaurant, and with each step her massive beehive hairdo swayed like the belly of a pregnant cow. There was at least one difference, however: should Wanda's coil of keratin explode, the cooties unleashed might devour half of mankind.

But true to her word, Wanda seated us in booth fourteen, which happens to be my favourite anyway, because the food there has the best chance of getting to one while still hot. She also knew better than to hand either of us one of the greasy laminated menus.

'You,' she said to Agnes, 'undoubtedly want the super-size Farmer's Skillet Breakfast with eight eggs, over-easy; cream cheese-stuffed French toast; the tall stack of pancakes topped with fresh creamery butter and dripping with thick maple syrup; and the usual meats, but also extra portions of sausage, bacon, fried ham, and home-fried potatoes, *plus* an extra basket of assorted pastries, in addition to the one that comes with your meal. Oh, an order of whole-wheat toast on account of the fibre it contains, as well as a bowl of raisin bran for the same reason, plus a bowl of oatmeal as a nod towards eating healthy. Am I correct?'

'Yes,' Agnes said. Then, quite unprovoked, she had the temerity to turn and address me. 'The Bible says: "Judge not, lest ye be judged."'

'Why, I never!'

'You were about to,' she said. Agnes turned back to Wanda. 'And peach pie for dessert. You make the best peach pie in the world. Which reminds me, Wanda, I want to personally thank you for toiling in that hot little tent behind the judges, cutting pies and serving up the slices. If you had entered your own peach pie in the competition, and that inconsiderate interloper of an author hadn't so rudely elected to die when she did, I haven't the slightest doubt that you would have won.'

'Agnes,' I said, 'aren't you being a bit unfair? There are others in this community capable of baking a passable peach pie.'

'But none quite as annoying as you,' Wanda said. 'What with your fondness for excessive alliteration, you should be writing nursery rhymes.'

Agnes squealed with delight. 'My uncles would love that!'

'It's a wonder that we're still all friends,' I said.

'Yes, it is,' Wanda shot back. 'Now, look, unlike the two of you, I don't have all day. Magdalena, I suppose you also want your regular order. That would be two eggs, poached hard; four strips of bacon, crisp on the ends, a short stack of three pancakes, so pale and undercooked that the batter isn't even cooked all the way through, an extra slab of rich creamery butter, and a double ladle of warm maple syrup. If your syrup isn't warmed to the temperature of the rat's armpit, you suffer a complete meltdown.'

'I do not!'

'How do you test the temperature of the rat's armpit?' Agnes said. The dear woman was without guile.

'Wanda keeps it in a cage in the pantry,' I said. 'The thermometer is glued to a long stick, and because the rat has four arms – uh, legs – any of which will do for the test, it really isn't that hard. You just toss in a bit of cheese, poke the stick thingy behind one of his legs, and presto, you have a reading!'

'Wrong!' Wanda said gleefully. 'Herman died last week, and I've had to send off to Pittsburgh for a new pantry rat.'

The woman with the wobbly hair may have been telling the truth. I had heard of folks keeping pet rats, and there was that memorable occasion when the Sausage Barn was shut down for three weeks on account of a new fry-cook (they quit as often as Wanda changes her underwear) found rodent remains at the bottom of the chips vat.

Wanda turned our orders over to Stanley, and was back in a flash with a carafe of orange juice and a thermos of coffee. Then she slipped into the booth beside me.

'OK, I'm all ears now,' she said. Unfortunately, with her hair pulled back in the twist, I could see that they were very dirty ears.

'Go ahead, Magdalena,' Agnes said, 'Spill your beans. Now that you have both of your "besties" here, tell us exactly what's going on? What are you doing with Toy's car? Has our new Chief of Police quit already? What a crying shame that would be! I haven't even had a chance to cook him my famous "meatloaf surprise" – you know, the one where I hide hard-boiled eggs inside? I was going to have him slice it at the table so I could enjoy the expression on his face when he sees those cute yellow circles surrounded by perfect white rings.' Agnes clasped her hands in delight; the dear woman is so easily pleased.

'Your famous "meatloaf surprise" is a cliché,' Wanda said. 'I did it first, then the entire world copied me.'

'Don't be hurtful,' I said to Wanda. 'And no, Agnes, the chief is not quitting; I thought I made that clear on the way over here. He's just very, very busy.'

'You mean handling all the tourists that have been pouring into town since our one, and only, genuine celebrity – and no, it's not you, Magdalena – is now deader than a doornail.'

'My, but somebody sounds bitter, doesn't she?' I felt compelled to say.

'Well, look around you, Magdalena,' Wanda said. 'Do you see any customers?'

'There were thirty-eight customers here when we arrived.'

'Yes! Day-labourers. I hardly break even feeding them. They order just one or two things from the children's menu. I need *real* American customers to come back, like in the old days, before the recession. I want customers with money to spend, who like to gorge at the trough. I want people who aren't ashamed to waddle in the door and back out.'

'Wanda, that's awful! If people knew that you felt that way they would never eat here. Some folks can't help their weight on account of thyroid problems.'

'Oh, give me a break, Miss Skinny Minnie. I have hypothyroidism, for which I take medication. But I also don't eat enough for ten people like Miss Bottomless Pit here – not that I'm complaining, Agnes.'

I had to kick sideways, but nonetheless the heel of my brogan connected with Wanda's shin. Much to my satisfaction she yelped like a whelp. I might have been born and raised a pacifist, and I would certainly never take a human life. In fact, we are not to exact vengeance of any kind. That said, please understand when I say that my swift kick to Wanda's shin was of a prophylactic nature, intended to make her think twice next time before she insulted our mutual friend.

'Agnes,' Wanda roared, 'was that your fat foot kicking the meat off my bone?'

'W-what?' Agnes said.

'How many times is it now?' Wanda demanded. 'Seven? Eight?'

I gulped. Oops. When would I ever learn to stay out of other people's problems? Agnes was my age, for goodness' sake, she'd been to college, and she wasn't seeing a therapist (although she had every reason to see one). Theoretically she was quite capable of taking care of herself.

'OK, so you busted me,' Agnes said. 'But I only kicked you six times. I think that what we should really be discussing is not my weight, nor your deplorable standards of hygiene; instead it is that fact that Ms Magdalena Portulacca Yoder Rosen is currently investigating the murder of that dead diva, Ramat Sreym, and that the two of us – her very best friends in the entire world – are on her shortlist of suspects.'

FIVE

FRENI HOSTETLER'S RECIPE FOR SHOOFLY PIE

Makes 8 servings

1 nine-inch unbaked pie crust
1½ cups flour
½ cup dark brown sugar
1 teaspoon cinnamon
½ teaspoon nutmeg
Pinch of ground cloves
¼ teaspoon salt
1 stick cold butter (½ cup)
¾ cup water
¾ cup unsulphured molasses
½ teaspoon baking soda

Combine the flour, brown sugar, cinnamon, nutmeg, cloves and salt. Cut the butter into pats and add it to the flour mixture. Using a fork, mash the butter into the flour mixture until you get a texture like coarse crumbs. Combine the water, molasses and baking soda. Pour into the unbaked pie crust, then spoon the crumb mixture onto the liquid. Bake at 375 degrees for thirty-five to forty minutes. Best served at room temperature.

SIX

'That's not true!' I wailed.

Wanda responded immediately. I can only think that at some point in her life she'd taken a correspondence course from the Vice President.

'I'm going to *hair-board* her,' she said, by way of explanation to Agnes, 'unless she explains herself.'

'Excuse me,' I said. Meanwhile, I'd scooted my bony behind so far over that I'd become one with the cheap plywood divide that separated booths one and fourteen.

Wanda cackled maniacally, as extremists are wont to do. 'What I am about to do is remove my hairpins, one by one. There is a child's game like this played with wooden sticks. In the game, eventually the little wooden tower collapses, and whoever pulled out the last stick is the loser. But this won't be a game.

'Oh, no. Eventually, my beautiful French twist, which you uncultured country bumpkins refer to as a hotdog bun and a rat's nest – this vestige of feminine fertility, what the Apostle Paul referred to as a woman's "glory" – this too shall collapse. And when it does, there won't just be a player out of the game, but all of Hernia – in fact, all of Bedford County – is liable to die from the Black Plague.'

Agnes, who was not being pressed into yet another layer of plywood, and who sat farthest from the vermin, chortled.

'You find that funny?' Wanda said. 'Maybe I'll aim my Toppling Tower of Doom in your direction when I come close to pulling the last pin.'

My fluffy friend gulped and turned the color of unbuttered popcorn. 'Gosh, no! It's not funny. It's just that I can't imagine how it is that you know all this stuff – the things we say about your – well, that thingamajig on your head.'

'Besides which,' I said, 'you've got it all wrong. We always alliterate. Copy-editors might hate that, but not readers. For example, dear: we refer to that Pitiful Pile of Parasites on top of your noggin as the Toppling Tower of *Terror* and the Disgusting Doughnut of *Doom*.'

'But not me,' said Agnes in her best teacher's pet voice. 'I never use the doughnut imagery because it makes me hungry.'

Personally, I think that our honesty should have counted for something with Wanda. Like Catholics in their confessional, one traditional Mennonite (*moi*), and one modern Mennonite (Agnes), had put everything we had right out there in the open on the cheap Formica tabletop in an even cheaper plywood booth of a greasy breakfast food restaurant. So how many points do you think Wanda gave us? *Nada*. Zero. *Zilch*. Zed.

'Well, girls, that was certainly enlightening,' Wanda said. 'Too bad it wasn't what I was after. So out comes the first pin.'

It was only a small exaggeration to say that Wanda's hairpins were the size of croquet wickets. But whether they were smaller or larger it's hard to remember, given the stress I was under. In any case, just the act of removing one was enough to start an avalanche of dandruff and assorted animal protein products, the likes of which I choose not to enumerate, lest I trigger a post-traumatic gag response. Suffice it to say that the chances that I would stay and eat breakfast at the Sausage Barn that morning were the same as those for the continued existence of an orb of frozen precipitation in a sinner's place of perpetual punishment. In other words, not much.

Let it be known that I did not crack until the fourth hairpin was pulled from Wanda's swaying stack of vermin-infested keratin. Then I cried 'uncle,' and just so as not to give her complete satisfaction, I added the name of Mama's brother to the word.

'Uncle Harlan!'

'So that means you give up?' Wanda said gleefully. The woman is a card-carrying sadist. Quite possibly she's even a card-carrying nudist – the English English have their quirks, you know.

'Don't press her,' Agnes begged. 'You know our Magdalena. She couldn't be more stubborn if she was the son of a two-headed mule *and* a US Congressman. Please, Wanda, just let her explain why she is investigating us while she is still willing to do so.'

'All right,' Wanda growled. Mercifully she snatched the hair-pins off the table and jammed them back into the structure of destruction.

I smiled pleasantly – as is my wont, I might add. 'Ladies, it is like this. I was living my life, ever so peacefully, like the meek and mild little housewife that I am—'

'Hardly little,' Agnes muttered. 'You're five foot ten.'

'Hardly meek, either,' Wanda said. 'You're like a wounded badger that keeps trying to hug a porcupine.' Actually, Wanda said something cruder, but my mind refuses to go there.

'That is so not true!' I declared. 'For your information, Agnes, I've already shrunk an inch, and I'm as docile as—'

'Ah, ah, ah,' Wanda said, wagging a greasy finger in my face. 'Lying will make your nose grow, and given your already out-of-kilter proportions, I wouldn't do that, Magdalena.'

'Agnes,' I implored. 'Aren't you going to defend me?'

My very best friend squinted before answering. 'Well, your nose is a little long and pointy.'

'*Et tu*, Brutus? OK then, here goes! I was going to spare your feelings, but not anymore. As you both know by now, that despicable – but may she rest in peace – bestselling author, Ramat Sreym was poisoned. Our earnest but not very experienced Chief of Police has asked me to assist him in interviewing a list of potential suspects.'

'Speaking of whom,' Wanda snapped, 'why did you essentially bankroll his transfer here from Charlotte?'

'Yeah,' said Agnes. 'Why?'

'I didn't bankroll anything,' I wailed. Oops. 'I *funded* it,' I said firmly. 'That makes me a *fund*amentalist, just like the two of you.' At that I chuckled pleasantly.

'I resent that implication,' Agnes murmured. 'I am a closet Democrat with such leftist leanings that I am thinking of leaving the Mennonite Church and becoming a Presbyterian.'

'But Jesus was a Mennonite!' I said. Right away I realized that I had misspoken; Jesus was Jewish. After all, Jesus' mother was Jewish, and so was Jesus' father. They even had a Jewish wedding, not a Christian wedding, much to the disappointment of some of his twenty-first century followers.

'Listen up, people,' Wanda said, 'we have to stay on track. At any minute more day labourers are going to come pouring in demanding to be served cheap but delicious children's lunch plates. Magdalena, are you saying that this boy-toy Chief of Police actually thinks that Agnes and I are capable of murder?'

'You and I are not on the list, Wanda, dear; just Agnes. And for your information, I only wanted pancakes.'

Wanda slid from the booth and was on her feet in a flash. 'What in the blazes kind of insult is that? Miss I-Never-Saw-A-Cheesecake-I-Didn't-Eat, Agnes Miller, is on the suspect list, but me, the woman who is so mean that everyone says that she puts gravel in her granola, doesn't rate being a suspect – tell me, how is *that* fair?'

I shivered. 'I don't write the news, I only report it. But for the record, I never heard that bit about the granola.'

'Oh, I did,' said Agnes. 'Jeb Peterson cracked a molar last July on a bowl of Wanda's granola.'

'Nothing lasts forever,' Wanda said, 'including body parts.'

'But a bad reputation lasts longer than a good one, doesn't it?' Agnes said. She was glowing like a Halloween pumpkin with *two* candles inside. 'I've never been a bad girl before. This is kind of fun.'

'Agnes, that's awful,' I said. 'You can't take pleasure in being a suspect in a murder case.'

Wanda's greasy index finger got a workout as she jabbed the air. 'If you get convicted they'll send you to the state penitentiary, where you will undoubtedly have a *boyfriend* named Scarface Sue, or Connie the Cruncher. How does that strike your fancy?'

Agnes clasped her plump hands (with the remarkably slender fingers) and closed her eyes dreamily. 'Well, you know, I have never been able to attract a *real* boyfriend, and now I am forty-nine years old. That's nearly half a century. Hey, maybe it *is* time to try something new.'

Wanda's forefinger ceased moving. 'Agnes may have a point there. After all, she isn't exactly – well, you know. What I mean is, a hard-bitten prison babe is more likely to find her fluffiness appealing. And society, even on the outside, is changing. Heck, the way my marriage is going, maybe I should give it a try.'

'Try, schmie!' I wailed. 'Just because society says it's OK doesn't make it right, and it certainly doesn't mean that you should go ahead and do it. If society said it was OK to jump off Lover's Leap, would you?'

Agnes opened her eyes slowly and smiled. 'Maybe. If Scarface Sue dumped me for Wanda, I might.'

I laughed.

'Hey, watch it.' Wanda laughed as well.

'Wanda,' I said, 'now be a dear and get our orders so I can begin grilling Agnes.'

SEVEN

'But I want to stay and listen,' Wanda whined. 'Please, Magdalena, can't I?'

'Sorry, dear,' I said, 'but this is semi-pseudo police business.'

'Whatever that means. Magdalena, I thought you said we were besties.'

'All right!' Wanda can be so exasperating. For example, I wear a white organza prayer cap because the Bible says that women should keep their hair covered at all times; at that moment, however, this little white cap was practically kept airborne by puffs of steam.

'Be right back!' Wanda raced off into the kitchen to check on our orders, made like a lightning bolt to lock the front door (just in time too) and then was back, seated in the booth beside me before I could perform a private function behind the privacy of a scalloped-edged hanky embroidered with violets.

'Yuck, that's really gross,' Agnes said.

'You had better get used to it, dear,' I said, 'because I'm afraid that you'll be seeing a lot worse than that in prison. Besides, you weren't supposed to look. I ask you, is nothing sacred any more?'

'Magdalena, I am referring to that humongous wad of chewing gum on the side of the booth just above your shoulder.'

'Ach!' Not desirous of dining next to a mound of someone else's masticated mucilage, I scooted all the way over to the aisle.

'What gives?' Wanda said when she returned.

'Your booth has cooties,' Agnes said. 'Really, Wanda, do you *ever* clean in here?'

'Oh, there you are, you little devil!' Wanda reached right over me and snapped that hunk of gum off the wall with a practiced hand. Cheeks bulging, she commenced chewing, but that didn't stop her from talking.

'Go on, Magdalena; grill Agnes like one of the proverbial weenies you're always yapping about when you conduct your silly little investigations.'

Believe me, if looks could kill Wanda would have toppled over dead. I sighed. A wise woman knows when to cut her losses; you know, when to hold them and when to run. I shared this knowledge with a guest who stayed at my inn eons ago by the name of Kenny Rogers. In my warbling soprano voice I even sang these thoughts to a catchy little tune I'd written. Mr Rogers said that he might quote me in a song someday, maybe even use my tune, but since I never listen to secular music I don't know if he ever followed through on that threat.

'Out with it, Magdalena!' Poor Agnes, I couldn't rightly blame her. I wouldn't want to be at the end of my weenie-roasting pole either.

'Calm down.' I took my time removing a small yellow tablet from my oversized, plain brown leather pocket book.

'My, but aren't you the technocrat,' Wanda said.

I smiled pleasantly. 'Really dear, you ought to list sarcasm on your menus as a side dish. As it so happens, I prefer to think of myself as traditional.' I cleared my throat as a symbolic way of cleansing my thoughts of Wanda's rudeness.

'Now, Agnes,' I said, 'in her ghastly tell-all novel, *Butter Safe Than Sorry*, the deceased depicts you as a somewhat-nervous-Nellie-like, anal-retentive roly-poly but fiercely loyal and exceedingly bright friend of the gracious, but less than comely, proprietress of the charming PennDutch Inn. Did that description in any way upset you?'

When Agnes is astounded, her open mouth forms a perfect but very small circle. Imagine a pink Lifesaver candy, if you will. Unfortunately, if she is to speak, this most attractive arrangement is but fleeting.

'*No*,' she said, 'what you just described did not upset me, because clearly *that* woman and I have nothing in common.'

'Harrumph,' Wanda said.

I treated Wanda to a glimpse of my bared and gritted teeth. 'Nobody actually *says* the word "harrumph," Wanda, except in British novels. One is supposed to just clear one's throat.'

'Then consider my throat cleared,' Wanda said. 'The Agnes

character in the book fits the real life one to a T. Ask the real one sitting here about her uncles.'

'What about my uncles?' Agnes said. I suppose that I would have gotten around to that question sooner or later, but frankly I was rather glad that Mrs Buttinski Hemphopple diverted some of the inevitable heat.

'Well, dear,' I said, 'there is the small fact that – no pun intended – both your uncles spend more time naked than Prince Harry.'

'If only they looked like His Royal Hunkiness,' said Wanda, waggling her eyebrows. Given that said brows resembled giant black caterpillars with their antennae intertwined, it was like watching them perform a mating dance. Surely Wanda's unplucked eyebrows are illegal in several Southern states.

'Lust does not become you,' I said to Wanda, merely by way of imparting information.

I turned my full attention back to Agnes. My best friend, my confident, my bulwark against the slings and arrows of whatever life would send our way since we were a pair of giggling lasses (perhaps she more than I), looked absolutely crestfallen. Given that we Mennonites of Amish derivation feel more guilt than Catholics and Jews combined, I wanted to crawl across Wanda's cheap laminate table and clasp Agnes's head to my scrawny bosom.

But I had a job to do, and besides, the same inbreeding that produced the overabundance of guilt genes in my people also made us even less physically demonstrative than the English English (perhaps even more so than the English English upper class), so that I would never actually hug someone in public. There is even a joke that goes: how can one tell if a Mennonite woman is having sex? The answer: she stops moving. Of course, I find that joke offensive and repulsive, albeit somewhat titillating. I knew for a fact that this scenario did not apply to all Mennonite women – well, enough said.

'Agnes,' I said, 'surely you were deeply embarrassed by the way Ramat Sreym portrayed you in her book. Not to mention the fact that she had your uncles leading a nudist parade through the streets of Hernia. A month after the book was published, and had been passed all around the county, you said yourself at the time that you couldn't go anywhere without people snickering behind your back. As I recall, didn't your minister even make some joke about it, like you being the most famous person in the congregation?'

Agnes grew shockingly, inhumanly red. I knew then that she was either going to self-combust with anger at me for reminding her of the horrible humiliation which Hernia had seemed more than happy to heap upon her, or else dissolve into a briny sea of tears.

'Of course, your minister was wrong to say *anything*,' I said quickly.

Agnes stared straight ahead in the way that folks do when they're trying not to cry. Unfortunately for both of us, that meant she was looking directly at me while trying hard not to see me. Trust me; that was a losing proposition given that my Yoder nose has its own zip code.

Meanwhile, Wanda, my second-best friend, tossed her ginormous glob of gum from tonsil to tonsil as if she had a pair of elfin basketball players living in her throat. Frankly, her silence hurt at a time like that. What good is a second-best friend if she can't swoop in and clean up one's messes? I used to do it for my slovenly, slutty sister Susannah all the time without being prompted. I did it because that's what sisters do – that and scream at each other, even if they are demure and quiet on the outside.

Finally, Wanda deigned to speak. 'Magdalena,' she said, 'how could you be so cruel to poor, sweet Agnes?'

'*What?*'

'Just look at how you've embarrassed her, and the dear woman doesn't have a brain in her head. How is she going to fight back?'

'Fight back? Against *what*?'

'Your insults, Magdalena,' Wanda said, 'that's what.'

'But I didn't say anything insulting. I was just—'

'Doing your duty, *jah*?' Wanda said, faking a German accent. 'You are my best friend, Magdalena, but at times like now you make me sick.'

'I don't want to be your *best* friend,' I wailed. 'I want to be your second-best friend.'

Wanda shook her head while the gum wad stayed put. 'No can do, Magdalena. That spot is taken.'

'By whom?'

'By Agnes, of course.'

I have often prayed for miracles, none of which have happened. Trust me, the Good Lord has showered upon me numerous gifts for which I would never have dared to ask. But as in the Hans Christian Anderson fairytale of the mermaid who gave up her tongue for a pair of legs, my biggest blessings came at a great cost.

While I was blessed with the most handsome husband in the entire world, the Babester and his beloved 'Ma' were a package deal. And yes, I am a very wealthy woman, but I earned my money by turning the family farm into a bed and breakfast for the über rich – those folks who think that they can actually buy a cultural experience rather than experience a culture. Tragically, the farm was not mine to transform in this way until *after* my parents died in a vehicle crash in the Allegheny Tunnel, squashed as they were between a tanker truck carrying milk and another truck containing a load of state-of-the-art running shoes.

So then, when dear, sweet Agnes turned her normal shade of pink and her lips momentarily resumed their miniature perfect bow shape, even though I was praying for a miracle I certainly didn't expect one. Even our gum-heaving hostess, Wanda, must not have, because she ducked the second Agnes began to speak.

'Magdalena, you might be the stricter sort of Mennonite, but I am a Mennonite as well. What's more important is that I believe that, as Jesus taught us, we should forgive seven times seventy. So I forgive you for all your manifold sins past and present.'

'You can't!' Wanda cried. At this the wad of gum catapulted from her mouth and landed, smack, dab on the head of an enormous housefly just as it landed on the table in front of us. The masticated matter pinned the unfortunate creature to the table in such a manner that, although it could not fly, it could spin in tight circles whilst buzzing annoyingly. If you ask me, it was the perfect metaphor for Wanda.

'But I can!' Agnes said. To my everlasting gratitude, she squeezed out of her side of the booth and hoisted herself to her feet. 'Come on, Magdalena. We don't need to eat here. I've suddenly lost my appetite for pecan waffles and smoked Virginia ham.'

'But you didn't order pecan waffles and smoked Virginia ham!' Wanda wailed, sounding disconcertingly like me. 'I don't even serve them. Where do you think you are – Cracker Barrel?'

No sooner did she say that than a buzzer attached to her apron sounded, informing us that our correct order of eggs, pancakes, warm maple syrup and sizzling bacon was ready for pickup. Pavlov's dogs had nothing over Agnes and me, who resumed sitting so quickly that our butts hit the benches almost before they left, making the collider in Switzerland redundant.

'Wanda, be a dear,' I said, 'and clean up that atrocious mess on the table. Then disinfect the table – in a spritely manner, of course – before you make haste to retrieve our orders. Cold eggs anywhere are disgusting, but when your pancakes get cold they're like hockey pucks. Just remember, however, that I am a wealthy woman who tips generously for services rendered.'

That last bit was quite true. While I am famous for pinching a penny until it screams, I do reward service people handsomely if they at least attempt to serve in a competent manner. The same holds true for managers who act as their own servers – even if they are old friends with hedgerow eyebrows and potentially hazardous hairdos.

Wanda's glare burned hot enough to keep the Sausage Barn's coffee at just the right temperature all through a delicious lunch. The pancakes were perfect. The bacon was the best that it could be, and even the eggs were exemplary. I was true to my word, and Wanda received such a fat tip that she was tongue-tied when we departed, and hence unable to invite herself along to the next bit of trouble I was about to find myself in.

EIGHT

In the narrow strip of farmland between Buffalo Mountain and Stucky Ridge lies Doc Shafer's farm. He too is some sort of multiple cousin – distant enough that legally we could wed, but on paper the math would have us being closer than siblings, despite the fact that Doc is old enough to be my father. While I hate to give her any credit, that unscrupulous author, Ramat Sreym, did pen something clever when she wrote: 'Oh what a tangled web they weave, when Amish-Mennonites conceive!' Indeed, this is true. The lines on my family tree crisscross over each other in a good number of places, so much so that I have had to use bits of brightly-colored embroidered floss to represent the various links between the branches.

Doc used to be a veterinarian – back in the days when Noah had his ark. He still goes by the title 'Doc' and keeps a few acres of pasture turned over to a lone Jersey cow named Latte and her companion, a black billy goat he calls Ramses. Until a few months ago he had an elderly hound named Old Blue who used to meet me at the top of the long gravel lane, and which, Doc claimed, could smell me coming a half-hour ahead of my arrival. That was a nonsense claim since I was often spontaneous and occasionally showered.

On this particular day it gladdened my heart to find Doc outside tending to a pot of chrysanthemums. When he saw the cruiser approaching with me in it he stood and waved, grinning like any old goat might. When he ascertained that I had Miss Goody-Two-Shoes, Agnes, in tow, the smile morphed into something only a 'Doc-watcher' might call a grimace. But Doc is ever the gentleman, and he would never hurt a lady's feelings. Besides, he is just as closely related to Agnes as he is to me, maybe even closer. The rumour that Doc and Agnes are one and the same person is just that: a rumour. Only a disturbed woman with an overactive imagination, and an impossible mother-in-law, could ever think up such a lame story.

Now where was I? Oh, yes – the old man was delighted to see me, and I him. Doc dropped his garden scissors and bottle of green insecticide, and threw his not-so-withered arms around me. When he was a veterinarian, Doc could shoe a horse, *and* throw a horse around with their shoes, so he's still pretty ripped for an old geezer. If you closed your eyes tightly you might even think that you were being hugged by a man in his forties, not an octogenarian. Doc even smells as if he's hung on to a bit of testosterone. Yes, I know, nowadays one can get a prescription from a medical doctor and roll the stuff under one's armpits like a deodorant, but Doc is a big believer in homemade remedies. If I were a betting woman, which again, I am not, I would wager that Doc and his billy goat, Ramses, smell rather much alike.

I was not surprised when the first words Doc said were, 'Ladies, you're just in time for dessert!' He didn't even mention Hernia's cruiser, but then, why should he? In recent years, it seemed, I'd spent more time in it than out.

Of course, we had just eaten pancakes soaked in syrup, but there isn't a Mennonite alive who will turn down dessert. Unlike Roman Catholics, we Mennonites never preached about the Seven Deadly Sins. When I was growing up the word gluttony sounded like a province somewhere near Tuscany. In those days, when Spandex was not yet invented but girdles were de rigueur, we ate until it hurt, and then we ate some more. We were even very fond of a dessert called Girdle Buster Pie.

'What are you serving?' Agnes said. The woman believes in staying informed.

'Girdle Buster Pie,' Doc said.

'Lead the way, old man,' I said.

Seeing as how the three of us were inbred Mennonites, we wasted no further time with unnecessary pleasantries like hugs, kisses or handshakes. Those are all ways of spreading diseases and, if you ask me, they should no longer be practised in casual situations.

As for the custom of shaking hands with someone just before a meal, or holding hands during grace, those customs should be outlawed, I tell you! Outlawed! The Good Lord gave us the sense to identify the cold virus and know that it is spread via hands, and then we turn around and mock him by spreading the virus while we thank God for our food? For shame!

'Earth to Magdalena,' Doc said. 'You almost tripped going up the top step.'

'Forgive me, Doc,' I said. 'I was off on another rampage.'

'That's why we love you,' he said with a chuckle.

'Well,' I said, 'you might not be singing the same tune when you hear why it is we've come.'

Doc opened the door with a flourish and ushered us in. His dear wife, Emma, had passed away eighteen years ago, but you wouldn't know it. The house is as neat as a pin. There is not a speck of dust – anywhere! Believe me; I checked using the hem of my white cotton slip when Doc went to get our desserts. And the overstuffed chairs still have doilies pinned to the backs and armrests. What man would do that, unless he was still in mourning for his wife and didn't want to change the look of things?

On the other hand, Doc is as randy as an old goat – perhaps because of the goat. Incidentally, Ramses is exceedingly randy: I have observed that billy attempting to do things with the Jersey cow that are certainly against the laws of nature! As for Doc's inclinations, about five years after his beloved Emma's passing, he started putting the moves on me. *Moi!* His cousin: his many-times-over-practically-himself cousin! True, I was in my late thirties then, the time in a woman's life when she is at her most desirable. At that age both her body, and brain, are in full bloom.

At any rate, when Doc returned with slabs – not slices – of pie, and mountains – not scoops – of vanilla ice cream, and we'd taken a few bites, raved and had a chance to put our sweets temporarily aside on wooden trays, I went fishing. Please do not think I am being mean, for I only report the facts: Agnes did not set her dessert even temporarily aside.

'Doc, dear,' I said, 'you are, without a doubt, the most intuitive man in all of Hernia.'

'Yup. Been that way for eighty-four years since May.'

'Wow,' Agnes said, her mouth full of pie, 'you don't look a day over eighty-three.'

Doc slapped his knee with delight. 'You hear that, Magdalena? Finally, your wit has some competition!'

Agnes swallowed, licked her finger and then ran it around her plate, collecting crumbs. 'On second thought, Doc,' she said, 'were you calling me a halfwit?'

Doc roared with laughter. 'This one's a corker.'

'Then maybe she should put a cork in it,' I said, perhaps a mite unkindly.

'Tsk, tsk,' said Doc. 'That sort of behaviour is beneath you, Magdalena.'

'Is it?' Well, yes, of course it was, but I was feeling ignored and rightly so. *I* was Doc's special friend; it was *me* who'd had to fend off his advances all these years, thanks to the goat juice he injected in himself. There I was, all decked out in what could pass for a policewoman's uniform – an outfit of authority – and he couldn't even pretend to flirt with me first.

'You know that it is,' Doc said. 'Now be a good girl and tell an old man why he should receive a delightful surprise after lunch when all his contemporaries are either dead or sleeping.'

'Or playing golf,' Agnes said. 'Have you ever been to Florida, Doc? I hear that you can play golf all year round down there.'

'Nah,' Doc said. 'Too many widows down there. I reckon the competition would be fierce. Besides, I don't much care for golf. Badminton – now that's a gentleman's game.'

'Ooh, I just love badminton,' Agnes squealed. What a falsehood. I knew for a fact that Agnes hadn't played the game since high school, which was over three decades ago. On the flip side, so to speak, I had just recently caught a glimpse of her naked uncles playing badminton, and the urge to poke out my mind's eye had yet to abate. I still shuddered to think where I'd seen that shuttlecock land.

Doc smiled warmly at Agnes – perhaps too warmly. He might even have leered.

'Terrific,' he said. 'There is nothing like a good workout. Shall we make it your place or mine?'

I stood and waved my arms like the person who guides the jets in and out of the gates at the airport in Pittsburgh. 'Hold it right there, you loathsome, lecherous lothario!'

'Magdalena, I'm shocked,' Agnes said. 'I can't believe you said such ugly things to an elderly gentleman like Doc Shafor.'

'You take that back, young lady,' Doc said with a wink.

'Yeah, take it back and apologize,' Agnes said.

'He's speaking to you, dear,' I said.

'*What?*' Agnes said.

'You just offended this sweet-talking senior swain who, as you'll recall, did the mattress mambo with the mother-in-law from you-know-where.'

'She means *her* mother-in-law,' Doc was quick to point out, 'not mine.'

'Oh,' Agnes said, and set down her fork. 'Yes, I remember now. You dated Mother Malaise, didn't you?'

Doc grimaced dramatically. 'Guilty as charged. But in my defence, she was Ida Rosen back then, and her elevator stopped at more floors than it does now.'

'I beg your pardon?' Agnes said.

Fortunately I am multilingual and butted in. 'He means that she wasn't quite as whackadoodle as she is now.'

'Oh.' Agnes nodded slowly as comprehension set in. 'But please, Doc, go back one step; how did I offend you?'

'You referred to him as elderly,' I said. I pretended to sniff the stuffy air of Doc's sitting room. 'Why, the scent of virility is positively overpowering.'

'Would that it were,' Doc said.

'Down, boy,' I said. 'My companion is a lady who has somehow managed to live a life even more sheltered than mine.'

'Not for want of trying,' Agnes said.

'Which is a pity,' I said, 'because she'll try just about everything.'

The old goat's eyes gleamed. 'I suppose that Magdalena has filled you in on my many attempts to woo her throughout the years.'

'Indeed, she has,' Agnes said.

Doc sighed, overly dramatic as usual. 'I always offered her food. *Plus*, I dished out wisdom whenever I had any to give.'

'You were always there for me, Doc,' I said.

'I could be there for you, Doc – I mean, *here*,' Agnes said.

'Spare me,' I groaned. 'You two should get a room already. This is obscene.'

'Whatever do you mean?' Agnes demanded, turning rhubarb pink. 'I'll have you know that I'm a good Christian woman and that I resent your insinuation. I meant just what I said, simply that I could be here to comfort him on his journey as a poor, grieving widower.'

'Oh, I see,' I said. 'You could clasp his hoary head against your ample, heaving bosom, all the while muttering sweet nothings into his mesquite-choked ears. Why, that's as plain as a winter's day above the Arctic Circle.'

'Your references are so arcane,' Agnes said. 'Someone who knew you as well as I do might conclude that you're showing off.'

'Heaven forefend, friend,' I said, feigning offence. 'I only wish that the widower with the wandering eye should find contentment with yesteryear's maiden, now blossomed into a full-bodied, voluptuous woman who is more than eager to grab life by the horns – oops, perhaps not the image I was going for, but I'm sure you get it.'

'Huh?' Agnes said.

'She said that she approves of us dating,' Doc said to Agnes.

A sly, happy, smile spread slowly across the space allotted for it between Agnes' apple cheeks. Suddenly Agnes remembered her manners; she was the lady, and must therefore always play the part of the prey on the verge of escape.

'Really, Doc,' Agnes said with a wave of a plump hand, but one with long, shapely fingers, 'you say the funniest things. And even if that were true, I'm sure that you have better things to do with your time. I know that I have work to do at my church, feeding the volunteers who are renovating the Sunday school rooms. These are big, strong men who are doing the renovating. Did I mention that some of them are young, strapping men with bulging muscles and abdomens that are rippled like Freni Hostetler's washboard?'

'Really, Agnes,' I said, 'it is one thing to signal to the male of the species that you are receptive to his advances, but quite another to build an autobahn that leads to your bed.'

I knew that the old geezer, forsooth, was finding our verbal sparring to be a great turn-on (to use the modern, vulgar expression). It would please me greatly if the ancient, but not yet decrepit Doc Shafor and the portly, but surprisingly not-so-prim Agnes Miller hooked up (another vulgarism) and did the horizontal hootchie-cootchie. Yes, of course, I would insist that they get married first, and that I be the one to give away the bride with the rhubarb complexion. Meanwhile, her uncles could watch the ceremony whilst wearing straitjackets from the front row of the church if they wished, or even in the altogether, but from closed-circuit television from over at the State Mental Hospital in Harrisburg.

I would also ask my husband Gabe, who is a doctor, to speak with Doc about discontinuing the use of male goat sex hormones. I was forty-eight when I gave birth to my eight pounds of bouncing joy, and that was cutting it close. Agnes is nearing fifty, and even if it is possible for her to get pregnant, she may see the wisdom in refraining from genetically reproducing. On the other hand, there is no accounting for human nature. It worries me to think of the myriad possibilities that could emerge from our limited, tangled family lines, coupled with the advanced ages of both parents. Add to that mix a black goat, whose unnatural love for a Jersey cow would surely put him in prison in the state of South Carolina, and possibly parts of Utah.

In the meantime, Doc had drawn up his dwindling pects (despite the goat injections) to their full extent, so that he looked somewhat like a cartoon drawing of a bantam rooster. Rather than cutting a pathetic profile, his head-on confrontation with his waning virility made him come across as a bit heroic – at least, in my eyes, on this *one* occasion.

'So, how about it, Agnes?' he said. 'Do you want to go out?'

'W-What? With you?'

'Ask him to bring his shadow along,' I whispered. 'It might spook folks if he leaves it at home, and besides, that way you'll have a chaperone.'

'Y-Yes,' Agnes said. 'B-Bring your chaperone along.' By now she was as red as a beet salad, and shaking like the paint-mixer at Home Depot. That simile, by the way, is an original Magdalenaism, even though I've read that it was a cliché.

'Then that settles it,' said Doc. 'We're an item.'

'Not yet,' I said. I stood, stretching my narrow frame to its full five feet and ten inches. 'Doc, since you are such an accomplished mind-reader, surely you know why I am here.'

Doc snighted, which is halfway between a snort and a sigh. 'Well, since you are driving the familiar cruiser today, I suppose you want to ask me questions about the recently departed, and oh-so-voluptuous, Ramat Sreym. The woman with a thousand graces, and whose face could launch a thousand ships. Now, as for her lips, they were like a thousand pillows of sweetness—'

'Stop!' Agnes cried. 'Magdalena, make him stop!'

'You heard her, Doc,' I said. 'That was disgusting. You went way overboard with your numbers. Next time, make it a "dozen graces," etc. You almost rotted my teeth with all that sugar.'

'Is that all you have to say to him?' Agnes demanded.

'No, dear, of course not,' I said. 'Doc, you obviously were very attracted to that woman. Did the two of you do the, uh, recliner chair rumba?'

Doc laughed so hard that his dentures slipped and he had to take a moment to fit them back into place. 'The recliner chair rumba?' he finally said. 'Now that one I've never heard of. For a woman who believes that sex standing up is a sin, because it might lead to dancing, you can be mighty creative with your positions. However, I'll pass on this one; it doesn't sound comfortable.'

'Don't knock it until you've tried it,' I growled. 'Now back to you and the deceased.'

Doc waved a well-weathered hand. 'A gentleman never tells.'

'He can, however, brag,' I said.

'Good point,' Doc said. 'In that case – and please forgive me, lovely Agnes – if one were to think of Ramat as a hill and me as a hiker, then allow me to say that the view from atop the hill was most disappointing, and I never mounted it again.'

I scribbled furiously into my wee yellow pad. 'I see. When was it that you went hiking?'

'That would be the first time she came to Hernia – the time that she left *alive.* About a week after she ensconced herself in *your* PennDutch Inn, I met her at Yoder's Corner Market putting the screws to our mutual cousin, Sam. So help me, Agnes, I had no control over what happened next; it was like lightning striking a dry haystack.'

'Hah,' I said. 'Agnes, wasn't I just saying the other day that using too much bleach will turn *any* mop of unruly hair into an unsightly haystack?'

Agnes giggled and nodded. 'You did, in fact.'

'Then make that as if lightning was striking twin haystacks,' Doc said and waggled his eyebrows.

'Don't be lewd in front of Agnes, Doc,' I said. 'Cruelty does not become you. My point was that a bleached blond is just that. The drapes don't match the carpet, and you know ding-dang well what I mean.'

'Well, I don't,' Agnes said. 'Why have we suddenly segued into home decorating?'

'Later,' I snapped, but not too unkindly. 'Doc, do you see what an innocent, sweet woman you're dealing with? You should be ashamed of yourself!'

Doc looked positively crestfallen. Creating sexual tension was his forte, even if following through on his near constant innuendo had never been tested by me. I'm sure that Doc did not intend to hurt Agnes, and when he realized that this was the case, he in turn felt bad. On the other hand, his inability to boast about his conquest of Ramat Sreym had to be painful for him. Bantam roosters live to strut.

'I'm not stupid, Magdalena,' he said. 'The late, not so great, author was clearly not shot, stabbed, or bludgeoned – thus the vehicle of her sudden and quite suspicious demise was undoubtedly some type of poison. I have no doubt that the Boy Wonder from Charlotte gave you a list of suspects of who might possibly have poisoned the infamous lady from who-only-knows where, and that my name is on the list. Yes, you don't suspect me in the least, but you had to satisfy His Youthfulness and pay me a visit and you brought your beautiful sidekick along because you want to brush her off on me, despite the fact that she is the second brightest person in Hernia and would make a very helpful addition to your team.'

'You hear that, Magdalena?' Agnes hissed. That time she did it without an 'S,' as just many other authors write – but quite wrongly so.

'I heard it,' I said.

'But wait,' Doc said. 'Like I said, you were hoping to dump her off on me.'

'I was not,' I said.

'You were so,' he said.

'Not,' I said.

'So,' he said.

'*So*,' I said.

'Not – hey, that's not fair,' he said. 'You can't switch like that.'

'I can, and I did,' I said. 'Look, it's obvious that the two of you are meant for each other, just like a pound of ground beef and a tin of mushroom soup. Add some macaroni and you have dinner for six.'

Doc snorted to let me know what he thought of tinned mushroom soup, but he edged closer to Agnes. She, by the way, was fluttering her eyelashes uncontrollably, and was *not* moving away.

'Agnes, dear heart,' I said kindly, 'no one has ever achieved liftoff using just their eyelashes; you'll need wings as well.'

Doc kept getting closer to Agnes but he was still looking at me. 'Just so you know,' he said, 'if I'd killed that woman, I wouldn't have been as stupid as to leave her body around where it could be discovered immediately. I'd have given her a much slower-acting poison, or else used another means altogether.'

Doc is mostly bald now, but what hair he has is snow white. Against the skin of his right temple a raised vein was throbbing. Perhaps I had gone too far by accusing him; perhaps this strong physical manifestation was from stress – he was going to *plotz* at any moment, and I would be charged with his death as well.

'Doc, I – I—'

He held out his hands. Given our shared ancestry, the gesture was meant to prevent me from hugging him first, not give me comfort. I immediately understood, and smiled my relief.

'Magdalena,' he said, 'you're such a bossy pants, and I'm such a stubborn old fool: I have to make sure that we keep to the same script.'

'Indeed; it would be folly to forget.'

'Who else is on your list?'

'Uh – well, it's funny that you just mentioned our mutual cousin, Sam. His wife, Dorothy, is on the list.'

Doc nodded vigorously. 'I'm surprised Sam isn't on there as well. You can't describe a man's wife as being so fat that a crane was needed to lift her from her bed, when all it took was a bulldozer to give it a gentle tap and out she rolled. I don't care how ravishingly beautiful that bleached-blond foreigner was, or how mesmerizing I found her honey-dipped tongue – or even the words it spoke. If that woman had written hurtful words of that caliber – because my Emma was an itty bitty thing – about my beloved wife, I'd have lassoed her, tied her up good and dipped her in a sheep tank. Then I'd have sheared those long, bottle-blond tresses off her head with my sheep shears and branded her tight little buttocks with a cattle brand.'

'Shame, shame, shame!' I cried. 'Doc, how could you?'

'Aw, come on, Magdalena,' Doc said. 'You know that I was only exaggerating to make a point. In real life I wouldn't hurt a flea – which is probably why some folks say I'm not the best veterinarian they've ever dealt with.'

'Oh, stop the pity party,' I said. 'I'm talking about hurting Agnes's feelings,' I said, jabbing the air in Agnes's direction. 'The Bible tells us not to covet thy neighbor's ass. I'm pretty sure we shouldn't be describing it to others in great detail either.'

'But Magdalena,' Agnes said, poking me and not the air, 'you're misinterpreting the word "ass."'

'Ssh!' I said. 'Quiet, girl; I know what I'm doing.'

'And doing it very well too, I might add,' Doc said with a wry smile.

'Thank you, kind sir.' I gave stout Agnes just the gentlest of pushes. Although she was far from weighing four hundred pounds like Sam Yoder's real-life wife Dorothy weighed, Agnes was not moved in the slightest by my gentle push. Trust me, I had no intention of ever toppling my bestie, but should push ever come to shove it would be helpful to know just how much force I'd need to apply.

If Doc was any the wiser, he didn't let on. Neither did Agnes. When I drove away the two of them looked as content as cats that had just finished licking out bowls of heavy cream. At any second I expected them to start licking each other; that's when my belly would roil. Don't get me wrong; we Mennonites are very sexual creatures. We'll submit to our husbands two or three times a year, whether it messes up our hair or not, and on a bad year, we'll even submit four times. Premarital sex, however, is a very big sin – not as bad as adultery (which is right up there with dancing), but a big 'no-no' nonetheless.

One thing I need to make as clear as the space between my ears is that I was not trying to push Agnes and Doc into bed with each other before the bonds of marriage had a chance to trap them into the purgatory that is marriage for all eternity. Marriage is sacred; it is certainly not for sissies, or repeat-offenders. What I was doing was trying to push them into holy matrimony. True, Doc was so old that he could remember when the rocks in his yard were still sand, but who knew, he could still have another eighty-five years left in him.

What I didn't do was pay much attention to the road after leaving Agnes at Doc's farm. There is a particularly sharp bend in it called Dead Man's Curve for a reason: six Amish children perished when the horse-drawn buggy that they were riding in was rear-ended by a motorist driving just fifty miles an hour.

When I flew around Dead Man's Curve that afternoon my speedometer read sixty-five, and when I saw the buggy in front of me I thought I was going to faint.

NINE

Tell me, what should one do if one knows unequivocally that one is going to plough into an Amish buggy and kill everyone in it, and most likely the poor horse as well? Should one just close one's eyes, pray, and pump the brakes as if one were inflating an air mattress?

When death is a *fait accompli*, perhaps all that pumping is unwarranted. Perhaps I should have kept my eyes open and enjoyed my brief time sailing through the air. After all, *Nearer My God to Thee* has always been one of my favorite hymns, and being airborne, as I was, I was substantially closer for a second or two. Besides, this was my first opportunity to observe the landscape from that altitude.

The amazing thing is, however, that I killed no one – not even the horse. Neither did I demolish the buggy. In fact, there was no horse and buggy. There was only my very fertile imagination *or* – and I beg you to consider this – the buggy and the Amish family riding in it were an apparition. These were not a product of my imagination, mind you, but ghosts. Genuine Apparition-Americans.

For the record, I am not the only person to have seen the Kirschbaum family and their horse after that tragic accident that claimed their lives eight years ago, either. To my knowledge there have been at least a dozen sightings reported by sober, church-going adults during daylight hours, and perhaps three times that many at night or when it's foggy. The rate is, of course, much higher amongst drinkers. In our community the only folks who drink are a handful of Baptists, nine Methodists, two Anglicans and our teenagers during their *rumschpringe*, which is a church-sanctioned period of rebellion.

When my borrowed police cruiser had screeched to a stop on the shoulder of the narrow road, I allowed myself a moment to recover my emotions. I will admit, even, to swearing.

'Ding, dang, dong!' I said. Usually that is as bad as I can

swear, but this time I was so shaken up that the Devil made me reach into the darkest part of my soul and add a new phrase to my compendium of evil expressions. 'Dang nab it!'

Having quite gotten all the bile out of my system I continued driving through the bucolic countryside of southern Bedford County. Mama – may she rest in peace – used to say that there was no scent more pleasant than that of road apples on asphalt warmed by autumn sunshine. Mama was two sandwiches shy of a picnic, if you get my drift. Cow pies have it all over road apples in the bouquet department; ask any farm girl, just not the rich horsey types who have somebody else shovelling it for them.

Now where was I? Ah yes, I was lulled into a peaceful state of semi-somnolence by the pervasive smell of thoroughly ruminated grass when at last I saw the handsome sign that announced Hernia, Population 2,103 and a half. Just beyond the sign was our sturdy new bridge that spans Slave Creek. Until very recently Hernia was a homogenous settlement of Amish and Mennonites of Amish descent. Then Baptists began to trickle in (they *cannot* be stopped!), followed by Methodists and even a few hip-waggling, dancing Presbyterians. Then along came an Episcopalian (which is American for Anglican), then another, and then even a family of Muslims. Soon we might have to admit Roman Catholics and atheists. The more the merrier, I say, but not everyone feels this way; there are some who think that we should evict the Presbyterian gal who started all the dancing. That last idea is a moot point because the guilty gal is no longer living in Hernia. She has run off, who knows where, and is aiding and abetting a man accused of murder.

Did I mention that the dirty dancer also happens to be my baby adoptive sister, Susannah? I know it was my intent to leave out the fact that her killer boyfriend (I know in my bones that he's guilty) was my biological brother, Melvin Stoltzfus. Although we emerged from the womb of the same evil Elvina Stoltzfus, I more or less resemble the common human being, whereas Melvin is an almost exact copy of a praying mantis – a bit larger perhaps, and a few shades less green. It wasn't the bony carapace of his chest, his wire-thin neck, or his tiny nub of a head that I found so disturbing, but the fact that his bulbous eyes were capable of moving in opposite directions simultaneously.

What is it about truly evil men that some women find so attractive? In my brother's case, he has dozens of women who call themselves Melvinites! The truly sad part is that many of these are ex-Mennonites – although two of them used to be Baptists, and one even claims that she started out as an atheist! Ha! I should think that it would be the other way around. At any rate, these poor, miserable, misbegotten souls literally worship Melvin. They claim to have started a religion that they call Melvinism, with its own set of religious rules, and they've actually assembled a book of hymns praising Melvin.

Just last week I read in the *Hernia Herald* that the Melvinite Missionary Society baptized its first two *male* members in Slave Creek. No circumcisions were required of these men either. The self-styled nuns at the Convent of the Sisters of Perpetual Apathy were anything but apathetic about this new development. My mother-in-law, Mother Malaise, flew into such a rage that for once I could discern immediately that she was upset about something that had happened in the outside world, instead of just expressing her intense hatred of me.

How ironic was that? The village of Hernia had been founded by my Amish ancestors who had fled religious persecution in Switzerland. Now a good many of their descendents were at war with each other, battling over false doctrines that were so ridiculous that it was amazing neither side had yet to field a call from the *Jerry Springer Show*. Just what business was this of mine? any sane person might ask. Why was I so hot and bothered by this *meshuggeneh* behaviour? *Because I owned Hernia*. That's right.

I was the little red hen who found the grain of wheat, who planted that grain, who watered and tilled the soil, who harvested and milled the wheat that grew on that stalk, who took the milled flour and kneaded it into dough and who baked the dough into bread. Then, because I was a good Christian woman, and humble to boot, I shared that bread with all the residents of Hernia. In other words, I had been fortunate enough to work my slender fingers to the bone, thanks to the PennDutch Inn, all the while fleecing the über rich who wanted to buy an authentic American folk experience. When all was said and done, having lined my pockets, it was expected of me to empty them for the good of others.

Thus it was that the citizens of Hernia received free utilities, police protection and an ambulance service, as well as regularly maintained streets and roads, and extra teachers and aids in the schools at all grade levels – courtesy of *moi*. I relate this not to brag; *au contraire*, with ownership came great responsibility. The death of that voluptuous temptress, Ramat Sreym, had clearly thrown our new Chief of Police Toy into a tizzy, and thus it had fallen upon my thin shoulders to ferret out the foreigner's killer.

Suddenly I had a terrible, chilling thought that sent shards of ice coursing through my veins. I mean that literally – in the same way that everyone else misuses this poor, tired word. What *if*, I thought, Miss Sreym's killer had been none other than the nefarious Melvin Stoltzfus? What if her murderer had been the slime-ball subject of a hundred hymns, the messiah to three hundred mush-brained New Agers who laughed at the Holy Bible, but then had the temerity to write one of their own? (And this long after King James is dead, mind you!)

The second I'd fully processed this thought I decided not to cross Slave Creek and enter my sweet little village of Hernia. Instead I pressed the pedal to the metal and virtually – not literally, for goodness' sake – flew the miles back up Route 96 to my farm and the PennDutch Inn. In a spray of paint-pocking gravel I skidded to stop inches from the kitchen steps.

'Batten down the hatches!' I cried as I burst through the door – again, not *literally*.

Unfortunately my poor family is quite used to my, uh, I like to think of them as heightened states of awareness. My husband, who was feeding the baby supper, barely glanced away from the spoon in his hand.

'Hi, dear,' he said. 'Supper's ready.' Then quite needlessly he added the following: 'As you can well see.'

As for Little Jacob, he opened his mouth wider and waved his arms in order to get his father's attention. The precious little tot didn't even look at me. The same thing went for the sweet, elderly cousin who had apparently decided to stay on for supper; she was too busy eating to turn around. Now that wasn't like Freni at all. Most probably she was having trouble again (in her mind, at least) with that 'too tall' daughter-in-law of hers, Barbara, who hailed from Iowa where nobody ever did anything right, least of all raise children correctly.

The first thing I did was to sigh dramatically to let everyone know just how disappointed I was in their responses to my dramatic arrival. In a world of 'tit for tat,' in which I don't know how to tat, and have a shamefully small bosom, I can at least sigh loudly. That is my forte.

The next thing I did was hook the strap of my handbag over a wooden peg before turning my attention to hooking the screen door and locking the sturdy main one. Being a strong believer in the 'more is better' school of thought, I grabbed an empty side chair and crammed it under the doorknob.

At that my Dearly Beloved put down the spoonful of peas that was headed toward my baby's yawning maw and gave me a closer look.

'You didn't wreck the car, hon, did you?'

'*What?* How did you get that from "batten down the hatches"?'

'Oh, is that what you said? I didn't quite hear you; perhaps because you just spoke four words, all of which were wasted on me. Anyway, you look a bit dishevelled.'

Dishevelled? Well, la-dee-dah! That was a bit harsh coming from a man who supposedly looked like the actor Cary Grant at the height of his film career, and who couldn't look dishevelled even if he'd been run over by a steam-roller whilst napping on a bed of nails. At that moment, while feeding the baby, Gabe was wearing one of Freni's crisply starched white aprons over a sky-blue shirt and cream-colored slacks. While there may have been food on Little Jacob, his high chair and the floor, my Dearly Beloved, as ever, remained annoyingly pristine.

'Your brand of flattery might not get you everywhere that you wish to go, kind sir,' I said. I've heard it said that sarcasm is the weapon of choice for the weak-minded; it's also been said that I have an uncommonly sharp tongue. I choose not to believe either of these two sentiments, nor a third which states that I might, at times, be a wee bit opinionated.

It was then that my dear, sweet cousin Freni Hostetler deigned to turn her stout frame and give me the once-over, except that it *wasn't* Freni! As I hope I have made very clear, normally I am not a swearing woman. Guests who swear are subjected to steep fines and the most unpleasant of chores. It is a sad and broken world that we live in, after all. That said, over the years in my career as an innkeeper I have heard just about every curse word imaginable, and sad as it may sound, absorbed a few of them into my vocabulary by the process of osmosis.

'Holy guacamole!' I cried, having been shocked – literally, this time – out of my shoes. I stuffed my boat-sized feet back into my enormous black brogans. 'You're not Freni, you're my mother-in-law! Mother Mayonnaise.'

'Her name is Mother *Malaise*, not Mayonnaise,' my Dearly Beloved said. 'Please, Mags, don't cause trouble. I asked her over because Freni had to leave early on account of a headache and I needed someone to watch Little Jacob while I finished getting supper ready – oh, and milked both cows.'

'Yah, und he milk de cows, vhile you vas off gallivanting wiz your fat friend, vhat dat has ze nekkid ooncles.' Mother Malaise, aka Ida spoke, all the while nodding with the rhythm and regularity of a sewing machine needle ploughing its way through leather.

When I look back on that moment, I am embarrassed to think that my first thought was: how lucky I am that I was not born into some nomadic tribal society that required hosts to be generous with their guests for three days. My second thought was: why is this self-styled Mother Superior not wearing her wimple? Had she finally seen the light and come back to the bright side? Those questions, however, could wait.

'Look, dear,' I said. 'You can't get away with calling my friend fat because she's not; she's horizontally-challenged with a pleasing spherical shape. You wouldn't like it if I called you short, when in fact you're merely squat and built like a bulldog on steroids – although you're a bit hairier and with a longer tail.'

Mother Malaise was not amused by my analogy. Quite possibly she would have huffed and puffed and blown my house down had not the Babester come to its defence, by first coming to hers. Oh, yes, my dear husband always picked his mother's side over mine in a squabble. When I told him that even Jesus said that a man should leave his mother to 'join with his wife,' my Jewish husband had the *chutzpah* to remind me that *his* Bible didn't contain such an injunction! *Oy vey*, what's a Mennonite wife supposed to do?

'Don't be giving Ma a hard time,' Gabe said. 'She's just helping out. So please, Mags, don't start anything.'

'"Don't *start* anything"? How is this *my* fault?'

'You started by calling her a name.'

'Mayonnaise? That was cute.'

'Cute my patooty, you knew that would get her goat.'

'I did? Are you sure? But speaking of goats, dear, I spent the afternoon over at Doc Shafer's house, turning the screws on his thumbs. Meanwhile, my bestie, you know, Agnes Miller, and old Doc fell head over heels in love with each other and started making the most pitiful, mewling sounds you ever did hear. They sounded like a box of newborn kittens—'

The more I embellished, the more I sensed Ida being drawn into my tale and the more I resented it. Well, if Ida wanted a tale, that's what she was going to get.

'So Jack had no choice but to trade them to the man with the magic beans. But when Jack's mother saw the beans, she got so angry that she tossed them out the window. The very next day, when Jack woke up and looked out the window, he saw a new car—'

'Stop it, Mags,' Gabe said sternly.

'Yah, *shtop*,' said his precious ma.

How can I maintain a gentle, peaceful heart when I have to put up with a mother-in-law who grates on me more than a thousand chalk boards and ten thousand fingernails ever could? I try, believe me, I do. Ultimately I know that the problem is mine, but still, as I have already intimated, I still can't help but think that my Dearly Beloved, who was once a renowned New York City heart surgeon, is still tied to his mother by her apron strings.

'Yah, so I *shtop* already,' I said.

'You see?' Gabe said. 'There you go again, making fun of her accent. That's just cruel; that's not the Magdalena I married.'

'The Devil made me do it,' I said. 'That's something you wouldn't know about, since you Progressive Jews don't believe in the Devil. But speaking of the Devil, the reason you shouldn't be sitting there, heaping coals of fire upon *my* head whilst shovelling peas into my baby's mouth is that I have reason to believe that the Devil incarnate may be back in town.'

'Like I alvays said, dis von is meshuggeneh,' Ida said. She

had the 'noive' to say this without turning around, and while making circles next to her oversized head with a stubby finger.

'Hey,' I said. 'I just noticed; why isn't that one wearing a wimple?'

'*That one* is my mother, Magdalena. She deserves our respect.'

'Zee vimple eez dare-tee,' Ida said. She paused to slurp whatever it was in the bowl in front of her. 'I vas tinking dat you vould vash eet for me.'

I was about to make a perhaps not-so-helpful suggestion when my sweet baby's father came to his ma's rescue. 'Mags, are you saying that your brother may be back in town?'

What a shame that it has taken me nearly half a century to learn that by gritting one's teeth, all that one truly accomplishes is wearing down the enamel, perhaps even piling grit on the floor which, of course, results in the need to vacuum. On the other hand, I would never truly say what was on my mind, seeing as how I really do struggle with what is right, and what is wrong, but even though I am wrong, more often than not I am right. At least I try to do right, and I don't judge others, like some people I know.

'Please do not call *him* my brother,' I said. 'We weren't raised together, and for his entire miserable life – ever since he was hatched from his mantis egg sac – he has been my nemesis. Besides, if you insist on a family connection, then remember that Melvin the Monster is also our son's biological uncle.'

'No vay!' Ida shouted. She still had not given me the courtesy of looking in my direction.

'Yes, Ma, it's true,' Gabriel said. 'I told you that fact before Mags and I got married.'

'Nu? I shlept since den.'

'Good for you, dear,' I said. 'I've been schlepping around all day; what does that have to do with anything?'

'*Dumkoph*,' Ida muttered. 'I *shleep* at night; I dun't *schlep* at night. I shlept since I herd dat you vas dee sister of Melvin zee killer.'

'Whatever,' I said charitably, as I hardly rolled my eyes. 'The point is that Ramat Sreym, the gorgeous, voluptuous, if somewhat vacuous beauty from a breakaway nation of the former USSR – or so I am guessing – stood a more than fifty-fifty chance of having met Her Maker at the hands of repugnant, repelling, rapacious—'

'Rat?' Ida said.

'Please, dear, I'm on a roll,' I said. I paused and counted to three. 'Rat,' I said. 'Ramat's book maligned Melvin's birth mother, his religion and, above all, his own sweetheart, my adoptive sister, Susannah.'

Gabe set down the silver baby spoon. 'What you say makes a great deal of sense. But tell me, hon, what were *you* doing across the road at the convent this morning, interrogating Ma? You scared her half to death.'

A faint snicker may have escaped my tightly sealed lips. Erring on the side of justice, I slapped my own face – albeit lightly. Surely, somewhere, someone gives me credit for being just about the only person on earth who lightly slaps their own face in chastisement.

'Puh-leeeze,' I said, 'Attila the Hun in drag couldn't scare your ma. For your information, dearest, I was merely observing formalities. Police Chief Toy gave me a list of individuals who he wanted eliminated as suspects right out of the gate, and your mother's name was one of them.'

The foregoing statement wasn't a lie; it was a 'shadow truth.' A 'shadow truth,' by the way, is a very clever invention of mine in which one is free to embellish a subject, just as long as the essence of that subject has not been fundamentally altered. Just think how much dimmer the fires of Hell would burn if we didn't try to force our politicians and teenage children to consistently tell the truth. Accepting a 'shadow truth' now and then from each other would make for a more peaceful planet. Oh, don't get me wrong; a 'shadow truth' and a white lie are not the same. The former is yellow at best, tinged as it is with a bit of cowardice.

Gabriel seemed to have bought my version of things, as well as the left-handed compliment of his precious mother – *if* that's how he chose to view it. 'So,' he said, 'who is next on this list of suspects? Am I?'

'Would you be disappointed if I said "no," darling?'

My Dearly Beloved can be very sexy when he wants to be, and much to my surprise things took a sudden turn in that direction. There I was, dressed in a long-sleeved white blouse, navy skirts that reached down beneath my calves, thick opaque stockings and the sort of clodhopper shoes that a farm girl of yesteryear would wear to, uh, break up the clods of earth turned up by her plough. Nonetheless, this very handsome, toned and tanned physician, in the sky-blue Lacrosse shirt and the sandstone Chinos, was lobbing pheromones at me with the accuracy of a Wimbledon champ.

'I'd be very disappointed if you said "no,"' he purred. 'If you say "yes," I can have the proof of our love bathed and in bed in half an hour. That should give you enough time to eat.'

'My, how romantic you are,' I squealed, barely able to contain myself. Trust me, after I gave birth to a baby whose head was the size of Kim Jong Il's aspirations, our foreplay has often been reduced to just three words: 'Brace yourself, Mags.'

Had I not been so tired, however, I might have predicted what happened next. The intruder with the broad back, topped by the cabbage head, pushed herself off her chair with her doll-sized limbs. Her mood was as dark as the black apron covering her habit; even without a cowl, Ida's scowl was truly formidable. Between the furrows in her brow I could see lightning flash, and when she opened her mouth to speak I was pelted with hail and brimstone simultaneously.

'Shtop mit der sexy-wexy!' she commanded, her stubby index finger pointed straight out in front of her or, in other words, about waist-high on Yours Truly.

That did it! That hiked my hackles up to my armpits. Who did she think that she was? The Almighty?

'My *sexy-wexy*, as you call it, is none of your ding-dong business.'

'Mags,' Gabe gasped. 'Don't swear at Ma!'

'Swear, schmare,' I practically screeched, and right in front of my baby too! 'She's trying to interfere in our love life.'

'No, she's not – *are* you, Ma?'

'Yah, of course I am,' she said, nodding that cabbage every which way but loose. 'Dis von eez no gut for you. Gabeleh, how many times do I tell you dis? Much better dat you marry Shoshanna Silverman, the goil mit zee face of an angel, and whose faddeh eez also single. Vee could haf a two-for-von vedding, yah?'

'Ma, *no*!' My husband might be slow to develop in the familial relationship department but, unlike his mother, his gray cells are human in origin, and not cruciferous. 'I'm so sorry, Mags, I had no idea – I mean, I forgot just how meddling Ma can be. Of course, my Little Vixen, my Little Minx, I want the sexy-wexy with you!'

'Judge not,' the Bible says. Amen to that. I am five foot ten inches tall and shaped like a hitching post. When a handsome, worldly doctor calls me his 'Little Vixen,' and his 'Little Minx,' the past is instantly forgiven; I am on him like white on a peeled banana.

Having uttered those erotic words, Dr Gabriel Rosen rose seductively from his genuine faux leather-covered dinette chair to approach me with his arms extended. What exactly occurred next, I will never know. Both Ida and Gabe deny any knowledge of the matter, other than that Ida stumbled on an untied shoelace. For a few aggravating seconds, Gabe looked like a human/octopus hybrid, his eight arms flailing about, as he tried to balance his top-heavy ma back on her undersized feet.

Somehow – which I'm betting only God and Ida can explain – in the ensuing fracas, their two sets of apron strings became inextricably intertwined. One might think that a thin-gauge knitting needle, or a greased nail, or *something* could have been slipped into one of the plethora of knots that had suddenly materialized, but *au contraire*. Either Ida, or Her Maker, had managed to pull off a good magician's trick in reverse, stumping at least two of us, and in the process bringing a sly smile to the liver-colored lips of the third.

'*Oy gvalt*,' the third party said. 'Look vhat happen! Eez wary funny, yah?'

'And about to get funnier, dear,' I said. While I may be built like a broomstick, my barge-sized feet render me anything but graceful, ergo I clomped over to the all-purpose drawer, which are found in kitchens everywhere, and extracted a pair of large, extremely sharp scissors. Then, humming a happy little ditty, I clomped over to the entangled pair, and with a couple of snips cut the apron strings that bound mum to son. At that moment a choir of angels filled the room, and I went from humming a simple tune to singing a rousing, operatic version of *Hallelujah* by Leonard Cohen.

Unfortunately, the mighty do not have far to fall, if they are unreasonably short. Hence Ida recovered in no time. By the end of the evening she had convinced my Dearly Beloved that it was unsafe even for him to drive her back to the Convent of Perpetual Apathy, because Melvin Stoltzfus could be hiding in the bushes by the entrance. When I countered with the notion that fear and apathy were incompatible emotions, she became angry; what did I know about apathy? she yelled.

Fortunately for me, my Dearly Beloved is never more amorous than when his precious ma and I are housed under the same roof. After we *finally* got her to sleep in one of the paying guest rooms upstairs in the inn, I gave Ida's son a night that he would never forget, and one that she would never have approved of – not in a million years. Enough said.

Karma is not a good Christian term, thus not a word to be used lightly, if at all. However, the longer I live, the more it would appear that good intentions attract good things into my life, and negativity begets unpleasant situations. The morning following my *Hallelujah* (in more ways than one) moment, I was in for a real letdown.

TEN

BROWN SUGAR PIE
(MILCHE FLICHTE)

Serves 8 normal people, but sufficient for only 6 people of Amish-Mennonite ancestry

1 unbaked 8-inch pie crust
1 cup brown sugar
3 tablespoons all-purpose flour
Dash of salt
1 12-ounce can evaporated milk
2½ tablespoons butter
Ground cinnamon

Preheat oven to 350 degrees. With your fingers, mix the brown sugar, flour and salt directly in the pie shell. Spread evenly. Slowly pour the evaporated milk over the mixture, but do not stir in. Dot with lumps of butter and sprinkle cinnamon liberally over the surface. Bake for 50 minutes.

The filling is supposed to be gooey. The pie is best eaten at room temperature.

ELEVEN

My investigation got off to a late start because I believe that a good wife should be subservient to her husband, as it is written in the Book of Ephesians. I served rather well, if I do say so myself. But even a meek and mild-mannered woman, such as me, is bound to have an opinion from time to time. That said, I am somewhat rankled by this particular chapter in Ephesians. I mean, the apostle who wrote this book was a tent-maker named Paul, a man never married, and who elsewhere comes across as misogynistic.

Yes, I know, the Bible was inspired by the Holy Spirit, and the Apostle Paul was just the scribe, and *yada, yada*. That's what my minister says, at any rate. However, the Gospel According to Magdalena is the following: occasionally the earthly scribes were unable to sufficiently turn down the volume of their mind's chatter enough to enable them to hear that small, still voice that is God's. This explains why certain customs peculiar to biblical times feel instinctively wrong to good Christians of today. I do not, for instance, own slaves, nor would I put Little Jacob to death should the day come that he curses me.

Ach, but just like the Bible, I have wandered again in my telling of what proved to be a harrowing tale. After servicing my husband, serving my child and swerving to avoid my mother-in-law, I headed back towards Hernia. Our village doesn't have a proper 'downtown,' but it does have a Main Street. Along this street, in the approximate center of the village, one will find an intersection fronted by the following four buildings: First Mennonite Church, Hernia Police Station, Sam Yoder's Corner Market and Miller's Feed Store. We have stops signs, instead of a stoplight, and hitching posts for horses instead of parking meters. The speed limit is fifteen kph because most of the traffic is horses and buggies.

I have found from a lifetime of experience that the best way to enter my cousin's store is via stealth. Yea, I am a homely woman. When I brush out my long brown mane each morning I am sorely tempted to rear up and neigh at the image reflected back in my full-length mirror. There is no way that I can objectively deny that fact. But is that truly how others see me? If so, how can I explain the fact that I have a drop-dead gorgeous husband over whom every other woman in Hernia drools and that I have both a widower, and a married man, chomping at the bit to get into my knickers – er, so to speak.

Main Street offers precious few parking spaces, so I parked in the lot behind the First Mennonite Church (*not* my church, by the way) and hoofed it over to Sam's little grocery store. Because this is the only place in a twelve-mile radius where the Amish can buy staples and not have to worry about having their horses spooked by trucks and speeding cars, the market does a brisk business. Sam was thoroughly distracted at the register, which suited me fine because I had business in the 'back room' – an office/lounge/storage area that took up nearly a third of the downstairs level of the two-storey building.

It was here that Sam had delivered my son, Little Jacob. I have been the recipient of many blessings in my life – too many to enumerate – but one of the greatest blessings bestowed upon me was that I experienced an extremely brief, albeit painful, delivery. At any rate, it wasn't memory lane that I wished to visit now, but Sam's cantankerous Methodist wife, Dorothy. In Ramat Sreym's scandalous book she'd been described as weighing seven hundred pounds. That was an out and out lie. Everyone in Hernia could vouch for that: at her annual weigh-ins, which took place at the stockyard and were well attended (entrepreneurial Sam sold snacks) the poor woman never, *ever* tipped the scales at more than four hundred and ninety-six pounds.

Dorothy is an extremely bright woman, who could converse on any number of subjects, if she wasn't always in attack mode. Perhaps this contentious personality is the reason why Miss Sreym chose to exaggerate my cousin-in-law's weight; perhaps the two women had *words*. Or, it could be that the witless writer was simply prejudiced against folks with fluffy flesh. However, in all fairness, Dorothy, being a liberal Methodist and *not* a Mennonite, was secretly flattered by being described as a 'strumpet without a trumpet' and a 'trollop who packed a wallop.' I know this because

Sam told me in confidence, and what is a secret if not something to be shared?

Dorothy also has the ears of a kit fox (my Gabe watches National Geographic), and could probably hear a fly sigh at fifty paces. Then again, she might have smelled my approach, given that some have dubbed me Yoder with an Odour, and suggested that I have the bathing habits of a European – possibly someone of French, or even Belgian, nationality. Oh how I resemble that remark! In any case, the Methodist menace met me at the door to the back room, where she'd apparently been waiting for me.

'What took you so long?' she said.

For the record, despite her bulk, Dorothy has the voice of a nine-year-old girl who has just discovered a nest of spiders in her pudding. Over the years I've trained myself not to show the slightest reaction to this anomaly. My training methods have involved prayer, tongue-biting, pinching my arm, pinching someone else's arm, biting someone else's tongue – you name it. Trust me, Dorothy's voice has got to be heard to be believed. The fact that Ramat Sreym made no mention of it in her novel was, to say the least, a puzzling thought.

'What's the matter?' Dorothy continued to squeal. 'Has the cat got your tongue?'

A little bit of irritation goes a long way to stopping the giggles. 'My pussy is at home in our barn chasing mice,' I said coolly. 'How is *your* pussy?'

Dorothy scowled, creating furrows on her brow deep enough in which to plant corn kernels. 'You have a filthy mind, Magdalena.'

'Why I never,' I protested. 'Well – maybe just that once – although I'm not sure what we're talking about. It isn't nail polish, is it?'

'Oh, for heaven's sake, you blithering Mennonite idiot,' Dorothy squeaked like a shrew on steroids, 'stop wasting my time and come in.'

She lumbered aside, allowing me to slip past her to claim my cousin Sam's chair, which is one of those sinfully comfortable babies that reclines at the push of a button. I realize that this might be a bit picky of me to feel this way, maybe even a mite sacrilegious, but when I get to Heaven, if my new digs don't have a recliner like that, I might ask to be shown to another room. Anyway, Dorothy's customary seat was the sofa – a very large daybed, really – that sagged to the floor in the middle. By the time she'd satisfactorily ensconced herself in the giant cup of broken bedsprings, she was no longer squealing. Instead she sounded rather like a bull sea lion on a mating frenzy (again, it was that ding-dong National Geographic channel!).

Normally, by then I would have already surrendered myself to the Devil by arranging my gangly limbs along the length of the heavenly recliner. *Normally*. However, on that particular visit, when I glanced down at Cousin Sam's much-coveted place of reposition, what did I spy but a pair of Dorothy's bloomers, laid out like the sails of the S.S. *Santa Maria*, the *Pinta* and the *Nina* combined. I half expected to see a miniature Christopher Columbus waving up at me.

'Go on, sit,' Dorothy said.

All right, but where? Surely she didn't mean on her floor. I try not to entertain mean thoughts in my head, given that I am a kind Christian woman, but truly, even germs wouldn't sit on Dorothy's floor.

No one likes to be yelled at, not even if that person has broad (albeit bony) shoulders like mine, and not even if the yeller has the voice of a nine-year-old. Folks think that I'm tough just because I'm quick-witted and sharp-tongued, but I have feelings too. What brains I have I got from God, and the sharpness of my tongue comes from having to bite down on it so much in order to keep from speaking what's *really* on my mind. That is to say, my poor tongue has been sharpened like a sword's edge against a whetstone, so what comes out of my mouth is really not my fault.

Allow me, therefore, to briefly meander this one time. I was born and bred in Hernia. I am a deaconess in Beechy Grove Mennonite Church, the conservative branch also known as Old Order Mennonite. I am related by blood to virtually every Mennonite person of Amish ancestry in the world, and every Amish person in the world. The branches of my family tree are so tangled that I have to share a shadow with my sister. On account of that, *plus* the fact that I am the best listener you may ever hope to encounter – and I say this with all humility – I am the gossip *maven* of Hernia. *Maven*, by the way, is a Yiddish word that I picked up from the Babester, and it literally means someone who is knowledgeable.

The things that I know about many a fine pillar in our community would light fires under the gossiping old biddies in Hernia. Thumbs would fall off willy-nilly from all that texting, especially in the case of Martha Gerber who really was born with 'all thumbs.' Even John Swartzentruber, with his extra pair of ears, will not have heard the tales that could be spun from my thin, colorless lips – *if* I was ever pushed too far, that is. And tales is not the right word, either, because my gossip is all *based on the truth*. It is rather what the Anglicans believe the Bible to be, although every *real* Christian knows that the Bible should be read literally, word for word. At any rate, when I gossip, I simply embroider the facts to make them more interesting, and leave out the boring parts.

Take Sam and Dorothy's marriage, for instance: it would have ended years ago, had it not been for—

'Sit!' Dorothy squeaked.

'I would, but your unmentionables are on the recliner.'

'Then move them, silly.'

'Uh – no offense, dear, but I am not about to touch something so personal.'

'Good heavens, Magdalena, what are you, a wuss or a woman?'

'I'm definitely a wuss.'

'Harrumph.'

'Again, I mean no offense, but the timbre of your voice does not lend itself to harrumphing.'

'Cuckoo, cuckoo,' Dorothy said, doing a fairly good imitation of a Black Forest clock. 'I guess you'll just have to stand while putting the screws to me.' She laughed, sharing another of her vocal inadequacies. 'If I were you, Magdalena, I'd get right to the point. As you know, one of the Yoder family traits is having ankles as thick as Redwood trunks. You, however, have legs like rubber bands dipped in plastic sauce. If a frog farts all the way over in Philadelphia, you just might topple over backward.'

I gasped. 'How dare you use the *F* word?'

'Get real or get out, Magdalena.'

'In that case,' I said, 'I would like to know why *you* weren't upset by the million extra pounds that the wretched interloper ascribed to you, yet Sam was?' Do you see how well I can exaggerate?

'Oh, that!' Then Dorothy's laugh reminded me of the sound of a dentist's drill, as heard from an adjacent room. 'How far was she off? Ten, fifteen pounds? Who's counting?'

'Three hundred pounds, and *I'm* counting, since I'm the person assigned to investigate this case.'

'That certainly explains your crazy get-up. I was thinking that either it's Halloween again or Cousin Magdalena is back to playing Miss Marple amongst the maples.'

'For the record, dear,' I said, 'I am your cousin-in-law, not your cousin, and what I am wearing is a genuine facsimile of a pseudo-policewoman's uniform, as per the regulations of the Hernia's Helpers Handbook, written by none other than the very generous citizen who pays our Chief of Policeman's salary.'

'A policewoman's uniform, no matter how well it is tailored, does not flatter a bean pole.'

'That hurt my feelings,' I said.

'I bet it did,' Dorothy said.

'No, really, it did. Besides, this really isn't a genuine facsimile of a uniform; it's a cobbled together hodgepodge of my own things to suggest a *uniform*.'

'Then perhaps that explains what's wrong with it. Listen, Magdalena, you will never in a million years convince me that a pipe cleaner like you minds being teased about her weight – or in your case, lack of weight and absence of shape. You know absolutely nothing about discrimination, or having your feelings hurt.'

'I'm Yoder with the Odour, or didn't Sam tell you about that?'

Dorothy snorted derisively, but given the timbre of her voice, that sound was surprisingly pleasant. 'You didn't think that we heavy people have our own problems with that?'

'OK, I capitulate,' I said. 'You have had a much more difficult life than I, which is really my point, dear.' I paused just long enough to let her swim up to my baited hook – metaphorically speaking, of course. 'I can totally understand why you decided to poison that awful woman with a piece of homemade fruit pie. I might have done the same thing if I was in your boat-sized shoes – then again, who am I to talk, considering that my sturdy brown brogans have been certified as sea-worthy vessels?' Rest assured that I would never kill another human being. We Mennonites, unlike Dorothy's Methodists, have been pacifists for over five hundred years.

'Why, you presumptuous little fruit fly,' Dorothy said. As her temper soared, so did her voice. At any second windows would shatter, neighborhood dogs would howl and perhaps even satellites would begin crashing to earth.

I did the only thing I could think of to stop the scale-topping trollop from trilling off the top scales. I plopped atop her panties, sat on her skivvies, set my bum on her bloomers, dug my derriere into her drawers – all in hopes of scaling things back a notch. Much to my ongoing amazement my strategy worked and – this I add cautiously – to this very day Dorothy Yoder, the English woman (*not* from England, but merely a Methodist) speaks in a tone well within the normal range.

'There, now aren't you just as pleased as punch with me?' I said.

'I beg your pardon?'

'Your voice, dear,' I said. 'You sound like a regular person now, not a canary. But really, there's no need to thank me; simply arrange for me to shop in your store without having to pay – let's say for three days, and we'll call it even-steven.'

'*What?*'

'So call me greedy,' I said. 'How about two days? I'm giving you a thirty percent discount, which is mighty generous if you ask me.'

'You're crazy, you know that?'

'You better believe it! OK, this is my last, and best, offer. I'll give you two days off this deal; that's more than a sixty percent discount.' I shook a finger at her in mock earnestness as I simultaneously attempted to waggle an all but non-existent eyebrow. 'Trust me, dear,' I said seductively, 'someone is making out like a bandit on this deal.'

'Oh, I'm sure of that,' Dorothy said.

I sighed dramatically, although I was far from beaten. 'Final offer: give me one hour to fill one of your wimpy little basket carts and I promise never to mention the mellowing modulation of your vocal membranes, *or* the fact that you forced me, the sweetest of souls, and the kindest of kin, to sit astride the most objectionable object one could ever imagine. Honestly, Dorothy, you should write to President Obama with the suggestion that "bloomer-boarding" replace "water-boarding" as the US method of interrogating terrorists.'

Dorothy glared at me for all of three seconds and then smiled. 'OK, you'll get one of my little wimpy basket carts to fill, but you have just half an hour to shop and you'll have to stay away from the spice rack.'

'We have a deal,' I said. Now was the time to ambush her. 'So how come you didn't mind that this *real* outsider – because you really aren't an outsider, you know, having been born in Bedford, just up the road – portrayed you as a prostitute? And don't deny it, either, because my source is impeccable. Really, Dorothy, such an admission is beyond the pale, if you ask me!'

Dorothy's normally ruddy complexion took on the waxy tones of a plucked chicken. 'How on earth did you know – I mean, *who* told you that?'

'I can't reveal my sources, dear. If I did, I'd have to kill you both.'

'Sam! Why, I'm going to wring his scrawny neck,' Dorothy said, without even chuckling at my pathetic pacifist attempt at irony.

'Give Sam a break,' I said. 'He loves you so much that he defied his parents' wishes and married outside the faith, and then for the last million years he's remained faithful to the most unpleasant woman I know, and that's including Wanda Hemphopple.'

Boy, did that little speech have her attention. 'What do you know about Sam's faithfulness?'

'Consider the evidence: *moi*. Your Dearly Beloved has been trying to infiltrate my bloomers since I was a wee lass of ten, and he a lad of only nine – he was an early-bloomer you see, pun quite intend—'

'Oh, shut up, Magdalena. You don't expect me to believe for a minute that Sam finds you attractive, not when he can have' – she then gestured crudely to herself – 'all this – the Dorothy buffet. And another thing: I have serious doubts that you really are a Mennonite, much less an Old Order Mennonite, which is just a skip and a hop away from being Amish. You have the most worldly and sassy tongue I have heard on anyone – except for Joan Rivers. You know what, I bet your husband secretly converted you and that you're Jewish now, or maybe you're a Universalist Unitarian.'

Trust me; it is quite hard to produce an enigmatic smile with a severe under-bite. Mona Lisa I am not, but I did my level best to emulate her timeless expression.

'Magdalena,' Dorothy said in response to the Mona Lisa look, 'the lavatory is the second door on the left.'

'I don't have to go,' I said.

'Actually, you do,' Dorothy said. 'Maybe not to the lavatory, but you have to go from here. My favourite morning television show is about to come on, and besides, I need my rest.'

It has been said that the Devil is in the detail. Frankly, I was happy to attend to a few of his minutiae for him.

'When I was eight,' I said, 'Sammy,' as he was called then, pushed me down in the coat room and stole his first kiss. When I was eleven, he dropped a pencil by my desk just to look up my skirt. When I was twelve, we were riding the school bus when suddenly he jammed his hand down the front of my blouse—'

'Oh, stop it,' Dorothy said. 'He was a precocious little boy experiencing new thoughts and urges that he needed to explore. They were all very normal and you'd know it if you weren't so repressed.'

I prayed for the Good Lord to stop my tongue from speaking evil. Is it my fault then that this prayer, like so many of my prayers, went unanswered?

'Sammy – I mean, Sam – wrote me a long, passionate letter the week before your wedding, imploring me to reconsider his multitude of marriage proposals. This was back when we were both young and nubile, and dare I add fertile as well? He thought we should immigrate to Australia and start a Mennonite colony in Melbourne; he thought that this particular alliteration had a certain melodic ring to it. I told him I was opposed to the idea – oh, I wasn't anti-Antipodes, mind you – but it was the thought of cleaving my Yoder flesh to his Yoder flesh, as the Bible instructs us, in order that two shall be one.' I held up a large, albeit shapely hand. 'Most unfortunately, it is incumbent upon me to breathe. So I shall now pause for a couple of seconds.'

Dorothy was as quick as a striking cobra. Her voice, however, which had once been so high-pitched that only angels and women could hear it, now sounded like a foghorn.

'Get out, Magdalena! You're a husband-stealing hussy, and I want you out now! *You* are the strumpet and harlot. In fact, you are *worse*.'

TWELVE

My, what a glorious day it was shaping up to be: the strumpet with the trumpet had called me, arguably the homeliest hausfrau in all of Hernia, a 'husband-stealing hussy.' If only Mama could have heard Dorothy. Mama would have been shocked – *mortified*, is how she usually put it – by such sinful talk. But perhaps it might have served Mama right for repeatedly referring to me as 'a carpenter's dream,' on account of my flat-as-a-board chest, or the fact that Mama said that I had a 'horsey' face. I feel that the latter statement was cruel; even though on two occasions, upon getting a close-up glimpse of Yours Truly, Amish horses had pulled free from their traces and followed us home.

Yes! It's true – never in the history of Hernia, Pennsylvania was a girl born who was so unlikely to find a suitor. In fact, my parents – may they rest in peace up on Stucky Ridge – were so convinced that I was doomed to a life of spinsterhood that they left the controlling share of their estate to me. It was this very lack of faith in me that allowed me to preserve the farm and turn it into a thriving bed and breakfast. In the meantime, my pretty sister Susannah – she with the bubbly personality – bubbled herself into all kinds of trouble, including, as I've said, into the bonds of unholy matrimony with a homicidal maniac of the mantis persuasion.

So, although Mennonites of my ilk don't have sex standing up, lest it leads to dancing, and we don't dance, lest it leads to enjoyable sex, and we seldom skip, because Heaven forefend it should be too enjoyable, late that morning, as I left Sam Yoder's Corner Market, I found myself skipping with joy. For the record, Hernia is a very pleasant village in which to skip.

The streets are lined with tall maples, oaks and sycamore trees. The wood-framed houses, two-story Victorian with fancy gingerbread trim, sport fresh coats of paint. Most of these historic residences have been kept white in keeping with the times, but here and there a soft yellow, or a robin-egg blue has crept in, and the result, in my opinion, is rather charming. In late summer, against the shady foundations of these lovely homes, one might expect to find billowing hydrangea bushes flanked by masses of ferns. If it were not for the fact that the PennDutch occupied the site of my family's homestead dating back to 1780, I would move into town in a heartbeat.

Then again, misanthropes, such as me, may not be cut out for village life. As I neared the church parking lot and saw that a small crowd had surrounded my car, my colon started dancing the polka. Since dancing is a sin, and I was in a public place, one can imagine my consternation.

'Stop it,' I growled.

My colon growled back.

'All right, have it your own way,' I said aloud.

Discovering what a pushover I was that morning, my stomach started in on a samba. A second later my bowels were doing the bossa nova. *That* was too much.

'Cut it out,' I snapped.

By then I was amongst the crowd, but not one of the women seemed to think that my words were meant for her. This was, of course, a relief for me but a sad commentary on our times. Now hidden mikes allow us to wander the streets, blabbing away on hidden phones, whilst all the while appearing like the mad folk of yesteryear.

These women, I soon discovered, were the members of Righteous Readers, the First Mennonite Church's book club for women 'of a certain age.' With them was their mentor, who was also their pastor, Rev Nathaniel Troyer. Upon realizing who they were, I briefly entertained saying nothing about my own bizarre babbling, or inventing a little white lie to cover it up. Instead, being the chronic and confirmed sufferer of *Veritas maximus* that I am, I confessed to the facts.

'My innards were misbehaving in lewd and licentious ways,' I said, 'so I had to give them a stern talking to. That said, good morning, ladies, Reverend.'

Several of the women twittered in the old-fashioned sense of the word, and a number of them twittered electronically. No doubt I had amused them yet again with my eccentric speech. Perhaps

I should wear a sign around my neck that reads: *Magdalena Portulacca Yoder Rosen, Catalyst for Gossip Extraordinaire.*

'Good morning, Magdalena,' Reverend Troyer said. He was a ruggedly handsome man in his late thirties, who had twinkling eyes and a winning smile. He also happened to be a 'confirmed bachelor.' The hens in his flock said that Reverend Troyer was a 'man's man' – by that they meant that he was *really* masculine – and so they flirted with him shamelessly. Our Chief of Police, Toy, on the other hand, had confided to me that his definition of a 'man's man' differed quite a bit from that of the members of the Righteous Readers Book Club.

Nonetheless, my knees knocked beneath my modest skirt and my belly continued to dance as I stood but an arm's length away from Pastor Nate, as he likes to be called. Although he held out his hand for me to shake, I declined to touch it, offering to bump fists with him instead. Nate knows me well enough not to take offense. Unlike many people, he is fully aware of the fact that the modern custom of shaking hands evolved from the medieval custom of proving that one was unarmed. Today we know that smearing sweaty palms together is a great way to spread colds and influenza, both treats I would just as soon pass up on.

Pastor Nate had been eyeing my faux policewoman's getup with a knowing smile. 'I see that you've been asked to help Toy with the murdered author's case.'

The gasps emanating from the gaggle of Righteous Readers were truly gratifying. 'Indeed, I have. Would you like to take a spin in the cruiser? We could drive up to Stucky Ridge with the siren on and the lights flashing?'

One of the twinkling eyes winked. 'Why, Magdalena, isn't Lover's Leap up there?'

The oral sort of twittering sounded like a flock of starlings had landed at our feet.

'I was thinking of the cemetery,' I said quickly. 'Or just the lookout part.'

'Magdalena was pushed off the lookout,' Lodema Short said, 'by her brother-in-law, who was also our Chief of Police a few years before Toy arrived.'

'Is that so?' Pastor Nate said, and winked with his other eye. 'It's a wonder that you didn't die. That is a wickedly high cliff.'

'I was saved by my sturdy Christian underwear,' I said, and then realized a second too late that my *Veritas* disease made me suddenly want to vomit. Sturdy Christian underwear, how corny was that?

'Please, Magdalena, expound,' Pastor Nate said. 'This is one subject we never got around to studying in seminary.'

There followed a chorus of agreement: cries of 'yes,' 'expound,' and even one misguided 'ex*pand!*' I have no intention of bulking up, so I ignored that last entreaty.

'Then listen up, folks,' I said. 'There is nothing secretive about sturdy Christian underwear. Simply remember that your body is the temple of the Lord, and the Lord wants a safe, clean, dry temple. That means generous cotton covers for both downstairs and upstairs furniture – if you get my drift.'

'*What?*' Marlene Schmucker said. Her parents are double second cousins, which helps to explain her confusion. 'How did furniture get into this conversation?'

'Just trust me,' I said. 'You want to use wide straps for the upstairs furniture – that's what saved me. And wear a petticoat – one that can catch the air if you sail off a cliff.'

'The woman's a genius,' Thelma Berkey said and nodded her head in admiration. I beamed expansively at her in payment.

'The woman is bonkers,' Marlene Schmucker said.

I treated her to one of my infamous 'one is not amused' looks; if it hadn't been for these icy expressions of feigned disdain, global warming would have been a done deal decades ago.

'Come on, ladies, let's go,' Lydia Graber said. 'We're just wasting our time playing her silly games. Lunch is on me at the Sausage Barn.'

Two centuries prior to her announcement, the North American bison thundered across the Great Plains in such numbers that the ground shook, rattling the tepee poles of the Sioux Indians. On this late summer morning, the ladies of the Righteous Readers Book Club thundered to their cars with such eagerness that the pavement shook, rattling the fillings in my aching head. Seconds later, engines roared. In a New York minute the companionable but oh so handsome Pastor Nate and I were all who remained in the parking lot of the First Mennonite Church of Hernia, Pennsylvania.

'Well,' Pastor Nate said, 'I hope you weren't too offended by what just happened.'

'*Moi?*' Offended, no; embarrassed, yes. My voice sounded like a rubber squeaky toy that had been stepped on.

'Would you mind coming into my office for a minute, Magdalena? There's something I'd like to discuss with you – that is, if you have the time.'

'Yes, of course.' I followed him silently, grateful as always that the voice in my head – the Devil, to be sure – could be heard only by me. 'Pastor Nate,' the inner Magdalena said, 'while I don't think that you bat for my team, you really are terribly easy on the eyes. If you were to ever bat those soulful hazel peepers simultaneously in my direction – well, I might consider dropping ten dollars in your offering plate some Sunday morning.'

I can't put my finger on it exactly, but there is a similarity in the smell of old Protestant churches across our great land. Perhaps it comes from casseroles toted in for potluck suppers in damp basements, or slightly mouldy hymn books stored in racks behind rock-hard pews. Add to those odours the human scents of sweat, given off in fear, heat, love and commitment, and sometimes doused in cheap chemical concoctions that immediately clogs one's nostrils.

The windowless basement of the First Mennonite Church was a bouquet of noxious but familiar smells. The large, damp room, with the linoleum floor and concrete walls, served as the social hall. The far end was taken up by a kitchen with a pass-through window, and a door that led to the lavatories. The opposite end was dissected by a plywood partition, behind which lay Pastor Nate's study.

'Tuna casserole,' I said as we passed through the open basement. 'And weak decaffeinated coffee. But definitely Girdle Buster Pie for dessert. I'd estimate that it was last eaten here yesterday evening at around half past six.'

Pastor Nate stopped dead in his tracks. 'How did you know?'

'So I was right?'

He nodded. 'Amy Stutzman brought it to the board meeting.'

I tapped my famously protruding proboscis and sighed. 'The Yoder nose is both a gift and a curse. I can smell if a melon is ripe without having to pick it up. If I'm out in a canoe and lose my paddle, all I have to do is lie on my back, face up, and the wind will push me back to shore. The flip side is that a sniffer as finely tuned as mine will, of course, pick up every scent – and not all of them are pleasant.'

Pastor Nate chuckled. 'I bet not,' he said and ushered me into what was a surprisingly warm and inviting space, given its location. This room did have a window, although it was at ground level. Still, some light is a whole lot better than none, and these walls were panelled and painted. Being a simple farm woman, I lacked the vocabulary to describe the décor I beheld, but I knew enough about the world to guess that this was what magazine writers described as 'professionally decorated.' I'd only seen pictures of rooms like this in the battered, and sadly out-of-date, women's journals in the waiting rooms of my doctor and dentist.

'Wow,' I said.

'I did it myself,' he said.

'*You* did it?'

'Yes. Why do you sound so surprised? Is it because I'm a man?'

'It's because you're a Mennonite, dear – and a man.'

'Well, I did have a little help – actually, quite a bit, from a friend. This is actually a good segue as any to what I wanted to talk to you about.'

I held up an immense, but somewhat shapely hand. 'There's no need, Pastor Nate,' I said kindly. 'I am not a judgmental woman; if Jesus didn't feel the need to comment on that particular issue, than who am I to judge?'

'Oh, dear,' said Pastor Nate, 'so the rumours are true? You really do stay so slim by *jumping* to conclusions left and right?'

'And sometimes forwards and backwards. Are you saying that you are not – I mean, that you did not – bring me down here in the belly of the whale to confess to a torrid tryst with Toy?' I stared at the poor man for a few seconds before continuing. 'Oh, my, I can see that I should add *running*-off-at-the-mouth to my list of weight-loss exercises.'

'Your words, Magdalena, not mine.'

'B-But, you're not married, for crying out loud!'

'Neither was our Lord. Are you suggesting that he was gay?'

'Certainly not!'

'Oh, then was he heterosexual?'

'Ick! Not that either,' I cried. 'He was asexual. He never had a sexual thought in his entire life.'

'Not once in all of his thirty-three years and yet we are supposed to relate to the human side of him?'

I clapped my hands over my ears. '*Na-na-na-na-na-na* – I can't *hear* you!'

Pastor Nate smiled. 'I'm sorry; I'll stop teasing you now. It's just that I find it fun to yank your chain. I really do have a secret love interest – just not Toy. Although I suppose that if I did swing that way – which I don't – the police chief would be very handy, and he is gosh darn handsome.'

'Stop toying with me,' I said.

Pastor Nate groaned. 'Good pun.'

'It was accidental, dear, I assure you. Now please continue with your fascinating tale before the odours of your basement do me in.'

'It was that lovely foreign woman, Ramat Sreym.' Pastor Nate even rolled his 'Rs' in the guttural French way.

There are moments in life when something happens that is such a huge departure from the normal that it takes us a while to process the new information and file it properly in our brains. September 11, 2001 is a case in point. This same phenomenon happened to me again when I heard this mild-mannered Mennonite minister neighbor confess to dating the bouncing blond bimbo from Baluchistan – or wherever she was from.

I jiggled pinkies in both ears to make sure that the passageways were clear. 'Let's try that again,' I said. 'For a moment there I thought that you said that you had been dating the recently deceased. You know, the woman who tore Hernia to shreds in her novel, and then had the temerity to show up at our prestigious, annual pie festival as a judge, and then if *that* wasn't enough, she had the unmitigated gall to topple over dead – plop – right on top of *my* apple pie.' I gasped for air. 'That pie was going to be my winning entry in the fair. That was my one and only chance – but a sure one – for a trophy.'

Before he would respond, Pastor Nate had us sit in a pair of espresso-colored imitation leather chairs that faced his faux mahogany desk. Rest assured they were all of retail quality and not the cheap stuff one might ferret out from the piles of junk at a flea market.

Pastor Nate sighed dramatically. 'Magdalena, do I detect a severe case of xenophobia?'

'Not on your xylophone, you don't! I'll have you know that as an innkeeper I have hosted folks from around the globe. Why, once I even hosted a lithe and lovely, albeit lackadaisical, lady from Lapland who didn't lift a finger to help with the chores, even though I offered to charge her the most exorbitant rates imaginable – you know, my ALPO plan.'

Pastor Nate shook his handsome head. 'Why do you always insist on joking? I only took one college course in psychology, but I'm guessing that your constant attempts at humour stem from some deep-seated sense of insecurity. In any case, I find it annoying, not funny. Forgive me for hoping that we could have a real conversation.'

Most unfortunately, the good pastor's sharp criticism of my best asset wounded me to the quick. Therefore, I cannot be blamed for rising to my own defense, especially when I had scripture on my side.

'If *real* is what you want, dear, then perhaps you should consider the facts: Ramat Sreym played Queen Jezebel to your King Ahab.'

The young pastor's expressive face appeared to be momentarily frozen. No doubt I had shocked him with my reference. Jezebel was a queen who lived in Old Testament days. She was so wicked that God decreed that she be thrown off the castle walls and consumed by dogs. There wasn't to be enough left of this evil monarch to bury, lest she be in any way memorialized. Jezebel was married to a king (of course) whose name was Ahab. Being a man, Ahab was utterly powerless – complete putty in her hands. She led him astray, just like Eve tempted Adam.

Pastor Nate was quiet so long that I felt the need to jog his memory. 'You will find the story in the Second Book of Kings.'

He blinked back to life. '"Judge not, that you be not judged." The Gospel of Matthew, chapter seven, verse one.'

I snorted – quite accidentally, but it was to be expected, given my rather horsey head and the passion with which I approach my avocation. 'I could say the same thing to you, but since there is no point in stating the obvious, I wish to plough – I mean, proceed – with my investigation. When did you take up with the deceased?'

'*Take up?* What is that supposed to mean?'

'Well, you know—'

'No, I don't know,' he snapped. 'So why don't you tell me.'

'Uh – OK, but for the record I would like to state that I am a bit taken aback that a man of the cloth – especially a fine young Mennonite pastor such as yourself – would speak so sharply to a simple-minded laywoman like me.'

'Ha, you are anything but simple-minded. Now explain yourself.'

'All right, if you insist. What I meant is: when did the two of you begin dating? Or did it go beyond that?'

'The answer to your first question is about a week after she showed up in Hernia on her initial visit. That's the time she stayed at your inn while doing her research. The answer to your second question is: none of your business.'

'How rude!'

'Forgive me, Miss Yoder, but you are the one who is being rude.'

'*Miss Yoder?* Has it come to that?'

'Friends don't accuse friends of murder, and they know when not to cross the line. You know, Miss Yoder, you would do yourself a favor by rereading *Butter Safe Than Sorry*. I'm sure that you can find a used copy on Amazon.com in the event that you have thrown yours away – which I highly doubt that you have. Anyway, in it you will find that Ramat wrote about an innkeeper named Magdalena Yoder, a woman who was as wise as Solomon, as bright as Einstein and as brave as a Navy Seal. What's more, that woman was also a fantastic mother; her consummate love for her son is what drove the plot forward. The woman sitting here today possesses none of those qualities.'

I popped to my oversized feet. 'That hurts! How dare you say that I'm not a fantastic mother? No one loves her son more than I do.'

'Is that so?' Pastor Nate said. Despite being a man of God, he smirked – well, just a little. 'Then how come you're not home right now with your kid? Shouldn't you be feeding him lunch or changing his nappy?'

I have been called many things in my forty-nine years on planet Earth, but 'unimaginative' has never been one of them. 'The reason I'm not home right now is because Little Jacob is having a Bar Mitzvah lesson.'

'I beg your pardon?'

'Beg away! You do recall that my handsome hunk of a husband, Gabe the Babester, is Jewish, right?'

'Yes, but—'

'You are correct: his buttocks are some of his best assets, but please, try to stay focused. You see, I promised my husband that we would raise his son in his father's faith, and when a Jewish boy is Bar Mitzvah, he becomes a man in the eyes of his religion. Now, who better to prepare him for that than another Jewish man? Of course, you're probably thinking that Little Jacob is a trifle young to be studying Hebrew and learning how to chant trope, but he's a brilliant boy, if I do say so myself. He takes after his father, you know.'

Pastor Nate was on his feet as well. Was it my fault that his face was the color of rhubarb jam? Was I to blame for the spate of sparks in his eyes, or that both temples had suddenly sprouted veins the thickness of pasta? I think not.

'Your time is up, Miss Yoder,' he said.

'What a coincidence, seeing as how I was already leaving,' I said. At the door that divided his plush office from the dank, odoriferous social hall, I paused to grace him with a 'smile for another while.' That is to say, the smile was genuine, but it was intended for a different occasion. 'I will be praying for you, Pastor Nate.'

Trust me, under the circumstances those were loaded words. The implication was that he needed to see the error of his ways, vis-à-vis his affair with that foreign woman. There isn't an honest person alive who enjoys having their sins acknowledged by someone else, much less taken up with the Higher Power by that person. This is especially true when the *buttinsky* is a laywoman, and the *sinner* holds a degree from a theological seminary.

I knew for a fact that Pastor Nate was not about to let me have the last word. His jaw twitched, his Adam's apple bobbed and his lips parted. Fortunately, his insistence on the last word allowed me, the mere laywoman, to sin anon. This time I was wilfully rude; given my stilt-like legs and feet the size of jumbo jets, I was able to gallop out of earshot before his first utterance escaped him.

Once outside the church, in the fresh warm sunlight of a late summer's day, I considered what had just transpired. A young Mennonite pastor, previously presumed by me to be gay and closeted, was actually mourning the death of that awful Ramat Sreym! Talk about abominable behavior. What were the good folks of the First Mennonite Church of Hernia going to think about their Big Kahuna doing the Horizontal Hula with the hootchie-mama from Timbuktu – or wherever it was that she was from?

You can bet that they were as blind to these sins as a litter of newborn kittens. I can safely say this because within five minutes of anyone at the church becoming privy to gossip this juicy, said person will make a beeline for Yoder's Corner Market, stake a post by the cash register and remain there until everyone in town has heard the news. Believe me, this isn't malice in action that I describe; rather, it's a way of keeping the community informed, as well as a way for the gossiper to jockey for position in society – but in a gentle sort of way. At any rate, Cousin Sam would have called me immediately with news like this.

Needless to say, I was rather shaken by this smarmy revelation, not to mention my earlier conversation with my cousin's caustic wife. It is a good thing that I have long been considered a nervy woman, for many of my nerves had just been shot. So what exactly should a grumpy, gangly, galoot of a gal do at a time like that? Well, I don't know what she *should* do, but what I did was open my purse and extract a jumbo-size Snickers candy bar. The peanuts perked me up with their protein and, as always, the chocolate coating held a party in my mouth.

The identity of Ramat's killer was still a mystery, but God's in His Heaven and all is well in the world, just as long as a lady can cram an ooey-gooey and oh-so-chewy snack into her mouth and feel that sugar rush.

THIRTEEN

I try to be the best person that I can be. When I was in fourth grade, Miss Kuhnberger drilled it into our heads that we should strive for excellence in everything that we attempted. It didn't matter if we were writing in our notebooks or tying our shoelaces. Every task was equally important, no matter how trivial. If Miss Kuhnberger sensed that we had not sufficiently applied ourselves to our respective jobs, she was more than happy to dole out a variety of punishments. Writing sentences was one of her favourites.

Therefore one can understand why I might feel the need to be *the* crabbiest woman in all of Hernia, or *the* most judgmental person in three counties, but I struggle against these temptations hour by hour, moment by moment. It is, I think, only because I own up to having these evil thoughts that I have garnered the reputation of being somewhat hot-headed and cantankerous, with a tongue that could slice through cold cheese. The truth, however, is that I'm a pussycat who, although too skinny to be cuddly-wuddly, is nonetheless in love with the fruit of her loins.

When I sailed through my back door and into my kitchen, I headed straight for Little Jacob. The love of my life was in his high chair, gumming a disgusting, salmon-colored paste. Globs of this particularly odoriferous baby food dotted Little Jacob's bib, the tray of his chair and his father's face and hair. When the Babester, the big man in my life, saw me, he practically dropped the small spoon he was using to feed our baby.

'Thank goodness you're back, Mags! Little Jacob won't swallow; I think he hates this stuff.'

'It's no wonder; your mother brought it over. It's something they made at the Convent of Perpetual Apathy. They want to test the market for a line of boutique baby foods. They were thinking of calling this one Babyhood Blahs. It contains liver and rutabagas.'

'Yuck!'

'I'll tell her it was a huge success – in the blah department. Where's Freni?'

'Mose came by and took her home in the buggy. He said he doesn't want her coming back to work until you stop playing snoop woman. He said last time she nearly took a bullet on account of your shenanigans.'

'*Snoop* woman? Those were his exact words?'

Gabe laughed, thus so did his son. Pureed liver and rutabagas never looked so disarming, nor yet so disgusting.

'You know those Amish,' he said. 'They have quite a way with words. This reminds me – speaking of wordsmiths – today is the day our own little Alison comes home from summer camp.'

My heart pounded and my mouth turned as dry as Nora Goodwin's pie crust. What kind of mother was I – *really* – if I could forget to pick up my thirteen-year-old daughter from her first-ever experience at an away-from-home camp? Perhaps all I was fit to do was to snoop – that, and maybe also fit to be tied.

'Mags,' said my Dearly Beloved, for he was a mind-reader, as well as my stud-muffin, 'you have had a lot on your mind. As soon as I wipe this slop off Bruiser's face we'll saddle up the horses and collect his big sister.'

Bruiser was the Babester's pet name for our cute *little* boy. It was totally inappropriate, if you ask me. Alison insisted on being called Alison; she always had. Alison had come into our lives just two years ago, but she is now our legally adopted daughter. A nosy person might ask about our daughter's origins, and if they did, they would get an earful. We happy hicks of Hernia are always delighted to speak at great length on topics of intensely personal stuff.

For instance, as I've said before, I was an inadvertent adulteress. It is, however, important that the word 'inadvertent' be stressed. I didn't know that Aaron Miller was married, much less had a child, until long after his horse broke loose from the barn – so to speak. Even now I shudder when I recall that awful night and my first glimpse of a totally naked man. To this day I am unable to look at a turkey neck without blushing. Thanksgiving is forever ruined.

As for Aaron, after he'd had his way with me, he suddenly remembered his much younger, prettier wife that he'd left up in frozen Minnesota. So then the lying lowlife lolled lazily back up north to do the Lindy with his lass in the Land of Ten Thousand Lakes. Well, one might ask, how low could two lowlifes go? The answer would be so low that they ship their only daughter off to stay on a 'farm' with the pseudo-ex-wife of the very *inadvertent* adulterer.

Call me crazy – the list is already incalculably long – but Alison was literally dropped off in the middle of the night. She was eleven years old with a note pinned to her collar, and she was clutching a pillow case containing an extra set of clothes and the Miller family Bible. She was clueless as to where she was, or who I might be. She had been under the impression that they were driving from Minnesota to Disneyworld in Florida – a trip of over fifteen hundred miles – and suddenly she was put out of the car. 'Here you go, sweetheart, Auntie Magdalena will take care of you for a while.'

Of course, I called the police. Back then Hernia was served by 'Melvin the Mantis' Stoltzfus and his sidekick Zelda Root. Together they were as competent as a pair of garden slugs on tranquilizers. I called children's services in Bedford, and they asked me if I could possibly keep the child for another night – long story short, I fell in love with a spunky kid whose mouth was more than a match for my own. Sadly, the reason for that is genetics.

Aaron Miller grew up on Hertzler Lane, the farm directly across from ours. He was every sort of cousin to me – except a first which, some would reckon, made him either my brother or a member of the British Royal Family. Hence, his daughter Alison was a cousin of some rank as well, although since she was harder to force into a bath than a cat, sometimes she was just plain rank. But we got along famously – just as long as we weren't talking about boys (her favourite subject) or religion (mine). When Gabriel came into the picture, it was mutual love at first sight and when Little Jacob was born – well, Alison was over the moon with joy!

Alison slid into the role of doting big sister, even changing his dirty nappies. What truly astounded us was that rather than feeling threatened by the arrival of the baby, she seemed to feel more secure. It was as if adding an infant sibling was the cement that solidified the family. This is not to say that raising a teeny-bopper was a bed of roses, especially when said child was a state champion eye-roller. (Much to her shame, Alison placed only second in the Pouty Face Division.)

Now I will admit that I was disappointed when Alison decided to follow Gabe's religion instead of mine. She had been raised without any religious instruction, and perhaps I should have been happy that she accepted the idea of one God, but that's where she stopped. Try as I might, I could not coax her into believing in the concept of God in three persons: the Trinity.

'That's *three* persons,' she said. 'That's not *one* God. You're supposed to believe in one God.'

'That's *three in one*,' I said. 'That's like rain, ice, fog – they're all forms of H_2O.'

'*What?*'

'Well, if you don't believe in Jesus—'

'Mags,' Gabe said, 'you're better off letting her make up her own mind. You're not going to brow-beat her into your idea of Heaven.'

So that was that, I'm afraid. Gabe found a Reform rabbi who performed a *bris* – a ritual circumcision – on our son, and *voila*, suddenly this Mennonite woman of Amish heritage was now the mother of two Jewish children. *Ach du Leiber*, as Freni would say. Was this the American 'melting pot' or what?

Of course, I hadn't a clue as how to raise a Jewish child, and if he were honest, Gabe would admit that Alison really didn't know her own mind at that stage of her life. Nevertheless, he did a little research and found a Jewish camp for 'tweens' just outside of Pittsburgh called Camp Hora Galore. Initially, I didn't know that the hora was a Jewish folk dance (of course, the Babester knew) and was '*hora*-ified' when I heard the camp's name. At any rate, Gabe had signed Alison up for six weeks, and even though she claimed to be homesick I couldn't pry her out of there.

But all good things must end, even Camp Hora Galore. 'How long is it until next summer?' Alison asked, before we'd even driven as far as the turnpike.

'Ten years,' I said. In my defense, I thought she was joking.

'Mom!'

'One year, honey,' Gabe said over his shoulder, but with a wink to me. 'Why do you ask?'

Alison sighed so hard she sent a flurry of dust motes into the front of the car. 'Geez Louise, do I hafta tell ya everything?'

'You do if you're going to swear, dear,' I said.

'Never mind the bad grammar,' Gabe said.

'Geez ain't hardly swearing, Mom,' Alison protested. 'Ya'd know that if ya ever went out anywhere except for Mennoniteville.'

My first reaction was to reach back with a long, gangly arm and brace the baby's car seat, which was already buckled in securely, because the Babester immediately stomped on the brakes and swerved to the shoulder of the road. It's a good thing that we enforce a seatbelt rule, or else we would have instantly become a buzzard buffet, having been tossed out of the car like so many rag dolls. After our heads stopped bobbing and we'd all managed to catch a modicum of breath, Gabe released himself and turned his full attention to our daughter.

'Now apologize to your mother,' he said.

Alison's eyes narrowed and her bottom lip projected a finger's-width in front of its companion.

Gabe waited a few seconds, but the only sounds to be heard were the purring of the engine, our continued heavy breathing and some rather noisy cicadas in the trees outside. 'I said "apologize,"' he said again.

Her eyes opened and rolled upwards until mostly the whites showed. 'Oh, all right. *Saw*-reeee!'

'Again.'

'*What?* I said I was sorry.'

'Now say it like you mean it.'

'Darling,' I whispered to my husband, 'you can lead a horse to water but you can't make it drink.'

'Hey! Don'tcha be calling me no names, Mom! Last time I checked it was you that had the horse's head – not me. And just so ya know, everyone thinks that ya laugh like a horse, too.'

I turned away from my dear daughter and focused my attention on a smudge of something on the dashboard upholstery. It was supposed to be fine-grain leather and it had cost an arm and a leg – well, not one of my gangly arms and legs; we couldn't have bought even a cheap plastic dashboard in exchange for one of my spindly limbs. Why, I once had a guest check into the PennDutch who owned a yacht (nothing new there). However, this gentleman's yacht came equipped with a bar, and the bar stools were upholstered with the foreskins of unborn whales. He claimed that whale foreskins were the softest leather on the planet, softer than the softest chamois . . .

'Earth to Magdalena; come in Magdalena.'

'Earth to Mom, come in Mom.'

I shook my head and rubbed my eyes. When I turned I could see that my sweet young daughter had replaced her doppelgänger in the backseat. Hair, forehead, nose, chin – they were all the same. It was only the eyes and the set of the mouth that were different, and oh what a difference.

'Alison has something to say,' Gabe said without further ado.

'Mom, I'm sorry that I was such a stinkpot,' Alison said, and I could feel that she meant it.

I smiled. 'Welcome back.'

We pulled back onto the highway and had driven all of five miles when I felt another sigh blow across my neck. 'Mom, ya know, like I'm so in love. Ya ever been in love, mom?'

'I is now,' I said.

'Huh?'

'Alison, dear, your grammar is atrocious. Is that the way the other children spoke at camp?'

'So then ya ain't never been in love!'

'Hold it,' Gabe roared. 'Her lover is sitting right here.'

'Gross,' Alison said. 'Yinz are my mom and dad; that don't count.'

'Just for that, daughter,' Gabe said, 'I will quote my favourite biblical passage, which I memorized when I was just about your age. It's from the Song of Songs.

"How fair and how pleasant you are
O love, with your delights!
This stature of yours is like a palm tree,
And your breasts like its clusters."'

'Oh, sweetheart, how romantic,' I said.

'Double gross,' Alison said. She was quiet for all of two minutes. 'Doesn't anyone want to know about my boyfriend?'

'Of course, dear,' I said. 'Tell us all about this nice young fellow.'

Alison chortled. 'Yeah, well, he ain't so young. Sheldon is

like twenty or something. Like a real adult who has to shave every day, and he doesn't forget to use deodorant either.'

I glanced over at the Babester. To his credit, he was keeping a steady foot on the accelerator, but the movement of his jaw suggested that he was chewing rocks. Also, I feared for the steering wheel, which was made of some polymer material, and therefore not good old-fashioned steel like the Good Lord intended. At any moment Gabe's grip might snap the ding-dang thing in two as he subconsciously did a number on Sheldon's skull.

'Are you sure,' I said. '*Twenty?* I thought the camp was for children aged twelve to fifteen.'

'Mom, I ain't no kid! Them counsellors called us "young adults." And if ya gotta know, Sheldon weren't even one of us young adults, on account of he was a *real* adult. Sheldon had him an official badge and everything.'

'You don't say,' the Babester said.

'Hey Mom,' Alison said. 'Dad just used sarcasm. I recognized it because you're always using it on me.'

'And you just spoke correctly. I am pleased to acknowledge that.'

'Whatever,' Alison said sarcastically.

I found the last number dialled and put it on speed dial. I made sure it was on 'speaker.' Our family rule is that a passenger may use a phone; the driver may not unless the car has stopped and the engine is off.

'Sheldon,' was the immediate response.

'Hi,' I said. 'This is Alison Rosen's mother. We just picked her up from camp, um, about half an hour ago.'

'Yeah, I remember. You're the Amish lady with the little white hat and the good-looking dude for a husband.'

'Good memory, son,' Gabe said.

Alison, who was by then rolled up in a ball like a hedgehog, groaned. 'I'm so embarrassed, I think I'm gonna die.'

'What was that?' Sheldon said.

'Your summer crush,' Gabe said. 'She thinks she's going to die.'

'Oh *that*,' Sheldon said.

'Yes, *that*,' I said. 'Alison is only thirteen; I demand to know what went on.'

'Mom, *pleeeease*,' the dying girl pleaded from the rear seat.

'No problem, Mrs Rosen. There's no need for you to worry; I have a girlfriend whom I met at the University of Pittsburgh. She was a counsellor here as well. We're finishing up some paperwork – as a matter of fact, here's Deborah now. Would you like to speak with her?'

'No,' Alison wailed.

'Yes, please,' I prevailed.

'Good afternoon,' Deborah said.

'Hello, dear. Did you have a good summer?'

'Umm, pretty good. Kind of busy, really. Frankly, I can't wait until classes resume – and I have a double major, so when school starts I don't have a second to spare! But that's nothing compared to Camp Hora Galore. I'm not meaning to *kvetch*, Mrs Rosen, but teens today – whew!'

'I'll say.' I bit my tongue until my toes curled. 'But I hear that you and Sheldon are a couple. If you don't mind me asking, how do you find time for dating?'

'Well, we – uh—'

'We live together off campus,' Sheldon said, getting back on the phone.

'No way,' Alison moaned, her hands over her ears.

'My kid's freaking out,' I said. 'She thought that you two were an item.'

Sheldon laughed. *Laughed.* Fortunately Deborah had the good grace to take the phone from her boyfriend's hand.

'Mrs Rosen, you didn't get a chance to meet Sheldon properly, did you?'

'No, dear, I did not.'

'Well, it's like this: Sheldon Epstein is very hot. Every straight girl at camp wanted him for herself. It happened last year as well. He got letters, text messages and phone calls all the way to Christmas. But he's mine, Mrs Rosen, all mine.'

'Soon it will be "til death do us part,"' I heard Sheldon say in the background.

'*Mazel tov*,' the Babester said.

'Alison, dear, please quit kicking my seat so hard,' I said kindly.

It is my contention that a sullen peace is better than no peace at all, and I would have been content to count the freckles on my hands and speculate as to which ones were the likeliest to turn into bona fide liver spots – if indeed there is a difference – when I heard the sound of a cow expire in the rear seat. If you have never witnessed a head of cattle being slaughtered, then don't. If you wish to experience the sound, without the fury, then take a bored teenager with you on a road trip.

The air suddenly became impossible to breathe as our daughter sucked out all the oxygen. With that extra enrichment in her blood she let loose a bellow worthy of an elephant, much less a male bovine. It was a sound honored throughout time, and across species, as a warning to intruders that this turf, this mate, or these young were not to be violated. Stay away, a bellow of this caliber blared.

Alison, however, was prone to get her signals crossed. 'I'm *bored*,' was what she actually said.

Gabriel and I exchanged smiles of contentment. A bored child is a healthy child in today's world of constant stimulation. It was a sign that we were doing at least something right. Needless to say, we were careful not to spoil the moment by acknowledging it.

'Hey, you guys, didn't ya hear me? Can't ya turn on the radio, or something? Ya don't want me dying of boredom back here, do ya?'

'Of course not, dear,' I said pleasantly. 'That's why I packed some library books in that paper bag on the floor, in front of your brother's car seat.'

'You're kidding, Mom, ain't ya? How am I supposed to concentrate at a time like this?'

'Trust me,' Gabe said, 'it's the number one remedy we doctors prescribe for broken hearts.'

'You guys don't understand,' our dejected teenybopper wailed. 'I'm so over that creep, Sheldon. That was then; this is now. But what am I gonna do the rest of this summer? We ain't even home yet, and I am, like, majorly bored. B-O-A-R-D!'

Then again, a bored child who is healthy enough to whine incessantly is akin to a tiny pebble in one's shoes, a pebble that can't be located without removing said shoe, and one is in a place where footwear must remain on. The very thought of having a flouncing, flopping, flailing, faux femme fatal flinging herself about the farm for the next fortnight like one of the demented film stars of the silent screen of whom the Babester is so fond was too much to bear. I just broke down and got it over with. I caved, like a politician's morals the day after elections.

'You can help me solve the murder,' I said, throwing myself under the bus. *Her* bus.

'What murder?' Alison asked.

'Mags,' my husband whispered, 'there's still time to save yourself.'

What point was there in stalling for a few hours? Grandma Ida would spill the beans by suppertime anyway, and then Alison would be sullen for having been shut out. Yes, she would stop talking – temporarily – but her door-slamming would more than make up for that.

'Do you remember the beautiful foreign writer who stayed with us last year?' I said.

'Yeah, and Dad thought she was really hot and couldn't hardly keep his eyes from popping out.'

'That's enough,' the Babester said with a smile.

'Wait a minute,' I said. 'Just when did dad say that she was "really hot?"'

'Hmm, well let me see,' Alison said, ham that she was, 'could it be one of them times when that woman lay out sun-tanning with her store-bought parts rolling around like beach balls in a breeze?'

'Those were your words, by the way, Mags,' my husband said quickly, 'not mine. I barely noticed her store-bought parts.'

'Yeah, ya did, Dad,' Alison said. 'Ya even said that ya didn't see how that itsy-bitsy string bikini managed to keep 'em all containerized.'

'Contained,' I said.

'That's what I said,' Alison said. 'Ya wanna know something else?'

'Not if it has to do with her parts,' I said uncharitably. I know that the Good Lord said that we're supposed to turn the other cheek, but He said nothing that pertains to the bottom pair of cheeks.

'Nah,' Alison said, 'it's about Grandma Ida and the Convent of the Sisters of Perpetual Apostasy.'

'Do tell!' That 'apostasy' was no slip of the tongue either; the girl was far more intelligent than she let on.

'You mean *Apathy*,' Gabe growled.

'That's what I said,' Alison said, then leaned forward just so she could throw herself back into her seat with annoyance. Of course that meant that she wasn't buckled into her seat harness correctly.

'Buckle up,' Gabe ordered sternly, 'and what's this about your grandmother?'

At that point Alison played her next trump card, which was to mumble. As her father was fifty, sitting in front of her, and a man, she might as well not have spoken.

'Now speak up!' he said.

A parent would do well to remember who is ultimately in charge. Or put another way, a wise parent picks his or her battles and then resolves to be content with the outcome. After several attempts to get Alison to speak audibly, both her father and I decided that we could live, at least temporarily, without the information concerning Grandma Ida and her flock of dropout nuns.

'Fine,' Gabe said. 'Have it your way. I don't have to listen to your gossip.'

That got our girl's goat! 'It isn't gossip; it's the truth. Grandma Ida and the Sisters of Perpetual Pity were really pis— I mean, mad at that beautiful lady for the way—'

'Do you really think that she was beautiful?' I asked as I patted my tidy bun under its attractive organza white prayer cap. The Bible says that a woman shouldn't cut her hair as it is our 'crowning glory,' but we Old Order Mennonites also believe that we should reserve the splendour of this home-grown crown for our husbands alone.

'Are you kidding, Mom? She looked like a movie star!'

'I, for one, didn't notice,' the Babester said and he reached over and squeezed my knee.

'*Anyway*,' my clueless daughter said, 'they was all jealous of her – even old Grandma Ida, who's like a hundred years old – so they said that they was gonna tar and feather her. Ya ever hear of that?'

'My mother is eighty-two, and yes, I have heard of tarring and feathering. Just not to anyone I know.'

'Well, they was gonna do it, but then decided against it on

account of the tar having to be hot and someone had to heat it, and they was all too pathetic to do it.'

'You mean *a*pathetic,' I said.

'*Whatever*. So instead they decided to rub her all over with Vaseline. Do you know that stuff is almost impossible to get off? Especially from your hair, on account of the fact that soap and water and even shampoo don't affect it none. Then after they was done with that, they was gonna bring her over here and roll her around in our cow poop.'

'You mean manure. *What?* Oh my, that's awful! That's downright wicked. They need to change their name to Convent of the Sisters of Perpetual Punishment. If I had anything to say about it, they'd all be headed straight to You Know Where.'

'Thank God that we Jews don't believe in your Hell,' Gabe said. 'At least that leaves my mother out of it.'

'I'll be biting my tongue yet again,' I said. 'But before I do that, what changed their minds, Alison? Obviously they didn't smear Miss Sreym with that messy ointment.'

'Well, they tried! Grandma Ida invited her over to the convent to sunbathe in the courtyard there. She told the lady that she'd have more privacy, as you wouldn't be scowling at her and Dad wouldn't be making leech eyes her way neither. So she gets there and Grandma Ida offers to rub her down with this special suntan cream that's guaranteed to turn ya brown as a toad in an hour flat, so the lady says to bring it on.

'But when Grandma Ida starts rubbing it on the lady's back, the lady complains about the way it feels on her skin, and tells Grandma Ida to quit. Instead of quitting, Grandma Ida calls for reinforcements, and so there are five of them pretend apostates holding down this foreign lady and greasing her up like a roasting pig. But let me tell you, that woman was strong with a capital C! She done broke loose and hightailed it back to the PennDutch. Then she drove to Pittsburgh or someplace and had them folks at a spa remove that gunk.'

I knew that Alison was telling the truth by the earnest sound of her voice, but it was all I could do to keep from laughing. Ramat Sreym greased like a roasting pig, imagine that! Then I remembered Gabe's 'leech' eyes, and his refusal to believe in Hell, and nothing was funny anymore.

'You should be a writer,' I said to Alison. 'You have quite a way with words. But you'd have to work on your grammar.'

'Well, you certainly have the imagination,' Gabe grunted. 'Do you really expect me to believe that a frail old woman – an octogenarian, for Pete's sake – would organize what amounts to an assault with petroleum jelly and manure?'

'See?' Alison cried. 'And ya wonder why I don't tell you guys more! It's because ya don't believe me – that's why. Ya always believe the other person. *Always!* No matter who it is. Besides, how was I supposed to know that your mom had eight kids at one time? Ya never talk about it. And I don't see what difference that makes anyhow.'

'*What?*' Gabe said.

I translated for him. 'She's referring to the so-called Octomom; you know, that woman who had eight babies all at once?'

The Babester shook his handsome head. 'Whoa! That's a scary thought. No, Alison, Grandma Ida did not have a litter of babies, and let's say that I do believe you – it's still an amazing story. It might even be funny if it wasn't for the fact that they held that beautiful woman down in order to grease her up.'

'Yeah,' Alison said, 'but she broke away and got herself a nice spa visit. Aren't ya always telling me that all's well that ends well?'

'Touché,' I said, for that was indeed something my husband was fond of saying.

Gabe took his eyes off the road long enough to give me a dirty look. 'Hey, I just had a brilliant idea.'

'Yeah?' Alison said. 'Does it involve stopping at McDonald's?'

'*Oy vey*,' I said.

'That too,' Gabe said. 'But the main idea is a way to keep you from getting bored during the last two weeks of the summer holiday.'

'Ugh,' Alison said. 'Ya know I love this slobbering kid, but do I hafta babysit Mr Chubby Cheeks *all* the time? No offense guys, but I can't be expected to improve my grammar with my head stuck up a dirty nappy twenty-four seven.'

Gabe chuckled. 'I suppose not. OK then, in that case I'll babysit Chubby Cheeks and you go off and do what I had in mind.'

'Which is?' Alison and I said in unison.

'You'll help your mother look for that beautiful lady's killer.'

'Yippee!' Alison cried.

'That was my idea!' I said. 'How dare you steal my idea without asking me first?'

'Well, every crackerjack detective has to have a somewhat bumbling assistant, doesn't he? Or, in this case, she?'

'Which one am I,' Alison asked, 'the crackerjack or the bumbler? And what do those words mean?'

'Aha,' I said, 'I think I'll let your crackerjack-doctor Dad dig himself out of this hole.'

'In that case,' Alison said, 'I want to be the bumbler.'

'Sold,' I said.

But soon after choosing to be a 'bumbler,' Alison was uncharacteristically silent. I turned in my seat enough to see her fast asleep, head thrown back and lips only slightly parted. Forsooth, the daughter that was mine by virtue of inadvertent adultery was beautiful when she sleeps.

Buckled safely in his carrier, also fast asleep, was her brother, the son who was mine by the fervent, feverish fumbling of femurs and assorted body parts, which had nought to do with white satin and lace. It astounded me to think that ten fingers, ten toes and such *nachas* could result from something as unseemly, and unsanitary as all that – now *that* was truly a miracle.

'Praise the Lord,' I whispered, turning back to Gabe. 'They're both asleep.'

'I'll second that,' he said.

FOURTEEN

It was Alison who decided the next step in my investigation. 'You need to grill old Doc's weenie,' she said the next morning over a breakfast of French toast and turkey sausage. I'm guessing the sausage was her inspiration.

'Ahem,' Gabe said.

'Ya mean "amen," right?' Alison said.

'No, I think that he is trying to caution you,' I said.

'About what?' That was just an approximation of what our daughter said, because she often speaks when her mouth is full.

'You're supposed to call him *Uncle* Doc,' Gabe said.

'Yeah?' A spray of masticated sausage flew Gabe's way. 'How come? You don't call him that.'

'That's because we're adults. It's a sign a respect for a younger person in our community to address someone like Doc as "Uncle."'

'Yeah? Well, how come I ain't supposed to call him "Cousin"? Ain't he some kind of cousin of yorn?'

Yorn? Now she was really digging at the bottom of the grammar barrel. Last year Hernia welcomed a family of Mennonites from the state of Illinois who seemed to have brought that loathsome word along with them.

'And *yorn* too,' I said, although I knew that sarcasm, like Limburger cheese, was wasted on the young. 'Still, I want you to call him "uncle." But anyway, why do you think that he deserves to be grilled first?'

Alison rolled her eyes so far back in her head that I feared we'd have to get the toilet plunger to suck them out. 'Cheese and crackers! Don'tcha observe *anything*, Mom? He was over here like a million times when that lady stayed with us, and he gave her even more goggle eyes than Dad did, but she didn't even send him one fairy moan. Not a single one.'

The Babester, who was feeding warm baby cereal to his male offspring, set down the miniature spoon and scratched his handsome Hebrew head. Figuratively – but not literally, thank you – I scratched my large, horsey head. Alison's malapropisms were like the Sunday crossword puzzle: with practice they continue to get easier. This one, however, proved particularly difficult.

'Uncle!' I cried at last.

'OK,' Alison said. 'I get it, already. I'll call him *Uncle* Doc. Ya don't hafta beat me over the head with it.'

'No, I mean "uncle" as in "I give up." I know that you meant to say "google eyes," not "goggle eyes," but I haven't a clue about what a moaning fairy has got to do with anything.'

Speaking of eyes, Alison's pair rolled back into place, saving me the time to hunt for them. 'You're nuts, Mom.'

'That was insulting, but at least it was grammatically correct, dear.'

'Eureka, I've got it,' Gabe said. 'The word is pheromone – with a P and an H. Is that right, Alison?'

Our daughter smiled happily. 'Ya see? I ain't so stupid after all.'

'Well, strictly speaking—' I started to say, but Gabe stopped me with a wink and an upright palm, which was his way of asking me gently to put a lid on my preaching. We Herniaites are, by the way, a winking, blinking and nodding lot.

I swallowed my irritation – which was a goodly portion of my calories for the day – and smiled kindly at one and all. 'So, Alison, sweetheart, in your estimation why would Miss Sreym giving Uncle Doc the cold shoulder be grounds for making him a suspect in her demise?'

'Her rump,' Alison said, to express her impatience with my lack of mental acuity. 'First of all, I didn't know the lady had dim eyes, so I *didn't* think that she blamed Uncle Doc for that. What I'm saying is that I think it's weird that she didn't give him the "come slither" look that Auntie Susannah was always yapping about when she was here. Ya know, where ya wiggle ya shoulders like this, and like that, so that your boobies go— Only I don't got none, so it ain't my fault that they ain't bobbing up and down like fishing corks over on Miller's Pond. And don't ya laugh none, because it ain't my fault.'

I know what it's like to be a carpenter's dream: flat as a board.

'Don't worry, dear,' I hastened to assure her. 'I can tell by your shoulders that you'll take after your mother's side of the family in that department. Why, I'm sure that in five years from now you'll need an old lady's walker just to tote those things around for you.'

Alison's grin nearly split her head in two. '*Really?*'

'Would I exaggerate, dear? Never mind; I just want you to answer my question about Uncle Doc's motive.'

Alison shook her head sadly. No doubt she viewed me as a hopeless case.

'It's like this, see. Uncle Doc couldn't stand being flat-out rejected. I know that he's an old geezer and all, but it's kind of funny the way he hits on ya.' She paused, her eyes searching my face. 'Ain't it?'

'Pathetic is more like it.'

'Ya mean it bothers ya?'

'It bothers me that sometimes he doesn't seem to realize when he's crossed the line between flirting and harassment.'

'Oh, give me a break,' Gabe said. 'That old man is always putting you on. He knows that you've given your heart to me, and that I've given mine to you. We are truly a couple until death us do part.'

'Ooh,' Alison said. 'This is *way* too mushy for my young ears.'

I felt all tingly inside, from my scalp down to my toes. 'This,' I said to Alison, 'is exactly the kind of thing that your young ears need to hear.' Then I turned to the Babester. 'But darling, he's always telling me how beautiful I am, what symmetrical features I have, what long, lithe, lovely limbs – words like that hurt a gal like me.'

It came as no surprise when my husband roared with laughter. 'Face it babe, you *are* hot stuff. You're the best-looking woman in three counties, but you can't see it. You never will. You have a body image problem, and you know it on an intellectual level. You've already had a professional diagnose it, and I concur.'

'Oh, no!' I heard Alison cry.

I whirled to face my daughter. The poor dear looked as if she was on the brink of crying. Her bottom lip, which is usually stuck out defiantly, was trembling as if she'd suffered a stroke.

'Mom, you ain't gonna die on me from a disease, are ya?

Because if you are, I can raise Little Jacob by myself – with Dad's help, of course – but I'm gonna need a bigger allowance than the one I'm getting now.'

Despite the five centuries of Swiss Amish and Mennonite inbreeding that had rendered me incapable of expressing my emotions physically (essentially making a Brit out of me), I was all set to hug my precious daughter when she piped up again after a very brief pause.

'And ya know, a sixty-inch flat-screen color TV for my room wouldn't be a bad idea either.'

I smiled broadly. 'This must be your lucky day then, because both of your wishes will be granted over my dead body.'

'Aw!'

'Aha! You must know that I'm not suffering from a terminal disease, or you wouldn't be disappointed.'

The sneaky scamp scowled and turned to her dad. 'I need that raise,' she said. 'I can't buy the stuff I need for school without it.'

Gabe is such a pushover when it comes to his children. 'We'll see. Go help your mom solve her case – that can be your job.'

'Really?'

'Come on, Nancy Drew,' I said, 'before we both change our minds.'

The Good Lord knows that I am not a jealous woman. I certainly am not the type of woman who would be jealous of one distant cousin cavorting with another very distant cousin. In fact, both degrees of relatedness are so distant that said parties are permitted to marry each other, both in the church and legally. Therefore to suggest that even for a nanosecond I might have felt a twinge of unpleasantness upon espying my best friend Agnes's car parked in front of Doc's house – well, that suggestion would be sheer poppycock.

Yes, it is true: I am in possession of a rich and vivid imagination. Alas, since I am neither a painter, nor a writer, what is for some a gift has often been a curse for me. Yet, since I am not the jealous sort, I wasted precious little time imagining Agnes's plump, stubby, limbs fumbling for the old goat in a twist of dirty sheets. Nor did I spend much time trying to imagine their long, languorous glances over an inedible dinner that Agnes had insisted on cooking, in spite of Doc's legendary prowess with skillets, pots and all manner of implements that just might, coincidentally, raise one's temperature.

'Hey,' Alison said, 'ain't that old Agnes's car?'

'Please call her Aunt Agnes, now,' I said. 'Or Auntie, if you prefer.'

'*What?* But it ain't like she's a million years old like Uncle Doc; she's just old like you.'

'Thanks, I'll take that.'

I also had to take the fact that it was Agnes who answered the door. 'Come on in,' she said with a welcoming gesture of one of those short plump arms. 'Doc is occupied at the moment' – she paused to giggle behind the back of her plump hand – 'but he'll be out in a moment. Or three.' She giggled again with irritating familiarity.

There are times when I just can't help myself, when I simply must speak what's on my mind or risk spontaneous combustion. Given that I am so thin that, were it not for my rudder of a nose, I would all but disappear when viewed from the side, fire could consume me in mere seconds. No more bossy, opinionated Magdalena would mean no more Mama for Alison and Little Jacob. Little Jacob would probably fare better than his sister, because he has never been rejected. For Alison, however, who was dumped on my doorstep at age eleven, my sudden demise would probably be devastating. That said, I owed it to her to tell Agnes exactly what I thought of her shameless behaviour.

'Hush, you shameless hussy, hush!' I said, sounding curiously Portuguese. 'Can't you see there's a child here?'

'I ain't no child,' Alison said angrily, and flounced over the threshold with her arms crossed.

Agnes's giggles turned to peals of laughter. Happy laughter at that!

'Oh, Magdalena, for once you've jumped to exactly the right conclusions, and your judgemental paranoia is going to be richly rewarded. After you dropped me off here yesterday, Doc and I talked for hours – all day, really – and then we, uh, got to know each other better all night. Doc has asked me to move in with him and be his kept woman, and I've accepted. How exciting is that?'

Exciting? Yes, in the sense that my heart was racing and my legs had turned to rubber. If it hadn't been for the still-strong arms of old Doc, who had finished his business by then, I would have had an unfortunate meeting with his coffee table. Instead, he managed to catch me. Then he carried me over to his personal recliner, which has a remote control, and had me lie back in it. Well, of course, I wouldn't stand for lying prone. I promptly righted myself.

'You can't do this to me,' I wailed. The ensuing silence was deafening; my ears screamed like sirens, the blood roared through my body and my heart beat like a bass drum. Oh, horse manure, I thought to myself, now I have really done it. I have gone too far. Everyone in Hernia and the surrounding County of Bedford is going to think that for two decades – ever since his wife passed – dear old Doc and the strumpet without a crumpet have been doing the 'bump it.' It wasn't true, of course, but throughout history folks have found it more fun to pass along gossip and slander than to speak the truth.

At any rate, while I was left hanging in this noisy breeze of silence, Alison was sitting on the edge of the couch, elbows on her knees, chin in her hands and staring at me with something akin to wonder in her large hazel eyes. As for the new lovebirds, they were exchanging little glances and mouthing words that might have made me sick, had I been able to hear them.

'Well,' Agnes said at last, 'it's always good to clear the air, don't you think?'

'But what will people *think*?' I protested. 'You both come from good Amish-Mennonite stock who came over on the Charming Nancy in 1738. The best families in Hernia; your ancestors are listed in Gingerich and Kreider's genealogical reference book, the best of its kind. You have ancestors who settled the area as pioneers, which means that you can be buried up on Stucky Ridge.'

'You can see for ten miles in every direction from up there,' Alison said. What a dear she was for trying to help her mama at a time like this.

'Let us not forget,' I said, 'that cohabitation outside the bonds of marriage is a sin. This saith the Lord, and not just Magdalena.'

'Whoa,' said Alison. 'Mama, you lost me there with them big words.'

'It means that they're fornicating,' I snapped. Understandably,

I was stressed, seeing as how my two best friends were sinning with each other, and not with me. This is not to say that I would ever, in a zillion years – not even in 'God's time'– want them to sin with me, but still, the mental image of their entwined limbs rankled this poor wretch's soul something awful. This is something that the amazing grace of God can help one overcome, but I wasn't ready just yet.

Sometimes it feels good to stew in one's own juices. Ask any rankled wretch and they'll tell you I'm right. We pick away at our scabs, we scratch dangerously at our itches, all because we are mortal. On our own, we are helpless to control our baser instincts. 'The Devil made me do it,' is the truth, and it's something that agnostics and atheists are just too blind to see.

'What does "fornicate" mean?' Alison said. 'I don't see them doing nothing right now except looking kinda goofy.'

'The "kinda goofy" look,' Agnes said, 'is because we're in love.'

'No sh—oot! Ya mean I look like that too when I'm in love?'

Agnes let loose with a string of her disgusting giggles. 'Even worse. Once, you—'

'Doc,' I said angrily, 'how can you stand there and let her say that you're in love when all these years you've been mourning your dear, departed wife by still setting a place for her at the table?'

My oldest friend squared his shoulders. 'That place setting was for you – in hopes that you would stop by, which you sometimes did.'

'But then you'd add another,' I said.

'Magdalena, you were always such a prim and proper lady – so buttoned up in your self-righteousness. There I was, a randy old widower, burning with desire for you – what was I to do? I did everything but hit you over the head with a club and drag you off to my bedroom. You may have thought I was just an eccentric old man and that it was harmless flirtation, but I was seriously trying to woo you.'

'Woo, woo!' Alison hooted, sounding quite like the Great Horned Owl that lives in the giant oak tree at the end of our pasture.

Meanwhile, poor Agnes was picking at her cuticles and fighting back tears. As for *moi*: I was immensely flattered by the heartfelt confessions of one friend, but at the same time feeling terrible for the other. If only I had the heart of stone that some have accused me of possessing; how much easier life would be then. As it stood now, I wanted to beat my breast in agonized dichotomous confusion, but lacking significant breastbone flesh, such an action would be unduly painful, and no doubt result in bruises that would be hard to explain to my Dearly Beloved.

The saying is that you can't have your cake and eat it too. Well, I had eaten many of Doc's cakes – and pies. He was a fabulous cook. The fact is that I had never thought of Doc as a serious marriage partner. He was over thirty years older than me, for crying out loud! He was, to put it frankly, a wizened, grizzled geezer. A lech. He'd been a contemporary of my parents, and was first cousin to Mama and second cousin to Papa. Grandma Yoder's ghost – er, Apparition American – would have looked down her long (née Hostetler) nose at him and sneered, because when Doc was a boy he was always getting into trouble of some sort or another (as bright lads are wont to do).

Well, that ship had clearly sailed, as another saying goes. It was time for me to let go of half-baked fantasies and ill-defined dreams, and to quit being arbitrator of moral law. Besides, who was I to throw the first stone, anyway? I am, in fact, so awful at throwing balls that any stone that I would throw would most probably circle back and hit me like a boomerang. I would probably deserve it, too.

I'm afraid that I took a bit too long, taking stock of my judgmental self. I do, after all, tend to meander down the irregular hallways of an unorthodox mind. Now it was time for me to redeem myself.

'I have just two words for you lovebirds,' I shouted. '*Mazel tov!*'

'Yay!' Alison shouted as well and jumped up and down, clapping excitedly.

Agnes looked up from her nails. '*Really*, Mags? You mean it?'

'I mean it with all my heart. The two of you are my dearest friends. What else should I want, except that you keep each other safe and healthy and happy?'

'Well done, friend,' Doc said. Under normal circumstances he would have hugged me after a highly charged moment such as that, but it was just as well that he remained where he was, framed by the doorway of the hall.

'OK,' Alison said, 'now that we have all the gooey stuff over with, it's time to get down to business.'

I stared at her with amazement. We all did, in fact.

'Some assistant, I have, eh?' I said, feeling a mite embarrassed.

Doc cleared his throat. 'She's the cat's pyjamas; no doubt about it.'

'Hey, wait a minute,' Alison blurted, arms akimbo. 'Is that a good thing or bad?'

'Decidedly good,' Agnes said with a weak smile. 'OK then, I acquiesce. Commence your infamous grilling, Torquemada. The sooner you've checked us off your list of suspects, the sooner we can get on with our wedding plans. By the way, I hope you realize that I want you to be my matron of honor.'

It may not be possible for a forty-nine-year-old woman to squeal like a nine-year-old girl, unless she has done something truly horrible like placed her hand over the top of a palm-sized spider while getting up to use the ladies' room at night, or chanced to come upon her mother-in-law naked. Both events left that poor woman badly shaken and as skittish as a colt in a rattlesnake den. This time I squealed out of genuine, unbridled joy for the bride-to-be. I have always wanted to participate in a wedding, without having to worry about those three minutes of inconvenience which every woman must endure on her wedding night.

'*And*,' Agnes went on to say, when there was a chance that she might be heard, 'Alison, I would like you to be my bridesmaid.'

Alison put one hand on her heart, but the other up in front of her as if to stop a runaway stagecoach. 'I can't!' she protested.

'Why can't you, dear?' I said. 'It's a great honor.' I lowered my voice to a whisper. 'Besides, Auntie Agnes will be hurt if you don't accept.'

I should have known that I would raise a child who is a stranger to guile. 'Oh, Auntie Agnes,' Alison said, 'I just can't be seen clomping around in high heels while trying not to step on a frumpy dress in some hideous color that has a bow on the back bigger than the one Minnie Mouse wears in her hair.' She said that all in one breath.

Much to my surprise, Agnes laughed and clapped her hands. 'Oh, honey, you can wear whatever you want, just as long as it comes down to your knees and covers your shoulders. And any color except for white – *that* is reserved for the bride.'

I cleared my throat. 'Now, Agnes, strictly speaking, isn't white—'

'Shut up, Magdalena,' Agnes said. She wasn't smiling, either.

'Now that we have those details taken care of,' Doc said, with a glint of approval in his eyes, 'how about we celebrate with a piece of homemade chocolate peanut butter pie?'

'In the middle of the morning?' I said. 'Won't that spoil our appetites for lunch?'

'So what?' Doc said. 'What's the worst thing that will happen? You'll eat less for lunch. Big deal. Instead, let's just be thankful that we have the opportunity to spoil our taste buds with something this delicious. Did I mention that you can have as much real whipped cream on your slice as you wish?'

'OK, Doc, you've twisted my arm. But now I'm going to show you my gratitude by telling you a secret.'

FIFTEEN

DOC SHAFER'S RECIPE FOR GREEN-TOMATO PIE

Makes 8 servings

6 or 7 medium-size firm green tomatoes without blemishes (and without wrinkles if you want to peel them), approximately 3 cups when chopped
2 tablespoons lemon juice
½ teaspoon salt
¾ teaspoon cinnamon
¾ cup sugar
2 tablespoons cornstarch
Top and bottom pie crusts
1 tablespoon margarine or butter

Wash the tomatoes. Peel them if you want, but it's a lot of trouble and not really necessary. Cut the tomatoes into bite-size pieces. Combine the tomato bits with the next three ingredients in a saucepan. Cook for about fifteen minutes. Mix the sugar and cornstarch together and slowly stir into the tomato mixture. Cook for a few minutes, until the sugar and cornstarch become clear. Add margarine and allow to cool slightly. Line a nine-inch pie pan with the bottom crust and pour in the tomato mixture. Put on top crust and seal the edges. Crimp narrow strips of aluminium foil around the edge to prevent it from getting too brown. Poke numerous holes with a fork across the top to allow steam to escape. Bake for 40 to 50 minutes at 425 degrees. Some people like to eat the pie warm, but Doc much prefers it cold.

SIXTEEN

Doc makes his own pie crusts. They always turn out tender and flaky, but for the chocolate peanut butter pie he makes a graham cracker crust. Let's face it, I enjoy being the center of attention, and I enjoy drama, just as long as I don't suffer financially from it. Ergo, I studiously mashed every speck of graham cracker onto the tines of my fork, and made a great show of licking them off before I commenced to spill my promised secret. But by then my little audience was properly primed; which is exactly how it should have been.

'You know that very handsome new minister at the First Mennonite Church?' I said.

'Well, of course,' Agnes said. 'Pastor Nate's *my* minister; you know that's why I go to church.'

'Quite so, dear. Then you might enjoy this little titbit of harmless gossip all the more.'

'Hold it there,' Doc growled. 'Gossip is seldom, if ever, harmless. We've been over this before, Magdalena; even if it hurts no one else, gossip always diminishes the teller.'

'Yeah,' Alison said. 'What's a teller, Uncle Doc?'

'Magdalena,' Agnes said in her patient voice, 'it was you who got me to see that Jesus came down very hard on the subject of divorce, but he had nothing at all to say on the subject of homosexuality.'

Doc laughed. '*One man, one woman* – folks who want that to be the law of the land, although they still want the right to get remarried after a divorce – those folks are the epitome of hypocrites. One of our venerable statesman, for example, has been married three times. There you have the perfect example of one man, and one woman, and another woman, and another woman.'

'You are both absolutely right,' I said. 'However, the secret which I am about to divulge has nothing to do with Pastor Nate being gay, for the simple reason because he isn't.'

'Now *that's* a surprise,' Agnes said. 'I thought you got most of your information by sticking your long Yoder nose into other people's beeswax. Now I'm beginning to doubt that. Because if you really did, then you might come to the same conclusion that the rest of us already reached a long time ago: that Pastor Nate *is* a gay man, who is very good at suppressing his true nature and passing himself off as straight.'

'Is that so?' I said.

Agnes gave me a pitying look that was probably well-deserved. 'You poor dear, and you call yourself an amateur detective? Just because Pastor Nate is so handsome, virile and rugged, and – uh – looks rather like Hugh Jackman, minus the wolverine claws, you think he's heterosexual?'

'What about you, Agnes,' Doc said, sounding more than a mite miffed, 'do you want to jump his bones?'

'Why, Doc Shafor,' Agnes said, 'I am shocked by your language! Need I remind you, fiancé of mine, that there's a child present?'

'Hey,' Alison said, 'how many times do I hafta remind ya that I ain't no child?'

'*People*,' I said, 'a word, if I may. Alison, you are a young woman, so act like one. Doc, I've made my peace with you loving Agnes; go for it. Agnes, your pastor is definitely *not* gay; so theoretically you *could* jump his bones. Now, what I wanted to say is this: Reverend Nathaniel Troyer, pastor of The First Mennonite Church of Hernia, Pennsylvania was carrying on a secret affair with the trollop who packed a wallop that sent our little village flying to bookshelves across America, and in the process exposed our foibles and made a mockery of our noble way of life.'

Both adults appeared stunned, whilst the teen's face lighted up with renewed interest. 'Yeah? That's dope!' she said, using her latest dopey slang word. Then seeing my look of disapproval she added, 'I mean, like, what's this world coming to anyway?'

When Alison trotted out that hackneyed phrase she'd learned from me, which has been used by adults from time *in memoriam*, we three grownups couldn't help but laugh. But for Agnes, the laughter was short-lived.

'Magdalena,' she said, stretching as tall as she could, and thus no longer forming a near perfect sphere, 'you better be darn well sure of this. You could be sued for libel.'

'How well do you know your Bible?' I said. It was a rhetorical question: even liberal Mennonites, like Agnes, try to read through the entire Bible once a year.

'Get to your point,' Agnes snarled.

'My source was King Ahab himself.'

'What? That doesn't make sense – unless you're trying to say that Pastor Nate is supposed to be King Ahab and Ramat Sreym is the wicked Queen Jezebel. Therefore it was Pastor Nate who told you this news himself.'

'Bingo,' I said. 'In fact, he told me down in his basement office, just off your social hall, with its delightful scents of tuna casserole and weak, decaffeinated coffee. I am quite certain that the word "bingo" has been uttered more than once down there.'

'You are so vulgar!' Agnes's eyes burned with fury.

'She meant the *game*,' Doc said.

'Oh, well, still, she's trying to get my goat.' Agnes turned back to me, eyes still ablaze. 'We're not Catholics; they're the ones who play Bingo. We're Mennonites; we *eat*.'

'I didn't know that Auntie Agnes had a goat,' Alison said. 'Why can't we have – oh, yeah, it's just an expression.'

'Agnes,' Doc said, 'it seems to me that you're inordinately bent out of shape by the thought of your pastor and Ramat having an affair. It sounds like you're taking it personally.'

My stout friend spun; it was like watching a top. 'Of course I'm taking it personally. I feel betrayed. That woman ridiculed me in her book, and this man – my spiritual leader – was being intimate with her? And it's not just me; it is anyone else who might have come to him for premarital counselling, etc. – and meanwhile he was fornicating. *Forn*icating.'

'There's that fancy word again,' Alison said.

'Now,' I said, 'please consider the following. Before most of us have actually read Ramat's ding-dong book, Sam asks her to be one of the judges for our historic annual apple pie contest. It was a brilliant move on her part to accept because, as you know, the Hernia Heritage Days Apple Festival lasts a week, with apple dunking, cider, sauces—'

'Mags,' Doc said, 'you usually mean well, but you're as long-winded as a Baptist preacher.'

'Amen,' Agnes said.

I glowered kindly at her – so to speak. 'Well, anyway, I think that it's entirely possible that Pastor Nate is the one who poisoned Miss Sreym. After all, she was sitting between him and Wanda Hemphopple on the judges' platform. The only reason that Toy didn't grill him like a weenie at the time is – well, because Toy is a Southern gentleman. In the South, the clergy are put on pedestals where they reign like demigods. Then every decade or so it seems they invariably give in to the sins of the flesh, or the temptations of the offering plate.'

Doc nodded. 'Hmm. Why do you reckon that seems to be more of a Southern thing; those dramatic falls from Grace, followed by televised appeals of slobbering evangelists begging for forgiveness?'

'I know!' Alison had her hand raised like she was in school, although I doubted that she ever raised it there.

'Do tell, dear,' I said.

'Because Southern women dress sexier, and that makes them prettier, just like that Ramat lady, who was some kind of beautiful.'

'She was not!' Agnes said sharply.

I smiled at poor Alison, who looked as if she'd been slapped. 'Anyway, Alison, you didn't address the issue of money. Why does it seem like more of the high-living, mega-church ministers live in the South?'

'That's easy too,' my daughter sniffed. 'It's the accent, see? It sounds much nicer to be asking folks to be coughing up money for God when ya sound just as poor as they is. But ya can't be begging for no money if ya sound like Pastor Nate. That don't sound right, ya see? I mean, why would ya give ya money to a college man?'

'That kid has a good head on her shoulders,' Doc said.

'Ya think so?' Alison said. She was beaming. ''Cause I got me another possible theory about who mighta killed that beautiful author lady.'

'Is that so?' Doc said. I could tell that he was tempted to reach out and pat her on the head. 'Who would that be?'

'You, of course. You, *and* Auntie Agnes.'

'Alison!' I was genuinely shocked at her bringing Agnes into this.

'Mom, don't look so fierce! You was saying to Dad that Uncle Doc and that gorgeous foreign lady had themselves a roll in the haystack.'

'I said no such thing!'

Tears immediately spilled from Alison's eyes. 'Mom, there's no need to make a liar out of me just because you're embarrassed about what you said. Auntie Agnes, go ahead and ask Uncle Doc if he thinks I'm a big fat liar, like my mother wants you to believe.'

At that point, it is doubtful that Agnes even heard her, so focused was she on Doc. Most certainly, Agnes was not paying attention to Alison's shifting grammar.

'*Snickerdoodle*,' Agnes said, 'did you sleep with that two-bit tramp of an author?'

Doc appeared genuinely rattled, I'll grant him that. 'Two-*bit*?' he rasped. 'Do you think that is all that she cost me? Just two bits? She demanded that I take her to Smokin' Joe's Steak House up the highway in Bedford, and then shell out $11.95 *each* for a proper steak meal with all the trimmings. Each! And that is not including gratuity. I'm telling you, those people on the other side of the Pond, don't know how lucky they have it not having to tip wait staff.'

Despite her impeccable Mennonite-Amish lineage, I thought Agnes was going to haul off and punch Doc so hard that he'd be forever planted on the surface of the moon, along with an American flag and some famous foot prints. Instead, her voice raised another octave as she swivelled back to face Alison, her accuser.

'I can see why you might think that *he* is guilty, given how low he can stoop, but why do you paint me with the same brush?'

'Huh?' Alison said.

'She means,' I said, 'why do you put her in the same category as Uncle Doc?'

Alison responded first with a very loud, and long, belch. She was, after all, just a young teenager who had stuffed her face with pie. While I do wish that she hadn't behaved in this manner, neither was I mortified, as perhaps someone thought I should be.

'Well, say something to her,' Agnes directed me, after a minute or so had elapsed.

'Alison, please answer Auntie Agnes's question: why do you think that she could be guilty as well?'

'Not *that* question,' my friend said, and angrily stamped a foot.

I nodded. 'OK, then, let me try again. Alison, what is the capital of Oklahoma?'

'Oklahoma City,' she said proudly. State capitals were something we'd worked on together when she first came to stay with us.

This answer was correct, but not what Agnes wanted, and that fact incensed her. An incensed Agnes is a fearsome beast – not one to be trifled with. My Alison, however, unlike me, is not a coward, and does not back down from a position she has taken when she knows that she is right.

'You can get as mad at me as you want, Auntie Agnes, but ya should be getting mad at Uncle Doc and my mom. They're both lying to ya. If ya don't believe me about Uncle Doc, just look in them beady eyes of his, and ya can always tell when my mom is lying because she sticks a finger under that silly bun on the back of her head and starts scratching something fierce.'

I yanked my finger out of my bun so quickly that I ripped my nail on a bobby pin. 'I do not do that!' I wailed.

'Anyway,' Alison said, 'all I know is that she did say that Uncle Doc and that gorgeous dead woman was dating for a time. This makes me think that maybe you wanted her dead, so that she was out of way, and then you could date this old man.'

'Why, you little imp!' Agnes cried.

'No ma'am,' Alison said. 'Both my legs work just fine; I don't limp at all. Now it could be that you is innocent, and it was Uncle Doc who wanted the beautiful writer lady dead so that he could date you, but that don't exactly make sense now, do it?'

'*What?*' Agnes said.

'What I mean is: why would he give up a chocolate cake for a piece of broccoli? Even if he did, ain't no jury gonna buy that.'

Dear, sweet Agnes. She was a smart cookie – uh – floret of broccoli, and as such, immediately understood Alison's analogy. She is also, essentially, a kind, Christian woman, and I could see her attempt to swallow her irritation until I thought sure that the poor dear was going to explode like an overfilled balloon.

Then suddenly, much to my horror, it occurred to me that Alison had a valid point. The Bible extols the wisdom of babes, and whilst my daughter was a mite beyond that age – perhaps even capable of producing her own babe – I would do well to give her views more credence. Especially when they made sense.

'I don't think that either of you are capable of murder,' I said carefully. 'Oops, let me start over,' I said even more carefully. 'I know for a *fact* that neither of you are capable of murder. Doc, when you were a practicing vet and had to put down one of my cows, I saw you weeping.'

'That was sweat running into my eyes,' Doc growled. 'I'd been up all night trying to help the darn calf survive its birth.'

I laughed pleasantly. 'Sweat, tears – they're both salty liquids, right? And you, Agnes, have trouble stepping on ants. Try denying that!'

Agnes gave a long, exasperated sigh, which thankfully deflated an otherwise dangerous situation. 'Magdalena, I have trouble stepping on ants because I have trouble seeing them. I've been putting off seeing my optometrist for far too long.'

'Nevertheless,' I said, 'can we agree that if the two of you were to be suddenly extracted from this scenario – excised if you will, by a giant pair of scissors – and another pair of players inserted in your stead, that these new players would be suspect?'

'I most certainly would not agree!' Agnes snorted. 'To do so would be to admit to plausibility, and you ought to know, Magdalena, that my character is beyond reproach.'

'You're treading on dangerous ground, Mags,' Doc growled.

'Puh-*leaze*,' I said, 'get it through your thick skull, Agnes; I can't conceive of you murdering anyone. I'm saying that to someone on the outside – to someone like Chief Toy, for instance – it could appear that you had a motive.'

'Only if your little brat brings up her cockeyed theory in the first place.'

That did it; that raised my hackles like nobody's business. It raised them from my scrawny chicken legs up to my featherless armpits. Nothing gets this old crone's juices going like a direct attack on her children.

'Agnes Delores Miller,' I hissed, there being sufficient S's in her name to make it sibilant. 'If you intend to remain my best friend, let me warn you, you are standing on perilously thin ice. If the ice starts to crack and push comes to shove, I'll push you off my ice floe and then give you an extra shove out to sea – if that's what it takes to keep Alison safe from drowning. Don't ever make me choose between my little seal cub and my best friend, the polar bear.'

'*Brava*,' Doc said. 'I find expanded metaphors to be downright sexy.'

'That was really gross,' Alison said, 'the way you spat all over me when you said Auntie Agnes's name.'

'Polar bear?' Agnes raged. 'Is *that* how you see me? Big, white and furry?'

I smiled noncommittally. 'Hmm. More like fluffy than furry. Now, dear, let us take a page from our friends across the pond—'

'Hold it right there,' Doc roared. 'I've been a pretty good sport, considering your accusation, but now you want us to take a page from the Perpetually Pathetic Sisters in that sham convent across from you on Miller's Pond?'

'Not *that* pond,' I said, 'but the Big Pond.'

'She means the "ocean,"' Alison said. 'Like Atlantis, for instance.'

'Yes, or another instance,' I said. 'And on that page would be written *Keep Calm and Carry On*. So in that spirit – which I'm sure we can all agree upon is a very sensible way of conducting business – I shall herewith carry on calmly. Agnes and Doc, the facts of the matter speak for themselves in this case. We have an aged lothario and a libidinous Lolita of uncommon beauty, carrying on what could only be described as a torrid affair, especially when judged by community standards.

'Then along comes a premenopausal spinster, of extraordinary intelligence, but whose face, alas, can barely launch a dinghy, much less a ship – no hurt intended, dear. The lothario immediately espies the value that the homely woman offers him over the two-bit trollop who lolls about in his bed, and he fiercely desires to be twain with the brain – but lo, he cannot, lest he be blackmailed.'

'*Blackmailed!*' Alison said. 'Cool. Hey, Mom, what exactly does that mean?'

'Well, dear, when you blackmail someone, you make them pay you in exchange for you not telling one of their secrets.'

'Ah, I get it. Just like at camp when Tracy snuck in two hours after curfew and I made her pay me fifty bucks for not telling.'

'Alison,' I said, 'I am ashamed of you; I would have asked for a hundred bucks and then settled for seventy-five.' I knew, by the way, that she was kidding. My daughter always tugs absentmindedly on her left earlobe while she's trying to pull my leg.

'Huh?' Three people looked in danger of having their eyes pop out.

'Hey,' I said, 'what is that old saying? Shoot for the moon, and if you miss, at least you stand a good chance of hitting a star. Right? Fifty bucks was way too low. But back to you, Doc. You didn't want Hernia to find out that you'd been dating the likes of that worldly floozy, and she was threatening to tell. For some incomprehensible reason, women find you attractive. Even *physically* attractive.

'I know what you're thinking: who am I, Magdalena Portulacca Yoder Rosen, that I should judge that? Fair enough. Just look at me. Agnes might be pressed hard to launch a dinghy with her face, but I could bring a hot air balloon down just by smiling at it. On the last day of October when I flew down to Tampa to visit my cousin Bertha, airport security told me to remove my Halloween mask. My point is that I'm no looker, and neither are you, but women sure do find you attractive.

'So, instead of giving me grief, it would be in your own best interest if the two of you stepped up to the plate and helped me find the real killer. The *real* killer, Agnes – not you. Get it? Because I don't think that it's you.'

'Harrumph,' Doc said, and rubbed a gnarled, liver-spotted hand over a sparse scalp. 'What about me? Do you feel as strongly about my innocence as you do your girlfriend's?'

Alison, bless her heart, had had enough of Uncle Doc for the day. 'Oh, Uncle Doc,' she said, affecting a light tone, 'put a sock in it.'

'*Ach du heimer*,' I squawked, reverting to my ancestral Pennsylvania Dutch. It's a meaningless phrase invoking a hammer, but I wouldn't be surprised if it substituted for something more sinister. Nonetheless, it's a handy thing to say when all else fails.

'Going all "Dutchy" on me, are you now?' Doc demanded. He's a good man, a kind man, but I'd never seen him so angry. Then again, Doc wasn't used to hormonal teenage girls – well, except for the ones he's dated.

I looked at my watch. It was a simple analogue watch: the same Timex I'd been given as a baptismal present when I was twelve years old, nigh on to thirty-seven years ago. We Mennonites, and our close relations, the Amish, are Anabaptists. So are the Baptists, of course. This means that, unlike Anglicans and Roman Catholics, we do not baptize infants, who haven't the slightest idea what is happening to them; we only baptize people who have made a conscious decision to accept Jesus into their hearts. To baptize a squalling baby who is still incapable of caring one whit about her salvation is absolutely ludicrous – not that I'm judging, mind you. That is merely common sense; any thinking person can come to that conclusion.

I tapped my trusted Timex. 'My how time flies,' I said, 'even when you're not having fun.'

Agnes grunted. 'You can say that again.'

'Are you kidding?' Alison said. 'I had the best time ever; watching the two of you squirm was even better than camp. An ancient man like Uncle Doc and a fluffy woman like you doing the nasty, and trying ta cover it up like ya didn't do nothing. And ya getting so jealous of that gorgeous writer that ya turn green around the grills – ya can't make this stuff up, I'm telling ya.'

They say that when the going gets tough, the tough get going. That is supposed to mean that tough people then 'step up to the plate,' as it were. They get the job done. Sometimes, however, tough people can simply be tired and literally just get going. That is what I did.

I grabbed Alison by the wrist and in a not too unpleasant voice I said our goodbyes in a number of salutations I'd picked up through my business as an innkeeper. '*Sayonara,* baby; *adios*; *hasta la vista*; *ciao*; *shalom*; see ya later, alligator; after awhile, crocodile; over and out.'

SEVENTEEN

If you ask me the only way to decompress – at least when you have a minor in tow – is to put sugar in your mouth. I base this philosophy on firsthand observation: to wit I have never seen a crabby butterfly, or an out-of-sorts hummingbird, and both butterflies and hummingbirds spend their days sucking sweet nectar out of flowers. One can be sure that both of these creatures were under a goodly amount of stress until their current incarnation, the butterfly having begun as a caterpillar, and the hummingbird as an egg the size of a jelly bean. There is, to be sure, a mountain of evidence that proves that sugar leads to all kinds of disease and disastrous consequences but, as a short-term solution, it is God's gift to the human tongue.

That said, when we pulled up to the police station, which is directly across from Yoder's Corner Market, and Alison begged to go get a 'nosh,' I shocked the poor child by instantly agreeing.

'No way!'

'Way,' I said.

'But like, you're kidding, right?' she said.

'I'm dead serious,' I said. 'Just not deadly. But whatever you're getting, get me one too. I'm hungry as well.'

'Yeah, but Mom, what if ya don't like what I choose – ya know, what with your old lady taste buds and all.'

'Surprise me, dear. My old lady taste buds will just have to stretch.'

'Yeah? Well, don't let them stretch too much, Mom. I weren't gonna say anything about this on my own, see, but now that you bring it up: ya show a lot of them gums when ya smile.'

I clasped my hands together in mock joy. 'I *do*? Oh, happy day!'

'Mom, that ain't a good thing,' Alison said warily.

'You're right, dear; it's a wonderful thing,' I said.

Alison leaned as far away from me as she could. 'Mom, ya ain't sick, are ya? Because ya sure ain't acting right.'

'I'm quite all right, dear,' I said with a wide, gum-baring grin. 'I assure you that I am. It is my firm conviction that excessive gumminess is a sure sign that one has noble blood in their veins. You see, there has always been a rumour in our family that we are descendants of the male offspring of a Swiss count. He was kidnapped by the family maid who then fled with the child to America. Now, thanks to you, and your keen powers of observation, we may be another step closer to proving it.'

'No way! Ya mean I'm cousins with that to-die-for cute Prince Harry, and that I can't marry him after all on account of your stupid gums?'

I smiled so wide that I proved that I was related to all of Europe's aristocracy, including some who had been dead for three hundred years. 'No, you silly billy,' I said with great affection. 'Like I said, the kidnapping was just a rumour, and the gum thing is just something I tell myself in order to keep from feeling depressed every time I look in a mirror.'

Then my bundle of sticky hormones leaned in quickly and gave me a peck on the cheek before scooting out on the passenger side. 'At least ya have a chin, Mom,' she called over her shoulder, as she headed over to the market to buy my mystery treat.

Until that morning I had never seen an angel, a Martian or a pornographic video. When I stepped into the police station and saw all three of the items on that list, my brain had trouble filing the information. I can only imagine that the feeling I had was similar to what the inhabitants of the Caribbean Islands felt when they saw the first Spanish ships sail into view back in 1492 – no rhyme intended. I make no bones about the fact that mine are a homely bag of bones, but it would be a sin to downplay the exceptionally high intelligence quotient with which the Good Lord has blessed me. It was precisely because my neurons were already performing at an already elevated level that this sudden surge of powerful, yet evil and extraneous information was able to produce such a massive misfiring.

Unannounced, I'd entered the cosy little police station that is Hernia's, hoping to find Chief Toy at his desk – his car was parked outside – when lo and behold – I discovered him *and* Wanda Hemphopple watching a television program in the middle of the day! Since neither of them are Mennonites, and it was close to lunchtime, it might have been excusable if they had been watching something educational like *National Geographic*, or perhaps reruns of *The Beverly Hillbillies.* These two shows are, I believe, an invaluable study of the cultural differences to be found in America.

However, it was not something wholesome that I saw on the television set that I had so generously donated to the police department of my village. Instead, what I saw was two women doing that very thing that I have tried so hard not to condemn. That act of physical, and perhaps emotional, connection about which Jesus had nothing to say, although he criticised divorce in the strongest of terms. Don't get me wrong, I still believe that folks have the right to love whom they please, just not on my television, and not in public where my daughter can walk in and see it.

I felt lightheaded. I was nauseated. My legs had turned into thin rubber strips, unable to support a fraction of my weight. Time crawled. I was viewing everything on the television set in intense colors and in what seemed to be lurid slow motion.

'I'm going down,' I hollered. 'Someone catch me!' But as in any nightmare, my lips didn't move and I couldn't produce a sound. More importantly, neither Toy nor Wanda moved a muscle to help me. They didn't even bother to glance away from the filth that they were watching on the idiot box.

'Timber!' I cried as my five-foot-ten-inch frame toppled forward. Quite fortunately – or unfortunately – as I was standing directly behind Wanda Hemphopple, my prominent, pointed proboscis probed her pathogen-filled beehive on my way down. While I should be thankful, because her nasty, vermin-filled hairdo broke my fall, the screeches she emitted almost broke my eardrums.

Toy wisely, and quietly, switched off the television.

Eventually Wanda settled down enough to speak – or perhaps I should say squeak. 'You clumsy oaf! Look what you did! You've ruined years and years of lacquering. Next time you should watch where it is that you're going to faint!'

I made a mental note of her request, even as I gazed upon the current devastation. With her beehive undone, Wanda's hair hung in greasy knotted ropes. Some of the ropes were so long that they rested on the floor. What took the cake was that that act of undoing the 'do,' had released a small avalanche of various comestibles and other impossible to explain items. A partial inventory from off of the back of Wanda's noggin would include: a blackened, shrivelled strip of banana peel; two fuzz-covered wintergreen mints; three blue and white swirled glass marbles; four unsalted peanuts; six mega-jackpot lottery tickets; and seven cotton swabs.

I glared at her with righteous wrath. Glaring is an art not much practiced in the Mennonite and Amish Churches. I had to study it on holiday when I visited my friend Abigail Timberlake who lives in Charleston, South Carolina. Abby took me with her to visit a 'Bible beaters' church – her words, not mine. There, the very devout minister smacked his Bible every time he wanted to emphasize a point, and since his sermon dragged on for nearly an hour and covered every sin I'd ever heard of – and a few I had to look up – that poor Bible got severely beaten. I whispered to Abby that, if the Holy Scriptures had been a baby and not a book, I would have called the child protective services within the first five minutes of his sermon.

At least my look of righteous wrath was not wasted on my audience. Wanda immediately shut up, although it is possible that she was stunned into silence rather than intimidated. Toy, on the other hand, had been raised in the South, and he obviously recognized the look for what it was; I could see him cringe.

'It was her idea,' he said without missing a beat.

'Did Eve give you an apple as well?' I said.

'What?' he said.

'She means that your first impulse was to blame it on a woman,' Wanda said.

'Uh – sorry about that,' Toy said, remembering his Southern manners. 'I wasn't thinking. I'm equally to blame, of course. I was the one who suggested that you stay and eat the delicious lunch that you prepared for me.'

It was only then that I began to see beyond the television set, and beyond the potential pestilence that had been unleashed when I had pitched headfirst into the hair from Hades – pardon my French. Toy's desk was piled knee-high with dishes, glasses, pots, pans and even a small vase of semi-wilted flowers. The desk, by the way, was a sturdy little wooden thing that I had purchased lovingly with my own funds from IKEA.

'What on earth is going on here, Toy? Are you turning Hernia's police station into Sodom and Gomorrah? Is this the influence of that big city of Charlotte from whence you hail, or is it the influence of this wanton woman, Wanda?'

'Wanton woman?' Wanda waved wildly, like the crazed creature that she was.

Toy is fortunate in that he oozes charm. 'No, ma'am, it's neither. It's just that Wanda here has taken pity on this poor homesick boy, and has been bringing me meals from time to time. The woman is an angel. No, really, Wanda, you've been an angel.'

It was then that I realized that Wanda's manic gesticulations had been directed at Toy. From the expression on Wanda's face as Toy spoke, it became clear that he, like most of his gender, was from Mars, whereas, sadly, Wanda and I were both from Venus. In the interest of science, I jiggled pinkies in both ears to make sure that I'd heard correctly – in case the pathogens had already begun to work – and when I was satisfied that I could indeed hear, I attempted to make sense of the incomprehensible words that had spilled from the young man's lips.

'Toy,' I said. 'Is this the *same* Wanda who has been bringing you food?'

'Yes, ma'am.'

'And you think that she's an angel?'

'Well, she's not a *real* angel; she's not the kind that goes flapping around on her wings.'

'Hmm. So angels in the South "flap" when they fly?'

'Ma'am?'

'Never mind, I was being facetious.'

'Which is normal for you,' Wanda said. For the record, she is my second-best friend, albeit on a part-time basis. At other times, because we enjoy butting heads so much (in a gentle, Christian-sort of way) she slips down a number of rungs on my ladder of love hierarchy.

'Yes, and I can be fractious as well. Someone better explain exactly what has been going on – from the *very beginning*. Are the two of you having an affair? Is this what this is all about? Is that why you are watching lesbians on the television which I purchased with my own, hard-earned money? My husband – a physician, mind you – told me that it is commonly known that many men are, uh, titillated by the thought of two women performing the mattress minuet, although frankly, Toy, I shouldn't think that watching the wedding waltz with Wanda would do the trick for you.'

'*Lesbians?*'

I hadn't heard the door open, but of course it had, for there stood my pubescent daughter, mouth agape, eyes as wide as dinner plates. There are folks who say that the reason that I remain as thin as a clothesline is because I starve myself, or that it's because I got lucky when it came to genetics. Ha! I happen to eat more than a busload of basketball players and, as for my genetics, when my great-grandmother Mary Hostetler died at home she had to be carried out of the house through a window and was buried in a piano case. It is *stress* that keeps me razor thin.

I am not one to exaggerate, so believe me when I say that my gaze zipped right past her dinner-plate eyes and went straight to the candy bars that Alison clenched in her sweaty right hand as she reappeared in the doorway. I'd sent her in for two treats: something for each of us. However, Sam knows that she and I each have a sweet tooth, and that *she* knows that he is sweet on me. Ergo, Alison had a fist-full of assorted chocolate bars.

'*King-size Snickers*, please,' I said. For those unfamiliar with this confection, it has a gooey caramel center and is densely packed with peanuts. The whole shebang is covered with a thick coat of chocolate, making it a substantial bar. Just fitting an entire bar that size into one's mouth should be considered an Olympic sport, on a par with, say, dressage. Once you have this nourishing candy (protein from peanuts, antioxidants from chocolate) stuffed in your mouth, it is impossible to speak coherently. This was certainly the case for me.

'Thespians?' I said, affecting an innocent tone.

'Mom, that's gross,' Alison said and turned away. 'You're not supposed ta talk with your mouth full. Ain't that what you're always saying?'

'Yeth.'

'Eeew! I thought I heard ya say "lesbian," not "thespian." Ain't a thespian some kinda bird? Ya know, with a white ring around its neck, and a long tail?'

'That's a "thesant," I said.

'Yuck,' Alison said. 'I'm getting outta here and going back ta Cousin Sam's. Ya know where ta find me when ya grow up and get some kind of manners.'

'Thootles,' I said. I had meant to be ever so cultured and speak like a real English person (an English English) but caramel, the Devil, or both had got hold my tongue.

'*Whew*, that was a close call,' Toy said when the door closed behind my dear daughter.

'I'll thay,' I said. Then, using my left hand as a screen, I discreetly began to work my right index finger around and over my spacious gums.

A split second later, Wanda clapped hands in front of my face. She clapped them so close to my person that one of her fingers clipped my upper lip. Truly, I tell you, I was assaulted by the woman whose beehive I'd unwittingly unbound.

'Have you no shame?' she said. 'No decency? What is America coming to? It's all because of Obama and his Democrats, I'm telling you.'

I'd swallowed enough calories to finish out my day. 'I'm not a Democrat, dear.'

'Aha, a Republican! I knew it! You can always tell by the beady little eyes.'

'Nope, not that either.'

'So you don't vote at all? That's even worse! That's a lazy American; you're an uninvolved citizen who doesn't deserve to be here. Go back to England from whence you came.'

'I'm an Independent voter, not that it's any of your business, and my people all came from Switzerland three hundred years ago, except for the Delaware Indian branch that formally adopted my ten-year-old ancestor into their tribe – after massacring his mother and infant sister. The Delaware arrived on this continent as early as fifteen thousand years ago, although given that the earth is less than six thousand years old, I am, admittedly, having a bit of trouble with the math.'

Wanda used to stand five feet seven when she had her beehive. With her hair down, she's an even five feet – if that. I had no trouble towering over her like a telephone pole. Wanda knew that beneath my gruff exterior there beat a heart of tarnished silver, so she didn't exactly shake in her crepe-soled waitressing shoes.

'If you must know, Miss Nosey Yoder-Rosen, we were watching a scandalous but ever-so-delightful TV series set in a women's prison, and of course there are some scenes of women doing the "mattress minuet," as you so quaintly put it, given that you are *the* most sexually-repressed of all my friends. My Hubert won't watch it with me, and since Toy enjoys it and isn't dating anyone – well, I don't know why I even need to be explaining this. It is, after all, a free country.'

Cheese and crackers, how do you like them apples? Wanda had actually thrown me a bone of flattery; I was *the* most sexually repressed of all her friends! By the sound of it, it wasn't even a contest. In fact, Wanda, sweetheart that she was, had thrown me a 'two-for-one.'

'So I'm still your friend?' I cried.

'Was there ever any doubt?' Wanda said as she began twisting and winding her hair back atop her head like a garden hose that had served its purpose for the day.

'And I really do hold the distinction of being *the* most sexually repressed of all the friends that you have? Not even any of your Roman Catholic or Amish friends are more repressed than I am?'

'Not even my friend Mary Elizabeth, and she was a cloistered nun for sixty-five years.'

'Cool.'

Wanda jabbed several large hairpins into the temporary nest atop her noggin. She then shook her head. 'You are a sad case, Magdalena. It's a wonder that you have any friends at all.'

'I'm not a sad case,' I said. 'I'm just very self-aware. It's because I can see myself for who I truly am, warts and all – although I haven't any, I assure you – that I am able to see people around me so clearly. For instance, I can see that you are a tightly wound individual – ergo, the pseudo-French twist with a hotdog-eating hole in it.'

Wanda grabbed her faux crocodile-skin handbag, made from

purple vinyl, no less, and leapt for the door. 'I don't have to take these insults like you do,' she said. 'I'm not a "turn the other cheek" Mennonite. You may be my friend, Magdalena Portulacca, but that doesn't mean that I always have to "lacca!"' She roared at her silly pun, and scurried out the door before I had a decent comeback.

'Did you think that was funny?' I asked Toy, who'd been foolish enough to grin.

'Yes, ma'am – I mean, no ma'am.'

'Well, which was it?' I said.

'It was only funny because Mrs Hemphopple said it,' Toy said.

'What do you mean?' I said.

'Miss Yoder, what I mean is that Mrs Hemphopple adores you.'

'*Adores?*' I said. 'Isn't that a pretty strong word?'

'Maybe so, but ever since she's gotten it into her head that I'm a lonely bachelor who needs fattening up, she brings me meals, and all she ever talks about, when I see her, is you.'

'Why, shoot a monkey!' I cried. 'But not literally, of course. Tell me, what exactly does she say?'

Toy shrugged, in the manner of all men when asked to repeat a conversation. I heard somewhere that Valdemar Poulsen, who invented the magnetic tape recorder in 1898, did it so that he didn't have to repeat office conversations to his wife.

'Well—' Toy stopped right away to scratch his head. He scratched and scratched and—

'How about we make a deal, Toy?' I said generously. 'I'd be quite happy to scratch that mosquito bite for you while you talk.'

'Huh? I don't have any mosquito bites,' Toy said.

'Well, then, whatever that lump is between your shoulders that you've been clawing at for the last five minutes,' I said.

'Hey, now that's a good one, Miss Yoder! Sure enough, a guy's got to laugh at that.'

'*Really?*' I said. 'That didn't make you angry? Not even a little bit?'

'No ma'am. Was that your intent? That wasn't it, was it?'

'No,' I said, feeling a good deal of relief. 'You seem to be a very decent young man.'

I fear that I may spoken too soon, for Toy immediately flashed me a brilliant smile, a testament to American dental care. He also fluttered his long, dark eyelashes, which for the first time lent his baby-blue peepers a 'come hither' look. For the first time I saw the possibility of Toy the boy becoming Toy the 'boy toy,' and the idea was both repulsive and fascinating. In other words, it was sinfully attractive – for what is sin, if not at some point attractive in nature?

'Miss Yoder,' he said, 'when do you expect your daughter to return?'

My heart raced with repulsion and desire. The two emotions, so diametrically opposed, meant that my heart nearly stopped, never to beat again, like my old grandfather's clock.

'She's likely to return at any second when she needs money for chocolate; we'll never get away with it!'

'*We?* Do you expect me to share in the blame?' Toy said.

'You bet your bippy!' I said. 'And here I thought you were a Southern gentleman.'

'I am a gentleman,' Toy said. 'Tell me, what's in it for me?'

'This is all theoretical, mind you,' I said. 'But I've been told that when properly aroused, I exhibit more energy than a sack of cats in a dog-fighting ring.'

'TMI,' he said. 'That means too much information.'

'I know what that means, dear. I practically invented the phrase, seeing as how I *did* invent the habit of sharing too much in the first place.'

'I rather doubt that.'

'Harrumph. By contradicting me, you have put the kibosh on my wanton, and wandering libido. A heterosexual man would have put up with any amount of idiotic blathering on my part, just to have his way with me.'

Toy clapped his hands to the sides of his handsome, well-coifed head, as if to keep it securely in place. 'Miss Yoder,' he ejaculated. 'Are you trying to seduce me?'

'Well, I wouldn't have followed through with it,' I wailed. 'Besides, you are the one who was coming on to me, what with all your eye-fluttering and asking when Alison was coming back. What was that all about? Huh? Answer that!'

There are few things as humiliating as being given a look of pity by someone barely more than half one's age. It ranks right up there with having to wear a homemade frock to my eighth-grade graduation party, when every other girl in Hernia was wearing a brand-new frock picked from the pages of the *Sears and Roebuck* catalogue. To add insult to injury, my homemade frock was simply a shortened edition of one of Mama's. Whereas Mama had enormous bosoms, I was still as flat as a pancake. Thus the frock, which was white and had a fitted bodice, could have easily concealed watermelons. Instead the dress conveyed a week's worth of crumpled newspapers to the school gymnasium the night of the big event.

Given that I have a modicum of imagination, I might have been able to explain away the simple fact that I had grown bustier overnight. However, the Good Lord frowns on fibbers, and on the short walk from the car to the school, the heavens opened and a downpour of epic proportions drenched Yours Truly, soaking through to the newsprint, and for the rest of the evening every twelve- and thirteen-year-old boy amused himself reading the sports pages off my chest.

Suffice it to say, Toy took no prisoners. 'I was *not* trying to seduce you – ma'am. With all due respect, even if your sort were my type, you wouldn't be my type – ma'am.'

'Wow. That was certainly quite a bit of due respect, Chief Toy.'

'The question is, Miss Yoder, is it deserved? I'm not referring to your obvious attraction to me, either. I realize that a woman of your age might still have certain needs; my granny used to chase the old geezers around the Sunset Assisted Living facility back home in Charlotte. But she was like a fox kit in a henhouse; I don't know what she would have done if she'd ever caught one. You, however, come across as a woman of the world.'

'I *do*?' Take it from me; some flat-chested women will take flattery wherever they can get it.

'Yes, ma'am,' Toy said. 'You have that certain *je ne sais quoi* about you.'

'*C'est vrais?*' I asked.

'You certainly do, plus I've heard the story – many times, in fact – about you being Hernia's first official adulteress.'

Instead of screaming, I followed Gabriel's advice and grinned. 'Yes, and although the plaque I received was awesome, I thought I deserved a loving cup.'

Toy tried not to smile. 'You see, Miss Yoder, it is quips like that, and your quick mind altogether, which make it so hard for me to perform my job.'

'I understand, dear. From now on, I'll give you wide berth – just not a place in *my* berth. Oops, there I go again. There seems to be no stopping me.' I chuckled, and not unpleasantly either.

'Would prison help?' Toy said, sounding quite serious to me.

'I beg your pardon?' I said.

'Miss Yoder, I think that you said it exactly: there is no stopping you. *You* were the one who murdered Ramat Sreym, weren't you?'

'*What?* I'm sorry, Toy, but given all the pheromones wafting about this room like sparks when the coals have been stirred – hey, you're serious, aren't you?'

'I'm as serious as a bucketful of snakes.'

'My, but you Southerners are a colorful lot. Look here, young man, you are way off base. You're out of line too. I am the *one* person in this one-horse town – well, actually we have quite a few horses in our village, given our Amish population – but nonetheless, I am Magdalena Portulacca Yoder Rosen. I don't commit murder; it's one of the Big Ten, for crying out loud!'

Toy had the temerity to snort. 'Adultery is adultery, inadvertent or otherwise. You don't get the privilege of renaming things just because you're fabulously rich, married to a handsome doctor and think that you own the village.'

Tears of frustration began to force their way up and out of ducts that weren't supposed to be used in public. We Mennonites and Amish are known as the 'gentle people.' At some point in our genetic history an ancestor with a tart tongue attached himself, or herself, to the family tree, and this explains the anomaly which is me. One thing none of us ever does is cry in public. This has led some anthropologists to speculate that we may be, in fact, British.

'Crocodile tears will get you nowhere with me, Miss Yoder,' Toy said cruelly. 'I don't have enough evidence just yet, but when I get it I intend to treat you just like every other Tom, Dick and Larry under the law.'

'That's Harry,' I said. 'I believe Larry was one of the Three Stooges.'

He flushed. 'You *see*? You just can't help yourself. And since when does a good traditional Mennonite woman like you know the names of those goofballs?' He held up a hand, palm facing me. 'Spare me the details. For now, until I uncover further evidence, I don't want you travelling any further than back to your inn. I also want you to turn over the keys to the police cruiser.'

I gasped so hard that even the curtains were sucked into motion. This is only a mild overstatement, mind you. I made the curtains myself out of the cheapest material I could find, which happened to be a sheer, polyester material with a wide weave. Over the ensuing decades the police station curtains have decomposed to the point that they exist now almost more as a memory than a physical presence.

'*What?*' I said to Toy when I could finally speak.

'You heard me, Miss Yoder,' Toy said. 'Turn over the keys. *Now*.' He imperiously thrust forth a manicured hand that put my ragged nails to shame.

'Hold your horses, dear,' I said. 'How am I supposed to get home? Not to mention, what about my beloved urchin who is currently gorging herself on candy at yon Yoder's Corner Market? Do you expect us to hoof it home and perhaps get run over by a horse with four hooves? What if we were to be mugged by a mad Mennonite? You can't expect everyone to behave decently to others, you know.'

Toy laughed sardonically. 'Tell me about it, Miss Yoder. After all, it is you whom I suspect of murder.'

'Ach, does that ever get my dander up!'

'Like they say: the truth hurts,' he said smugly.

'I meant your sardonic laugh, you – you – juvenile. You make me so frustrated that I could just scream.' I screamed then to illustrate my point, as the lad is a bit thick in the head.

A faithful Christian should not believe in luck. However, permit me just this once to say that good fortune did indeed smile on me then. I had yet to reach my high note when the door to the police station opened, and in swept Toy's next big distraction.

EIGHTEEN

'Unhand her, you cad!' Sam's face was red from the exertion of running across the street. His brow was dripping sweat.

'But I haven't handed her,' Toy said. 'See!' He spread his pretty petite paws beneath my kissing cousin's nose for close inspection.

'Then why is she screaming bloody murder?' Sam demanded between gulps of air.

'Could it be that she's guilty of murder?' Toy said diabolically. 'I've been given to understand that this one is given to fits of what could be described as high drama.'

'That's not so,' I said.

'Oh, isn't it?' Toy said. 'Weren't you assigned a two-line role in your senior class play, *Who Cares About Ernestine?* but instead of saying your lines you launched into a fifteen-minute soliloquy that you wrote. It was something totally extraneous about the pain and trauma involved in the dehorning of cattle and the declawing of cats. Didn't this result in the entire production being shut down?'

'Who told you that?' I wailed.

'There she goes again,' Toy said, his smirk practically cutting his head in twain. 'She sounds just like an emergency vehicle, doesn't she, Sam?'

'You shut your trap, son, or I'll shut it for you,' Sam said. Sam started out as a peacenik, a pacifist Mennonite, but after doing the mattress mambo with a bona-fide Methodist for thirty years, there's not a soul in Hernia who's surprised that his views on fisticuffs have changed.

Toy shut his yap so tight that it looked like his face was going to pop.

'Good,' Sam said. 'Now, would someone care to explain what this is all about?' He looked at me. 'In a normal speaking voice, if you can.'

'I'd be glad to explain,' I said. 'This nincompoop from North Carolina wants to arrest me for the murder of Ramat Sreym.'

'What the Hades?' Sam hollered. 'Are you out of your mind, Chief? Have you what little sense God gave you? Magdalena is our most upstanding citizen!'

'She's a chameleon,' Toy smirked, showing his true colors at last. 'She has everyone in this town thinking that she is a saint, just because she's Miss Moneybags. Well, I'm telling you now that she's not a saint; she's a cold-blooded murderess.'

'I'm not a sexist, dear,' I hissed. 'That would be murder*er*.'

'You see?' Toy said triumphantly. 'She admits it!'

'I did no such thing,' I wailed. 'I merely instructed you in how to be politically correct – you of all people!'

'Toy, you idiot,' Sam said loyally, 'whatever put that dang-blasted idea in your head anyway? Magdalena has trouble killing flies; what on earth makes you think that she killed that so-called novelist from who-knows-where?'

Toy licked his symmetrical and really quite lovely pink lips. How terribly ironic that the Good Lord saw fit to house such ignorance in such an attractive package.

'Sam, you run a grocery store. Surely from the moment that book hit the stands you must have heard talk about the hatchet job it did to Hernia.'

Sam grunted. 'Some.'

'Did you read it yourself?' Toy said.

'Parts of it.'

'Did you find them disparaging?' Toy said, sounding almost kind.

'My wife was deeply hurt,' Sam said. 'If this was the UK, we'd sue for libel. In the United States, just about anything goes – except for nudity. It's a shame, really, when you think about it. Freedom of the press versus bare breasts, I'm telling you, Toy—'

'Stop it!' I said. 'Sam, if you want bare bosoms so bad, either be sweet to Dorothy or drive into Bedford and buy a copy of *Playboy*. As for you, Toy, in a mere fifty-one more years I'll be a century old, so please hurry up with your assumptions, assertions, allegations, or whatever else you have swirling about in that adorable little head of yours – no sexual harassment intended.'

Toy looked me straight in my watery blue-grey eyes. 'She thought you were ridiculous, and she made you come off as a gangly, bigfooted creature that smelled like a polecat. She described your personality as that of a badger that had been run over by a team of track stars wearing cleats.'

'Ouch,' I said, surprised to hear Toy quote the appraisal of myself I'd seen fit to share with Ramat during her stay at the inn. It was the God's honest truth. Besides, everybody knows about my big feet. I'd presumed that's why I wasn't on his list in the first place. 'I must admit that having someone you never liked say such positive things about one is— Well, I think that I shall endeavour to remember her more kindly from now on.'

'You're kidding,' Toy said. 'The old cow thought that you were crazy! Bonkers!'

'Aren't we all, dear?' I said.

'Speak for yourself, Magdalena,' he said. 'Anyway, just because I'm a Southerner, doesn't mean that I'm stupid. I've never once thought that you're as crazy as you let on to be. I come from Charlotte, the epicenter of eccentrics, remember? I can spot a real nut job, someone just enjoying life, and every shade in-between. And you, Miss Yoder, fall into a special category – the very same one employed by used car salesmen – that of having an exaggerated personality for the sake of business.'

I clutched my chest. 'Why I never!'

'You see?' Toy shrieked at Sam. 'That's just like her. When she gets into trouble, she deflects.'

'But it was a genuine deflect,' I said, 'unlike my genuflects, which are no good at all. I can't tell a genuflect from a curtsey. What if the Palace were to invite me to lunch? What would I do then?'

'You *see*?' Suddenly there were veins popping out all over Toy's temples. 'She's doing it again.'

'OK,' I said. 'Calm down. You're going to burst something and I don't want to be held responsible. So whatever you have to say, now is your chance. Spit it out.'

'You thought you could boost your business by murdering the writer, Ramat Sreym – *in cold blood—*' The last three words were spoken in what, to Toy, was supposed to be a posh English English accent. Instead, of course – given that he was an American and not Prince Charles – he sounded as if he was speaking whilst sucking on a frozen binky.

'Huh?' I was temporarily at a loss for words.

'You heard me,' Toy said. 'You are a cold-blooded killer.'

'Toy, I have more money than—'

'He doesn't need to know,' Sam said to me. He faced Toy like a silver-back gorilla, albeit a miniature one. 'Stand down,' Sam said to Toy. It was shocking to hear the extent to which television had corrupted my dear cousin's manner of speaking. And yes, the blame lay with his Methodist wife, Dorothy.

Toy's face suddenly resembled a peeled tomato. 'You're interfering with the law here, Sam. I could have you arrested as well.'

Sam is a compact man: lean, leathery – even his ears are no bigger than pepperoni slices. But when the former pacifist juts out his jaw, tenses his muscles and his stare turns colder than ice, you'd swear he was Vladimir Putin. He once looked an ornery horse square in the eyes, causing it to bolt and run as far as Maryland. I was very tired after that.

'Fire him, Magdalena,' Sam said.

'*What?*'

'*What?*'

Toy and I both responded with squeaks which, I am, told broke crystal in some of Hernia's finer homes.

'You,' Sam said, pointing at me, 'are still the mayor, Magdalena, right?'

'You're darn tootin' right I am,' I said. 'Pardon my French.'

'Which means,' Sam said, 'that you have the power to hire and fire the Chief of Police. Am I right?'

'Indeed, I do. I hired this very lad and funded his move as well.'

'Then fire his ass,' Sam said. 'Pardon *my* French.'

'Hold it right there!' Toy said. 'All this "pardon my French" is terribly disrespectful to the French. What have they ever done to us, besides giving us Gerard Depardieu?'

There was no time to waste. I certainly wasn't about to discuss the merits of French politicians.

'You're fired,' I said. 'Gather your stuff, *tout suite*, and skedaddle from this suite.'

'You can't do that,' Toy said.

'I just did,' I said. 'Listen while I do it again: you are fired.'

'*Brava*,' Sam said, and began hooting and clapping like a crazed English – which, in case you've forgotten, has nothing to do with an *English* English person.

Just then the door to our little police station flew open and my precious daughter burst in. 'Hey, yinz, what's going on?'

Sam turned and smiled. 'What's going on is that your brave mother just fired this guy before he could toss her bony butt into the slammer.'

'Why, the *chutzpah* of that remark,' I said.

Sam winked lasciviously. 'Beg your pardon, cousin. Trust me; I have nothing against bony butts. In fact, if you'll recall, I've been keeping my eye on yours since the fourth grade.'

'Sam, that was my *braid*, and you dipped it in my inkwell.'

'Whatever. I've always said that we could have a life together, and now seems the perfect opportunity, what with you on the lam, and Dorothy—'

'Mom, what does Cousin Sam mean?' Alison said. 'I don't understand any of this crap – I mean cud. And somethin' else: yinz sure do a whole lot of winking here in Hernia. Maybe yinz oughta get yer eyes checked.'

'Thanks for the cow-related correction,' I said, as I'd been working hard to tame my adopted daughter's vocabulary. 'Also, I appreciate the ocular advice. As for you, Sam, haven't you ever heard the saying: if they'll cheat with you, they'll cheat on you?'

Sam has less lip than a lizard, perhaps as a result of constant licking. 'Though,' he said, as a result of bad timing on the part of his tongue, 'are you trying to say that you'd cheat on *me*? On Sam the Magnificent?'

'*Ick*,' I said.

'Like, Cousin Sam is really weird,' Alison said.

'Y'all are both idiots,' Toy said. 'He's trying to distract you by pretending to be attracted to you. Give me a break, Miss Yoder. I mean, no offence, but have you ever taken a good look at yourself in a mirror? You're the only woman I know – besides my Aunt Gladys – who could walk through the North Carolina woods alone and not have to carry a can of bear mace. Bless y'all's hearts, of course.'

'Of course,' I said.

I know that I should have been terribly offended by Toy's implication that I was ugly enough to scare away bears. Instead, I was feeling curiously exhilarated. All at once, at age forty-nine, I had the possibility of a new career opening up in front of me; one that I had never even known existed. Still, one can see why I was always so confused about my body image, can't one?

Anyway, I could immediately picture my business cards. They would be printed on heavy stock paper, in a classy shade of ecru and embossed in a froufrou font that was just barely legible. In the upper left corner would be the silhouette of a tall, thin woman with a walking stick, and in the upper right corner the silhouette of a running bear. Between the two graphics, beneath slanted lines suggesting mountain peaks would be the following words: Magdalena Yoder, Professional Bear Chaser.

On the reverse side I would list some other uses for a mug as miserably ugly as mine. These include the fact that I can also scare curly hair into being straight and straight hair into being curly, induce labor, turn drunks sober and, sadly, cause sober people to drink.

Of course, I'd include my contact information. On second thought, since a picture is said to be worth a thousand words—

'Earth to Mom,' my urchin said.

'Well,' I said, 'to be honest, I was thinking of all the ways that I could put this hideous face of mine to work frightening things other than bears. Bears, you see, can be really dangerous when provoked. I would much rather be slapped by a mop of curly hair than mauled by a grizzly bear.'

'Mom, stop it!' Alison cried. 'You're not supposed to think of yourself that way. Didn't the psychiatrist say that you suffer from body diarrhoea disease?'

'That's body dysmorphic disease, dear. It means that my body image doesn't match what's really there.'

'Bingo,' Sam said, 'because you're a real looker.'

'She's a head case,' Toy said. A good Southern boy, born and bred, he tipped his head slightly in my direction. 'If you don't mind me saying so, ma'am,' he added.

'Oh, but I do mind,' I wailed. 'I don't mind you calling me a head case, because the Good Lord Himself knows that I'm nuttier than a five-pound fruitcake, but I do mind you calling me a cold-blooded killer. Ramat Sreym was an atheist – she told me this herself. Unless she had a so-called "death-bed" conversion, that poor woman is going to burn in the fires of Hell for all of Eternity. Have you ever burned your fingers on a match, Toy? Or on the stove?'

'Yes, ma'am, but—'

'But nothing, dear. You are a lapsed Episcopalian, are you not? And Episcopalians are the American form of the Church of England, right? You probably explain Hell as nothing more than a spiritual separation from God, but believe you me, it's much more than that: it's physical agony. It is flames eating your skin, licking it off your body with red-hot tongues, over and over again while you scream in pain. Like this.' I threw back my head and screamed like a banshee. 'So you see, young man, I would never murder an unrepentant heathen, lest the Devil – the *real* one, with the capital D – escort that poor woman's soul straight to you-know-where.'

I wasn't trying to be cruel; my intention was to convey the strength of my conviction. Granted, for a mild-mannered woman I can be bellicose at times, and for the shy, retiring woman that I truly am, I can be verbose upon occasion. However, we are none of us composed of just one trait, and that day, at *that* time, there was least one person there who believed in me. In this person's eyes I was not a murderess.

'Aargh!' Alison cried, or something similar to that. Her fists were balled and her elbows locked as she ran straight at Chief Toy, taking him by surprise.

Alison was tall for her age, but skinny. She was also very motivated, which counts quite a lot when one is intent on turning oneself into a human battering ram. Being knocked back on his Carolina butt was one thing that Toy had not counted on happening. He gasped as the air left his body, and once on the floor he floundered about like a fish on the end of a line. Clearly, he was going nowhere fast.

'Come on!' I shouted, grabbing Alison's hand. 'It's time to make tracks.' I stopped in the doorway. 'Sam, call the town council. Tell them that I just fired Toy and have them approve it. Also, notify Sheriff Crabtree. Oh, and you're a peach, Sam, but don't be getting any ideas. You're a first cousin, and in my book that's still too close for kissing.'

'But you were adopted, remember?'

'Yes,' I said, wasting precious time, 'but even then, we're second cousins on one side and third cousins on the other.'

'Oh, what tangled webs we weave, when Amish-Mennonites conceive,' Sam muttered disconsolately.

Do you see what I mean by wasting time? By then Toy was groaning and beginning to pat his pockets in search of his phone.

'Get his phone, Sam!' I shrieked in farewell, and then Alison and I flew out the door like hawks in search of new prey.

NINETEEN

Take my word for it, when one is the mayor of a village like Hernia, and one has paid for the police cruiser out of one's own pocket, then one is not stealing it – under any circumstances, am I not correct? If one asks a silly question, then one should expect a silly answer.

Nonetheless, I pressed the pedal to metal and, I say this shamefully, I drove twice the speed limit, all the way to the Sausage Barn. This greasy spoon eatery sits twelve miles north of Hernia, just south of the booming metropolis of Bedford, Pennsylvania (population 3,121). Don't get me wrong, I have nothing against ingesting grease, particularly bacon grease. I firmly believe that while Jews may be the Chosen People, God shows his love to us gentiles by permitting us to eat all manner of delicious pork products. Ham, pork chops, pork roasts delight my soul, but nothing makes my taste buds dance (in an almost sinful way) as plain, ordinary B-A-C-O-N.

That said, the last half mile to the Sausage Barn was so coated in pig grease, thanks to Wanda's wonky exhaust system, that I had to apply my foot to the brake rather than the gas pedal. That's normal for the course, and every time we pull up Alison squeals with glee. Gabe, who is a Reform Jew, does not see the need for him to keep kosher in today's world (I beg to disagree), and neither does Alison, who is, of course, still searching for her religious identity.

'Wow,' Alison said as she staggered out of the car and regained her land legs. 'Now what?'

'I'm glad that you asked, dear,' I said. 'The best way that you can help me in my detective work is to please just make yourself look like the specks on the inside of Wanda's walls.'

'Ooh,' Alison said. 'Gross! You want me to look like a bunch of dead flies?'

'Well—'

'Mom, she swats them things and then leaves them smooshed

on the walls until they fall off on their own accord. Once, one of them dead flies even landed on my pancakes.'

'How nice for you, dear.'

'Huh?'

'It's all in one's perspective, sweetie. We eat cow muscle and call it steak. Folks in other countries eat big fat palm grubs, thicker than your thumb, and are glad for opportunity to do so. For them, the grubs are protein. It's all in one's upbringing.'

My daughter gave me what she calls the 'stink eye.' 'You're weird, mom, ya know that? I ain't never ate no cow muscle, and I ain't never gonna, neither!'

'Ha! Last night you and Dad sat on the couch and each polished off a little tin of cow lips, cow cheeks, cow noses, cow tongues and who knows what else.'

Alison stiffened. Her cheeks drained of blood, and I could swear her hair stood up a smidge under its coating of 'product.'

'Whatcha talking about, Mom? We was eating them little Vietnam Sausages; we eat them all the time.'

'Read the ingredients list sometime. Read the label as well.' I grabbed her hand and led her around to the back of the restaurant where Wanda kept a vegetable garden. Pennsylvania is a Commonwealth that is overrun by whitetail deer, despite our regular hunting season. Many gardeners believe that growing a few castor bean plants around the periphery will keep not only deer away but other troublesome varmints such as racoons, opossums and voles. The beans themselves contain one of the deadliest chemicals known to mankind – ricin. It is believed that plants give off an odour that wild animals can detect, causing them to keep their distance. In any case, castor bean plants can grow to be seven feet tall in a single season and have large palm-like leaves, making them rather decorative, if nothing else.

'So,' Alison said, 'what are we looking at?'

'See those tall, gorgeous plants with the big leaves?'

'Yeah,' she said. 'How come we don't have any around our garden?'

'Because I'm responsible for guests,' I said, 'that's why. Those plants have seeds that are deadly poisonous. If you chewed and swallowed just two of them, you would die. Those are the same seeds that some people ground into white powder and tried sending to the President and other government officials.'

'No kidding?'

Oops. I realized that I had perhaps shared too much information with an angst-riddled teenager.

'The reason I'm showing you this,' I explained quickly, 'is because we can see these plants from the road when we approach from the south, now that they've gotten this tall. So I got to thinking while we were with Chief Toy—'

'Which you always do, Mom,' my cheeky daughter said.

'Right. *What* I was about to say is that it is entirely possible that Wanda ground up several beans into a pie and served just Ramat Sreym a slice of the poisoned pie while everyone else was given a slice of a similar pie baked by someone else. She was the only person working back there in the pie-serving tent, cutting up pie and serving slices, so that would have been as—'

'Easy as pie,' Alison said. 'Pun intended,' she said as she gave me a light tap on the arm with a loosely balled fist.

Although I was gobsmacked by her flash of linguistic, and possible literary wit, I am not the dullest knife in the drawer. 'Judy says hello,' I said, and punched her back.

'Mom,' Alison said, 'you're weird, but ya know what?'

'Let me guess: you love me anyway? Well, I love you too, Sugar Doodle.'

'Cheese and crackers, ya don't have ta get all mushy on me. I was only going ta say that I like having a weird family. It kinda makes me feel normal.'

'I didn't think that we were *that* weird,' I said, not unkindly. 'Now come on, dear, before the woman with the perfidious and pungent pile of pelt atop her noggin gets suspicious.'

It didn't surprise me to see Wanda Hemphopple, erstwhile owner, waitress and my number one nemesis standing stalwart behind the cash register counter. She was decked out in a red-and-white-checked apron that had seen cheerier days. Although her beehive had been reassembled since we'd last seen her, it now leaned like a certain tower in Pisa. In fact, it would not have surprised me if Wanda's less-than-lustrous locks had been hastily recoiled around a calzone and then had some dipping sauce poured on them for good measure.

All right, so I judge the woman a mite harshly – and the Bible warns me not to judge, lest I in turn be judged. But I put to you the following: Wanda Hemphopple is *always* judging me. *Always.* If I didn't judge Wanda in return, and give her some of the karma that she so richly deserves, then isn't it possible that the Good Lord – or God forbid, even the Devil – will come down hard on her in this life instead? The way I see it, my gentle Christian rapprochement of Wanda's errant ways is, in effect, a blessing in disguise for her. She should be grateful for my criticism; enough said.

'Hey,' Wanda barked as we finally made it through her stubborn, sticky door. 'You're not wanted here.'

'Money is always welcome, dear. We'll be in booth fourteen. Send Swivel Hips to take our orders, because you need to join us – police business – so your company is mandatory. Pronto.'

'In your dreams,' Wanda hissed. Trust me; Wanda is such an accomplished hisser that if she ever tired of being a restaurateur she could open an academy for snakes. Before she married a Hemphopple, Wanda was a Sissleswitzer, so hissing is hereditary in her family.

One of the few blessings of having feet the size of kayaks is that I can stop after moving forwards a yard, without having lifted a foot. Thus I was able to lurch to a standstill, whereas poor Alison, who possesses a normal size undercarriage, had to turn around and backtrack. At any rate, what I did next was to put my giant mitts up to my lipless mug – rather like a megaphone. Then at the top of my considerable lungs, I addressed the Sausage Barn customers, as well as the dead in the cemeteries for a radius of at least five miles.

'Pleasant patrons, puissant pundits, portly pashas, pliable pupils, pork purists, this patron's patsies all, I beseech thee, lend me thine ears.'

Wanda may be short, but she is an athletic woman, having grown up with five older brothers. She would have tackled me had not Alison stepped adroitly in front of me, her knobby fists raised in a defensive boxer's position. That was the Queen of Bacon's fatal mistake – so to speak.

'This woman's a liar!' she shouted. Alas, the phlegmatic diners continued to gnaw away at their sausages, having not even looked up from their plates.

'Wanda Hemphopple is a cold-blooded murderess!' I screeched.

Trust me, there has not been a person born with louder lungs than yours truly.

The diners briefly debated whether a free floor show was worth the price of cold pancakes and congealed bacon grease. With few exceptions, their answer was 'no.' The mastication of massive amounts of mammal muscle and carbohydrates continued.

As for Wanda Sissleswitzer Hemphopple, did she ever look fit to be tied! Her face was white while her ears and nose were red, and her eyes looked like at any given second they were going to pop out of her skull and sizzle on the floor like a pair of enchiladas dropped in a skillet that contained an inch of hot, melted lard.

'You win, Yoder!' Wanda virtually ran down the aisle of her own restaurant, her arms up over her head like she was an already convicted criminal.

Now I ask you, was her bizarre response the result of God whispering her guilt in her ear or what? Truly, there was simply no way that I could go wrong following my gut instinct at this point. If we are to be faithful followers of the Lord then we are to pray for guidance, and then trust the still, small voice inside us. That said, Wanda, who really did look rather fetching in stripes, had her wardrobe all picked out for her until the Angel of Death came along with his pitchfork to show her to more permanent quarters.

As for that still, small voice of guidance, she – it was definitely female – was surprisingly loud, louder even than the GPS on my new Elantra. It supplied me with a plan that was designed to frustrate Wanda to the point of a spontaneous confession – if only Alison didn't unwittingly sabotage me.

In the meantime, I was exceedingly grateful for whatever placating ingredient pork contains, particularly bacon, which makes folks zone out to events around them, because despite the ruckus we caused, it seemed as if we indeed remained invisible to the greater portion of the portly pacifist purchasers of Wanda's pungent patties. Once inside booth fourteen, which backs up against the kitchen, we were out of sight from most of the other diners, and since Wanda had neglected to give Swivel Hips any orders, I knew that I had only a few minutes to work my Magdalena Yoder magic. The trick, as one might guess, is to act tough. Be brassy. Don't let 'em see you sweat.

It might surprise you that such a timid, soft-spoken Mennonite woman as me can pull this off. Well, I can only do it through the help of prayer, *and* because in all but the hottest weather I wear a wool skirt that comes well below my knees, sturdy Christian underwear which includes a knee-length cotton slip, and thick opaque hosiery. This adds up to three substantial layers of natural fibers between my knees, the result of which is that when they knock together, they do so quietly, and thus do not tip off my adversary to the fact that I am obviously terrified. The English say: 'Keep calm and carry on,' whereas Magdalena says: 'Appear calm and carry on.'

'I ought to sue you,' Wanda said. At least she waited until we'd had a chance to maneuver our way over, and around, the grease blobs on the benches of booth fourteen. One learns not to slide in but to claim a spot and then keep it. This technique is helpful when it is time to launder 'post Sausage-Barn garments.'

'Sue away, dear,' I practically sang. 'Whatever floats your boat. I'm sure that if you're patient you can even learn to do it yourself; you're certainly not the stupidest woman I know. Lord only knows, you'll have plenty of time to earn a law degree in the big house.'

'What's the big house?' asked my wide-eyed protégé, Alison.

'The state prison,' I said. 'I heard that it has a great library, and that they even teach remedial reading to the inmates.'

'Very funny,' snarled Wanda.

'Is it irony when she uses the word "funny" in that context?' Alison said.

'Well done,' I said. 'Alison, why don't you talk like that all the time? You're a very intelligent young woman; there's nothing shameful in letting people know it. And by the way, Wanda was being sarcastic.'

'Right – that's it, sarcasm. But Mom, boys don't like girls that are smarter than them. It threatens their – you know.'

'Masculinity?'

'Hey!' Wanda snapped. 'Enough of the sickening family chit-chat. This is about *me*, remember?'

I smiled – in a sarcastic sort of way. 'How could I forget, dear?'

'What is *that* supposed to mean?'

'That fact that it's all about you is the reason why you murdered Miss Ramat Sreym.'

'Mom,' Alison said, 'nobody says "miss" anymore; everyone says "ms."'

'I'm not *everyone*. Now, please be a dear and study the menu.'

'*What* menu? We ain't got no waitress, thanks ta ya yelling bloody murder.'

Alison has excellent, uncorrected vision. Still, there are times when she couldn't find a missing elephant if it was standing right in front of her – not that this example has been tested often, mind you.

'Sweetheart,' I said, while praying for patience, 'the things that pass for menus here are those greasy, plastic-covered, thingamabobs tucked behind those sticky, syrup pitchers.'

'Get back to talking about *me*,' Wanda snarled.

'With pleasure,' I said. 'Wanda, am I your friend?'

'Huh? What kind of question is that? What does that have to do with me?'

'Yes or no?'

'Both, stupid. You're my friend, but sometimes I could wring that scrawny chicken neck of yours.'

I recoiled in surprise. I had no doubts about her being Ramat's killer, but as for wringing my scrawny chicken neck – now that was going too far!

'The feeling is mutual, pal,' I said in a huff. 'However, I do have other friends, and as for your neck – it's anything but scrawny. In fact, stumpy is more like it. It would take a winch and a thick chain to wring a neck like yours, so I guess that our feelings aren't so mutual after all.'

'Well I never!' Wanda said, crossing her long, muscled arms over her boxy chest. A charitable biographer might someday record that Wanda Sissleswitzer Hemphopple's proportions were more suitable to an orangutan than to a member of the Homo Sapiens species.

'As for you, Alison,' I said pleasantly, 'why have you reverted to talking like one of the people your Auntie Susannah hangs out with? You know, like thugs, dropouts, thieves, murderers – folks of that ilk?'

'Aw, Mom,' Alison said, before delivering a world-class sigh, one so strong that it actually caused ripples to form on the grease layer of our genuine Formica tabletop. 'Ya gotta quit with the nagging if ya want me talk right all the time. Besides, Auntie Susannah is in prison, so it ain't fair ta go comparing me ta her.'

'Susannah, bonannah, fofannah!' Wanda cried. 'Yinz supposed to be talking about *me*, you idiots. *Me, me, me!* I'm the one who killed Ramat Sreym, remember? It was so easy to add poison to the pie. She wrote about everyone in Hernia in that dreadful book of hers, except for me, the *one* person in this place who is at all interesting.'

'Yeah?' Alison said. 'What makes you so interesting, Auntie Wanda?'

'Hush, dear,' I said. The poor girl was a newcomer to the area; I didn't want her to stir the pot of a crazy woman, especially one who'd just confessed to murder.

'For one thing, your mom dangled me by my feet down into a well, so that a little girl could climb out by holding on to my hair. Actually, it was a pair of twins: Hans and Gertrude. It was covered by all the news channels. I'm surprised you didn't see it. Isn't that true, Magdalena?'

'Baloney,' I said. 'Yes, you lowered your hair – under great protest, I might add – but it was at a sinkhole, and it was a killer who climbed out on your locks of dread.'

'Just the same, smarty,' Wanda said. 'I was a heroine; I was the toast of this crumby little town. In fact, *Entertainment Delights* devoted a segment to me, and one of the late-night comedians even put me in a joke.'

'It wasn't you; it was Hernia. We were the butt of the joke for having such an unusual name. The supposedly funny host asked if we would be willing to change our name to Haemorrhoid.'

Alison chortled.

'Sweetie,' I said, 'do you know what a haemorrhoid is?'

'Nope. But it's gotta be funny if that guy said it was. They pay those TV dudes like millions, ya know. Yinz guys are always yapping about how we young folks are going to move away if this town don't have more to offer us. So, here's yer chance ta shake things up a little.'

'Ha,' Wanda said, 'your sassy-mouthed kid is on to something.'

Even Mennonite blood can boil if one's child is maligned. 'Don't you call my daughter names, you whackadoodle – dear. And as for *Butter Safe Than Sorry*, that novel was *literature*,' I said. Yes, I confess: I said it just to be cruel, and I didn't stop there in my taunting. Once the Devil gets hold of your tongue it's hard to shake him loose. 'Anyone who was *anyone* was featured in that great American novel.'

'Trash, trash, trash!' Wanda yelled, pounding the genuine Formica with both fists. 'Don't you ever say that again, Magdalena, or I'll have to kill you, too.'

Suddenly I could feel Alison's warm, skimpily-clad body pressed up against my left side. 'Mom, is she – like – *serious*? You guys aren't just joking around anymore, are ya?'

'I'm deadly serious, sister,' Wanda said. 'It isn't fair, I'm telling you; why does my life have to be so damn hard but yinz get it so easy? Huh? Tell me that!'

I try not to be a judgmental person, but there are at least three things with which I'll hold no truck. These things are: people who text while driving, people who spit their gum out on side-walks, and people who make snap conclusions about my life.

'Come again?' I said. 'I'm not sure I know what you mean.'

'Oh, yes you do, Miss Money Bags. Look at me, working my butt off running this grease pit, married to a broken-down, impo-tent, flat-footed bald lush who could take out half of North Korea with his morning breath, while here you are, married to a hand-some Jewish doctor – and everyone *knows* that Jews are rich – who is so fertile that he knocked you up when your womb was as dry as the Gobi Desert – your words, not mine – plus you're plenty wealthy on your own, what with that brilliant idea you had of turning that picturesque farm your parents left to you into a thriving bed and breakfast, which continues to attract Hollywood celebrities as well as high-ranking politicians from Washington, although, frankly— Now, where was I?'

'You're here in your greasy spoon, plumb exhausted, after delivering that record-setting run-on sentence, dear,' I said.

'Ha! There, you see, Magdalena? That's why I love you as well as hate you. You're as tart as a not-quite-ripe cherry. You're the kind of cherry that's too sweet to discard, but if one adds enough sugar then it's all right for pie.'

'How about some mud for your eye,' I said drily. 'That might help improve your vision, because Lord only knows that the romantic picture that you've painted leaves out all my back-story.'

Alison must have been feeling calmer on account of all our jibber-jabber, because she pulled away a fraction of an inch. 'Like what, Mom?'

'Hmm. Well, like the fact that I, like you, was adopted. However, I didn't even find out about my adoption until I was in my forties, and that was only *after* my birth brother threatened to kill me.'

Alison shivered. 'And then what?'

'Well, dear, obviously he didn't kill me.'

'Oh.'

'Anyway, the people who adopted me were kind but very strict. I loved them very much, and they loved me. Mama – your grandma – gave birth to your Auntie Susannah, and I loved her too. Then one day, when I was twenty years old, your grandparents were killed in a car accident. It happened in that mile-long tunnel under Allegheny Mountain. The car that Grandpa was driving got rear-ended by a milk tanker, and they were pushed into a semitrailer truck carrying state-of-the-art running shoes. As a result they were squished to death, flatter than a plate of Swedish pancakes.'

'Gross,' Alison said. 'Now I'm never eating pancakes again!'

'I should sue,' Wanda said.

'Hush,' I said, not unkindly. 'My point is that you've not been the only one of us to have a difficult life. Alison has had a hard life as well; her birth parents abandoned her, shipping her off to live with me.'

'But Mom,' Alison said, '*that* was a good thing! You and *this* dad are a million, gazillion times better than my other parents.'

'Who cares?' Wanda snapped. 'You're just some rug-rat from Minnesota, yet you still got mentioned in that awful book.'

Alison beamed. 'Yeah, that was sweet. That gorgeous Ramat lady wrote that I was a college graduate with a handsome husband,

and Mom left us to run the PennDutch Inn while she sailed off to the antidotes.'

'You mean "Antipodes," dear,' I said.

'Yeah, whatever,' Alison said.

'Shut up, both of yinz,' Wanda said.

'Mom,' Alison said, 'I thought ya weren't gonna let her talk to us like that no more.'

'She is a mite rude,' I agreed. 'Wanda,' I said, removing a pair of genuine, stainless-steel, police-issue handcuffs from my oversized handbag. 'Hold out your knobby wrists, Wanda, because I am hereby conducting a citizen's arrest of your person, Wanda Sissleswitzer Hemphopple, for the murder of the late Ramat Sreym.'

Alison gasped. 'Give me yer phone, Mom. I gotta get me a picture of this!'

Wanda, however, hardly blinked. In fact, I wouldn't be surprised if she didn't blink at all, given that reptiles seldom do.

'Ha! The joke's on yinz,' she said. 'Before either of yinz makes a move, yinz might want to consider the fact that one of my knobby wrists is connected to a stubby-fingered hand, which is holding a gun, which is pointed directly at your daughter's hoo-ha under the table.'

'Now *that* is rude,' I said.

'Mom,' Alison said, 'I don't want to die yet. I didn't wash my hair last night when I showered, and I'm pretty sure my lipstick got all worn off at breakfast.'

'I don't blame you, dear – about your hair, I mean – but you know how I feel about you wearing that color lipstick at your age.'

'Yeah, I know. "Only harlots and starlets wear scarlet." Something like that.'

'Excellent,' I said. 'Now, another one of my clever sayings that you may wish to commit to memory is this: "Only the hapless wear strapless."'

'*Stop it!*' One of the cords in Wanda's short, bullish neck started pulsating; that's how angry she was. With her free hand she retrieved a smart phone from between the depths of her compact yet ample bosom and placed a call. About that same time I could barely hear a phone ringing through the kitchen doors behind her.

'Leroy,' she said, 'I assume that you still want that raise you've been nagging me about. Yah? Here's the thing: I'll give you double that amount, but only on the condition that you take everything off the griddle, no questions asked. I said no questions, Leroy. I don't care. Just throw it all in the trash. Then exit through the *back* door and take the rest of the day off.

'Yes, Leroy, don't be such an idiot; of course you should turn the stoves off. And remember to exit through the *back* door. I'm right here in booth fourteen, Leroy. If I see you walking past me, you don't get any raise. In fact, you get a pay cut. Is that clear? And Leroy, don't tell anybody about this, because if you do, you'll be fired.'

At this point, what could I do but pray? The Bible tells us that God hears all our prayers, and clever preachers say that He answers all of them – although perhaps not always in the way that we want Him to. But make no mistake about it, when there was a gun pointing in the direction of my daughter, I wanted not only an immediate response, I wanted action. I'll even go so far as to confess that this lifelong pacifist, with five hundred years of nonviolence inbred into her genes, had temporarily gone around the bend – so to speak.

'Oh, Lord,' I prayed aloud, 'if it please Thee, may the roof of this greasy establishment crash down upon the head of a certain murderess, rendering her incapable of committing yet another heinous deed.'

'Harrumph,' said Wanda, much to my surprise, 'at least I'm *included* in that stupid prayer.'

I felt my hackles rise. How dare that pagan Presbyterian label my prayer – or any prayer – as stupid? If only her neck weren't too stout, and corded, to wring. Well, if being included was of paramount importance to her warped little brain, then that's what I would give her.

'But Lord, on the other hand, Thou knowest that no one can serve up pig parts like Wanda, even though Thou hast forbidden us to partake of them in Thy word, forever and ever, amen. Thus it would be a shame if indeed this pigsty – oops, poor word choice – should disintegrate, and cause the death of our dear sister, Ms Hemphopple, née Sissleswitzer. Therefore, Lord, I ask that you give this woman the courage of Joshua and Caleb, whose story we read in the Bible last Sunday – at least in the *Mennonite* Church.'

'Mom,' Alison whispered, 'ain't this an awful long prayer?'

'Shut your trap, kid,' Wanda said. 'It's about *me*, isn't it?'

It's been said that the best defense is a good offense, and I can be as offensive as the best of them. 'Did you hear that, Lord? Wanda Sissleswitzer deserves to sizzle you-know-where, although of course I don't make that call, sir; you do. But what I was about to say before she got super mean and slapped down one of your little lambs, is that Alison and I might be persuaded to forget about today's little misunderstanding *if* the foaming fruitcake here puts her gun on the table and her hands in the air.'

Neither Alison, nor God, nor the Foaming Fruitcake, made a sound for an unbearable length of time. We were, however, serenaded by a swarm of flies, whose musical repertoire was disappointingly monotonous given the size of their wings.

'Ding, dang, dong, dab nab it,' I said at last, having been reduced to swearing like a drunken sailor. 'How about it, Wanda? Do we have a deal?'

One positive thing that I *can* say about my erstwhile friend is that she certainly has *chutzpah*. Her response was to call Swivel Hips on her cell.

'Swivel,' she barked, 'we're closing. No, and it's none of your business why. The kitchen's already closed, by the way – Leroy's already been sent home so don't go back there bothering him.' She paused, and her face contorted like a rag mop put through a wringer. 'Well, then give them their stinking money back. I don't give a rat's hind end what they say. And I want you to get the *hel*-met out of here, too.'

To be honest, Wanda, being one of the more liberal types of Presbyterian, used language much stronger than that. Then again, if one is a confessed murderess, I suppose that one might not feel the need to hold back when it comes to language. I know that *if* I were ever to commit murder, which I would never, ever in a trillion light years do, I think I might experiment with the entire gamut of sins.

And why not? I could be like the Roman Catholics in those Mafia movies: I could commit a sin and then I could go to confession. Just as long as I could get to that little wooden booth before my number was up, I could have it made in the shade! Why, I could cavort, carouse, and I could even cuss while doing cartwheels in a carnival.

'Magdalena!'

It was that bothersome Wanda, always intruding on my imaginary sins. 'Get a hold of yourself, Magdalena. You look like you're daydreaming again. Just like you used to do in Algebra II class. *This*' – Wanda waved a short muscular arm – 'is supposed to be all about *me*. This is my crime, so it's my time.'

'Well, it is, dear,' I said. 'I'm just trying to help you with planning some of the details.'

'Details?' she asked coyly. 'Of what?'

Her mocking smile made me want to do something very un-Mennonite to her person. 'I am helping you to plan the details of our murders, dear. Already Alison here is the size of a small adult woman, and you could fit the entire village of Hernia in just one of my shoes. My point is that you are going to need to know how to dispose of us when we go to that final judgment in the sky.'

'Are we really going to die, Mom?' Alison said. She sounded eerily calm.

'You can bet your bippy that we're not,' I said. 'God will take care of us. Remember the story of Abraham and Isaac? God sent a ram just in time, before Abraham could sacrifice his son.'

'I've always hated that story,' Wanda said. 'No father should ever be willing to sacrifice his child. Besides, that would have broken several of God's commandments right there.'

'Just like you're about to do,' I said. 'Wanda, if you reconsider your plans, I could make you a very rich woman.'

'Yeah,' Alison said, 'my mom's rolling in dough.'

'Just like Scrooge McDuck,' I said.

'Huh?' Alison said.

'Scrooge McDuck was a comic book character when we were growing up,' I explained. 'I wasn't allowed to read comics, but when I had sleepovers at Wanda's house we would spend hours reading the stacks of comics that her older brother left behind when he joined the army.' My hope was that this childhood reference would jog a fond memory from back in the days when we were best friends *all* of the time.

'I didn't know that you had a brother,' Alison said. 'There ain't no Swizzlesticks going ta my school.'

'My maiden name was *Sissleswitzer*,' Wanda hissed, 'and my brother died in Vietnam.'

'Oops,' Alison said. 'My bad.'

'Say you're sorry,' I hissed. We must have sounded like a nest of disturbed snakes.

'I *did*,' Alison protested. 'I said "my bad." What more do you want?'

My eyes couldn't help but stray from our captor to my distraught daughter, and given that the Good Lord has blessed me with phenomenal peripheral vision, I noticed for the first time that Alison was holding her new cell phone under the table where Wanda couldn't see it, and that she was texting away like nobody's business. What a *Dumkoph* I was! Here I'd been, worried about the kookaburra sitting across from us with her supposedly loaded gun, when all along I should have been trusting in the Lord, like I was supposed to do. In the biblical story, the Angel of the Lord interceded with a ram to save Isaac's life, but in *my* story it was Isaac – er, Alison – who was interceding with a cell phone. All I had to do was to continue to stall the whacko with the wobbly French twist until the sheriff arrived.

'Wanda, dear,' I said, 'you must have loved your brother very much. Tell us all about him.'

My nemesis recoiled so fast that her teetering tower of doom nearly toppled. 'You ignoramus,' she said. 'How could you have forgotten? You must have a brain like a lump of overcooked noodles. Gilbert was a sadistic bully; he was the meanest brother who ever lived. Our parents doted on him but I danced a jig of joy the day he left for the army. You, *especially*, should remember that, Magdalena, because on one of your sleepovers at my house he ripped the head off your favourite doll and stuck it on a wooden stake. Gilbert claimed that he was a head-hunter and that your doll was a dead missionary. You bawled your eyes out after that for days.'

'Ga-waw, Gilbert,' I growled softly. Sometimes it is merciful to forget.

'So,' Wanda said brightly, having noticed my discomfort, 'shall we discuss the time that I stuck the "Yoder with an Odour" sign on your back in *Senior* High School and you went home crying?'

Alison stopped texting. 'Mom, you didn't!'

'Boo-hoo,' Wanda said. 'Your precious Mom was a world-class cry-baby.'

'The entire school was laughing at me,' I said. 'I have feelings too. Besides, the next day was when I— Uh, never mind.'

'When you what?' Wanda said.

'I forget, dear. But my, don't you look good in turquoise today, Wanda! You always did, you know. That color suits you to a tee; it really plays off your green eyes.'

'My eyes are brown,' Wanda snapped. 'Beady brown, you've always called them. Now get up, both of yinz, and move your lazy butts off out of my booth. We have someplace to go.'

'But we have yet to eat, dear,' I said quite reasonably. 'I realize that you sent the cook home, and that we're stuck here without a passable cook between the three of us, but couldn't we at least have some toast with jam and butter? And I'm speaking of real butter – not margarine, or some hybrid of the two, which in my opinion are worse for one than the good ole fashioned kind. Oh, and a nice hot pot of tea would really hit the spot. Again, I'm not speaking of those worldly herbal teas – their very names are meant to stir one's imagination and possibly even one's loins – but something Christian and sensible, like Earl Grey.'

'I prefer hot chocolate, if you please,' Alison said, doing a perfect rendition of the Duchess of Cornwall.

When we Americans pretend to be *la-de-da*, we '*la*' our way all the way up the ladder to the top rung. Frankly, I'd rather that the child continues to speak like a royal duchess than a low-class grammar school dropout, but I dare not encourage her. Push Alison a step in one direction and she'll push back three steps.

'Stop it!' Wanda cried. 'Enough!' Even though she'd been seated behind the banquette table of a booth, she managed to stand and clap her hands over her ears.

For the first time, that horrible handgun was visible. I am not a political woman, and no expert on guns by any means, but if Wanda was the person who actually bought that gun, then either the seller was completely distracted that day or was someone without a conscience. I state this because Wanda practically had the word UNSTABLE branded into the skin of her pallid forehead. Seeing Wanda with a weapon of a duo's destruction made me sick to the stomach.

Unfortunately, my equine features are both expansive and expressive, for Wanda's subsequent smile undoubtedly reflected her deep satisfaction at the horror registering on my face. She lowered her pistol and pointed it directly at Alison's chest.

'I have a name for this little baby, and I call her Fanny,' she said. 'Do you want to know why?'

'No,' Alison said. 'You bore me.'

'What a naughty girl,' Wanda said, caterpillar eyebrows arched to stratospheric heights in surprise. 'Really, Magdalena, if I were you, I'd spank that child.'

'Yeah, right,' Alison sneered.

Generally speaking, the kids who come into the Sausage Barn have plump sausage arms and legs, and their focus is lining up to the grease trough that passes for the All You Can Eat Bar every Saturday and Sunday between ten a.m. and one p.m. They dare *not* sass anyone, lest they be left at home with a babysitter, and the opportunity to nibble on a frozen dinner the next time their All-American family goes off to graze. Wanda, it was clear, had no experience of thirteen-year-old girls with empty mouths.

'Magdalena,' she said to me, 'are you going to let her get away with that?' Wanda's gun hand began to shake as her temper rose.

'Of course, dear,' I said. 'We don't respect murderesses in our family.'

'And *you* call yourself a Christian?'

'Wanda, just be glad she hasn't stoned you yet. That's very biblical.'

'Mom,' Alison said, '*can* I? Please? Just *one* stone – it won't be very big. I promise.'

I sighed. 'Would that I could, dear, but undoubtedly this evil woman with the gun has other plans.'

Wanda's lower lip was trembling; I was so close to victory that I could almost taste it. But I couldn't think what to say next fast enough, so she beat me to it.

'Move,' she barked. 'Get out of the booth. Now! Out! Leave your purses. Come! Move along.'

So, obediently, we slid across a conveniently greased banquette seat and tumbled out into the aisle of an eerily empty restaurant. Wanda then marched the pair of us – two hungry sacrificial lambs that we were – into the kitchen and bade us stand still while she unlocked a door at the far end of the kitchen. This door was equipped with a hasp with a rusty Yale lock stuck through it, and Wanda had to try at least several keys until she found the one that fit. She did that with her right hand, while her left hand waved wildly in our direction. I only briefly entertained the idea of throwing myself at her gun-wielding hand. BC (Before Children) I would have done so with no compunctions whatsoever; AD (After Dementia) I have a tendency to be less rash.

The door had apparently not been used in some time, and Wanda really had to tug on it to get it open. As I'm a fair-minded Christian woman, I believe in giving credit where credit is due, so I have this to say about the Hemphopple with the Tower of Doom: there are times when that woman sports a rather attractive bulging bicep. Now, where was I? Oh, yes, when this door finally became unstuck and swung open, it brought with it a rush of stale air. Chief amongst the foul odours was an acrid, chemical smell that was somehow familiar.

'Get in there! I want yinz to keep your hands up and get in there one at a time.'

'Speak now,' I said as I nodded at her gun, 'or forever hold your piece.'

'Stop it! How the heck can I kill you if you insist on joking all the time? Even we whackadoodle psychopaths require the correct conditions.'

'Pshaw,' I said. 'Or do you suppose that is something his urologist instructed him to do during his declining days?'

'*What?*'

'Piss. Shaw. Now see what you did, Wanda? You made me say two dirty words, and your name was one of them. A joke is no good if it has to be explained.'

'Cuckoo, cuckoo,' Wanda said, addressing Alison while making twirling motions beside her ear, all the while holding the gun in that hand. 'You much-loved Mom is a nut-job.'

'Perhaps so,' I said, 'but if that's the case—'

'Shut up, Magdalena,' Wanda said, 'or your frightened little squab gets it right between the eyes.'

'I ain't no squash,' Alison said. She was angrier than a two-headed snake with a one-toad dinner. I was afraid that if I didn't intervene, Alison was going to do something that would make Wanda actually pull the trigger.

'A squab is a cute little baby pigeon, dear,' I said. 'The Whackadoodle meant it as a compliment.'

Wanda fired her pistol.

Before I even heard the sound of the gun, I felt the breeze generated by the lead slug as it whizzed just above my scalp. My white organza prayer cap usually sits atop my coiled braids. However, the slug tore right through my braids, severing one in half, and pretty much demolishing my clean white cap. Whether or not Wanda meant to hit my head and missed, or was really aiming for my headgear, one thing was clear: the woman meant business.

TWENTY

FRENI'S BUTTERSCOTCH CHIFFON PIE

Serves eight English, four Mennonites or two Amish

½ cup cold water
1 envelope unflavored gelatin
4 teaspoons instant coffee powder
¼ teaspoon salt
2 eggs, separated
1 package (6 ounces) butterscotch pieces
½ cup firmly packed light brown sugar
1 cup whipping cream
1 baked nine-inch pie shell

Combine water, gelatin, coffee and salt in saucepan. Cook and stir over moderate heat until the gelatin dissolves and the mixture comes to a boil. Remove from heat. Beat egg yolks slightly; add the gelatin mixture gradually, stirring rapidly. Cook over low heat one minute, stirring constantly. Remove from heat. Stir in butterscotch pieces, reserving one tablespoon for garnish. Beat egg whites until stiff; beat in brown sugar. Continue to beat until stiff and satiny. Fold in butterscotch mixture. Whip cream; reserve half cup for garnish. Fold in remainder. Spoon into pie shell. Garnish. Chill until set.

TWENTY-ONE

'Mom, mom!'

I awoke in pitch darkness with a throbbing headache and a teenager screaming in my ear. Forgive me then, if I momentarily thought that I had died and gone to you-know-where. Yes, I know that my salvation is assured, but I am also aware that I quite willingly listen to, and accept, the advice of a therapist named Luci Feragamo simply because I like what she has to say. Granted, this is how most people behave, but Magdalena Portulacca Yoder Rosen is *not* most people: she is far more inclined than most people to have just plain rotten luck. Hell, I posit, is not much to write home about.

'Mom, I *order* you to stop being dead and get up!'

I chuckled. What a delightfully cheeky child I had! Imagine that: ordering her poor old mom to rise from the dead like Jesus did to Lazarus in the New Testament. Well, I would certainly give it a go.

'Oomph,' I groaned. But as far as rising from the dead, I fear that I only managed to get closer to that point. In my pitiful attempt I just succeeded in giving my noggin yet another nut-cracking whack.

'Blimey,' I moaned. It is possible that I said a word far worse than that because I thought that I'd heard one. But since I couldn't see anything, and my ears were ringing like church bells on Easter Sunday, I couldn't be positive that it was me who said it now, could I? Besides, even if I did say that foul, four-lettered word, it must be remembered that it has been part of the English language since 1680, and was derived from a Danish word that had to do with cattle breeding. As it just so happens I am the daughter of a dairy farmer and keep two dairy cows, which I breed on a regular basis for milk production. Therefore, I believe that I should be absolved of that one, uh, somewhat unfortunate slipup.

'Mom, that's awesome!'

'*What?* You heard that?'

'Aw, Mom, ya rock! Just wait 'til the kids at school hear that you said the—'

'Be a dear,' I said, 'and help your old mom sit up – if indeed I am lying down. I can't make out heads nor tails in here.'

'Yer lying down, Mom,' Alison said. 'Yer flatter than a pancake.'

'What happened?' I said.

'Ya really don't remember? Ya don't remember nothing?'

'Well, I do remember how to speak English.'

'Ya like fainted when Auntie Wanda shot your Jesus bun half off your head. But ya weren't hurt none; we both checked and then she went ahead and shoved ya in here anyway. It's so awful, Mom, and I'm so sorry ta hafta tell ya, but yer hair's lying out there on the floor.'

My hands flew to my head. '*All of it?* Where's the rest?'

Alison began to sob noisily. 'She cut it, Mom! And then she made me cut some of your hair too!'

For the first time in my life that I could remember, my hair was too short for braids. I felt violated. In a sense I felt as if I had been raped. Wanda Hemphopple had robbed me of the symbol of my religious identity and forced my child to participate in this fiendish act. Even worse than that, she was stirring feelings of revenge up in me. I wanted nothing more at that moment than to do something that would really hurt Wanda. I wanted to not only cause her pain; I wanted to cause Wanda *exquisite* pain.

Those were my initial feelings. There's probably not a child in the Western world whose mother hasn't told her, or him, to count to ten before responding to something negative. This advice holds for grownups as well. Those of us who are parents must be especially thoughtful about the examples we set in front of our children.

In the darkness I found Alison's arm and pulled her into an awkward 'Yoder embrace.' 'There, there, it will be all right,' I said. Those six words are obligatory in our family when giving comfort, as are giving back-pats. 'You did nothing wrong, dear. Those braids were hot. Where are we?'

Fortunately, 'Yoder embraces' are mercifully short, and we decoupled simultaneously like train cars. Alison has always run a degree warmer than average. Lately I've had sudden bursts of internal and spontaneous combustion of such intensity that, if wheels could be attached to my bony hips, and I used a child's scooter for steering, I could save a lot on my petrol bill. Perhaps I should also add that the room itself seemed to be stuffy.

'We're in her cleaning supply closet, Mom. She said that she's coming back for us just as soon as she makes room in her freezer.'

'She did?'

'Yeah. Bummer, right?'

'Bummer is an understatement. I can see the headlines now in the *Bedford Journal*: "Charming Innkeeper and Cherished Urchin Perish with Chapped Cheeks."'

'Mom, sometimes you're kinda geeky, ya know that?'

'That, too. Alison, have you felt around to see if there is a light switch in here somewhere?'

'Duh, Mom. I'm not, like, *totally* stupid. There is a light switch, but it's on the outside. Auntie Wanda said that the tins and boxes didn't need no light, which was a good thing, because it was cheaper installing it on the outside, and now look how handy it was when storing two *shlubs* like us in here. Mom, what's a *shlub*?'

'Unfortunately, a shlub is anyone who isn't Wanda. And Alison, there is no need to call Wanda auntie anymore. In fact, please don't.'

'Gotcha.'

'But speaking of light; do you still have your cell phone?'

'Aun— Wanda saw me with it, and put it down her industrial-strength garbage disposal. Geesh, Mom, ya really don't remember nothing.'

'Well, at least I remember who you are, and what a brave young woman you've become. That was really something the way you were able to text for help while you had a gun pointed at you under the table.'

Alison said nothing, which didn't surprise me. At first.

'I just hope that you didn't send the message to Police Chief Toy. I have reason to believe that he is involved up to his armpits in this case.'

'Ya think he slipped her the poison?'

'No – I don't know. Anything is possible, I guess. So who did you text? Sheriff Crabtree?'

Alison giggled. She had a right to giggle nervously; that's what I thought for the first few seconds. But a mother *knows* when her daughter is stalling.

'Well, dear?'

'Ain't that a funny name, like maybe a crabby tree, or a crab up in a tree?'

'Alison! This is important. *Who* did you text?'

'OK, ya ain't gonna get all, like, hyper about it if I tell ya the truth, are ya?'

'*Alison*, we *are* in a *life* and *death* situation *now*.'

'All right, don't get your panties in a bunch, is all. I sent Sheldon a photo of the gun pointed at my hoo-ha under the table. But just the gun is all, so don't, like, get mad and think I'm a pervert like that guy who ran for President of New York.'

I could not believe my ears! 'New York has a mayor, for crying out loud, not a president!'

'Y-Yes, but I should have texted the sheriff. We could die on account of I wanted Sheldon to pay attention to *me* for just one second, and I thought that maybe he would if there was a gun pointed at me.'

'Maybe he still will. Now all we can do is trust—'

My words of intended comfort were interrupted by the scraping of the lock being removed from the hasp once more. 'It's not my fault that it has to end this way,' I could hear her say. 'It's your fault, Magdalena, for being so darn nosy.' Of course, being a lapsed Presbyterian, Wanda used a stronger swear word.

By the time the door opened to near-blinding light, my right hand – my strongest – had closed around the handle of a heavy plastic jug. I lifted the gallon vessel and swung it at the silhouette coming through the doorway. How was I to know that the cap wasn't screwed on tightly? Not only did Wanda experience being hit in the sternum with a heavy object, but a good deal of concentrated cleaning fluid, which was meant for her sticky floors, splashed all over her upper body and may have gotten into her eyes.

One could only feel sorry then for Wanda. The poor dear screamed like a teenager without phone privileges. I had meant only to disable the woman, and then only just long enough for Alison and me to make our getaways. I'd had absolutely no wish to maim her. Thank the Good Lord, at least, that during that fracas Wanda dropped her pistol and Alison thought to pick it up. And, in a rare moment of maternal clarity, I thought to snatch it from Alison's hands and stuff it down my bra. Right cup – there's more room in there. In all honesty, in order to get the small pistol to fit I had to ditch the store-bought pad that it came with plus the two pairs of Gabe's rolled-up knee socks. (Decades ago this was a *Playtex Living Bra*, but ever since Little Jacob was born, this brassiere has been slowly starving.)

Now then, with Wanda's weapon under wraps, so to speak, I felt free to lend her a hand. 'Alison, grab an arm! Let's drag her to the kitchen sink and wash whatever it is out of her peepers.'

Wanda kept screaming. 'No, no! Just leave me alone. Go away.'

'Nonsense, dear,' I said firmly. 'We can't leave you like this, can we, Alison?'

'Uh, Mom, why the heck can't we? Wanda, like, was gonna kill us; or did fainting make ya forget everything?'

'Yes, but dear, "all's well that ends well," right?'

'Mom, them Jesus words sound awfully nice and all, but like Dad's always saying, ya can't just pick and choose. How about "it ain't over until the fat lady swings"? That means that we gotta get Wanda over to the sheriff in Bedford. She needs to be arrested and *hanged* for killing that beautiful author lady from Baluchistan.'

Baluchistan? Oh, well, by then we'd gotten Wanda's decidedly not-so-bony butt over to the sink. The entire time the wiry woman had been cursing so bad that even Alison could no longer translate. That was just fine with me; I have what is called a phonographic memory, and can recall conversations word for word, years later. That talent can be hazardous to a marriage, but in this case it merely meant that I would ask Gabe later about Miss Potty Mouth's plethora of putdowns.

'Do your best to hold the little varmint,' I said, not unkindly, 'while I hose her off. She's wiggling like a ten-pound mudpuppy, and I have to rinse these chemicals out of her eyes.'

'Stop it or I'll sue!' Wanda shrieked. Admittedly, the 's' word does give me pause. 'I'm not worried about my *eyes*, you idiots; but you might get my *hair* wet, and it isn't one of my hair-washing months.'

'Get her hair wet, Mom,' Alison chortled.

Oh, to be young again and able to chortle with abandonment! Alas, I was far too weighed down by incredulity, followed by a heaping helping of judgment.

'What do you mean by a "hair-washing" month?'

'Don't be dense, Magdalena. I take down my hair and wash it for spring on the first warm day in April. Then I wash it again in September. That's all human hair requires – no more, no less. This is the secret to my beautiful long locks which, as you know, are the envy of fertile young women everywhere in the county.'

Wanda has not been fertile since John Locke played with God as a child (take your pick as to who was the child). But who am I to challenge her statement, or her fertility, for that matter? I thought that my womb was as barren as the Gobi Desert, but then the Good Lord blessed me with the cutest baby boy in the entire world, including Justin Bieber.

'Pull Wanda's arm down to her side,' I directed Alison. 'And then throw your arms around her middle. Here, now get this other arm in there. Yeah, like that. Now start breathing through your mouth.'

While I spoke, I undid the masses of fetid hair and began wrapping it around and around the little woman, beginning at her shoulders. When I reached a point that was a few inches above her wrist, I stopped and reversed direction. That way, I was able to wrap Wanda's own wands of keratin around her a good six times, which I then tied off in one humongous knot.

By then Wanda was fit-to-be-tied, if you'll pardon the pun. 'I should have killed you both when I had the chance,' she said. 'Oh, why did I have to let my fond memories of us as best friends our entire lives get in the way?'

'Maybe that is because they were false memories,' I ventured. 'Agnes always was, and still is, my bestest friend; you were never more than second best. Not a month went by that you didn't threaten to rip out my tongue to feed it to your pet lizard, Iggy.'

'For your information, Smarty Pants,' Wanda said, 'Iggy was an iguana, not a lizard.'

'That does it,' I said, having lost what was left of my patience. My original intention had been to rinse the jug's contents out of Wanda's eyes, but now I just cared about getting her wet. I wanted to punish Wanda. As if *I* had a right to do that? Well, I didn't. 'Vengeance is mine,' saith the Lord, and I certainly wasn't He.

I have no doubt that I would have proceeded on this shameful path had not the sheriff and his minions burst into the kitchen through the rear kitchen door. Unfortunately for Wanda, at that moment Alison and I were trying to lift her up and into the industrial sink, which is the size and height of a laundry room tub. To be sure, we were startled. Therefore, as one might guess, we dropped the poor dear like a hot potato.

TWENTY-TWO

On the day that Wanda Sissleswitzer Hemphopple was arrested for the kidnapping of Magdalena Portulacca Yoder Rosen and Alison Lyre Yoder-Rosen, she was also charged with the murder of Debbie Sue Nelson, aka Ramat Sreym. Even Debbie's publisher didn't know what her 'real' name was, so you can imagine the surprise we folks in Hernia felt. Still, for some of us in particular, like Pastor Nate, it was a great relief to not only have one's name cleared of suspicion, but to have Debbie's killer brought to justice.

Of course, Toy's name was also cleared, but he never got over the fact that *I* thought that *he* might be capable of murder. I know I've said it before, but I'll say it again: as a faithful Christian, I don't believe in karma. Still, I can't help but think that he brought it all on himself, by hanging out with Wanda and watching filthy prison movies with her in the jailhouse that I pay for out of the generosity of stone-cold heart (as some would have you believe).

As for the tables being flipped the other way – that's like comparing apples and oranges; I *know* that I don't commit murder. Shame on Toy for even permitting himself the trace of such a thought. I have given him back his job, but he and I will never speak again, unless it pertains to village business, or matters of faith – or if that young whelp sees the light of day and comes crawling to me on his hands and knees begging for my forgiveness. Who knows, if Toy catches me on a day after I've had a good cuddle with Gabe, I've taken a nice long bath in Big Bertha with all her Jacuzzi sprays, the baby hasn't thrown food at me, Alison hasn't rolled her eyes in reaction to something I've said, and that crazy cult leader who birthed my husband doesn't try to stuff him back inside her womb – *if* all those things fall into place on a given day, then Toy won't even have to get down on his hands and both knees to beg. Just one knee will do.

As for Alison and myself: I think that we have both done a marvellous job of getting on with our lives. It goes without saying that I am extremely proud of that girl. Sure, she sent a photo to Sheldon instead of texting the sheriff for help, but the good news is that Sheldon had the smarts to call the sheriff. When the story about our little adventure hit the news – first local, and then even the national morning shows – Alison was entirely candid about what she'd done. Who knows, she may even have saved lives by advising her peers that they might still have something to learn from their 'ancient, like older than the dinosaurs' parents.

On a warm October day, when the leaves were at their peak, our little family drove up to Stucky Ridge for a picnic lunch. Stucky Ridge, which is the highest point in the county, is a rocky spur in the Southern Allegheny Mountains. From the crest, on a clear day, one can see forever – if it weren't for the interfering blue haze which denotes our neighboring state of Maryland. I haven't travelled to Maryland recently, but if one insisted on going, I would advise stocking one's vehicle with certain necessary provisions. (I have heard that the English English are particularly fond of Toad in the Hole and Spotted Dick.) Frankly, one would think that a really committed – and dare I say moral? – traveller would refrain from such unsafe practices and restrict themselves to enjoying the scenery. Keep the toad out of the hole until after the wedding, I say, and there will be no spotted dick!

Thank heavens that a hazy Maryland is not all there is to see from atop Stucky Ridge. There is Lover's Leap, for instance, where legend has it that a Delaware Indian maiden leaped to her death when her sweetheart was killed in battle; there is a fabulous view of my precious village of Hernia; one *could* see the bathroom window of one of the guestrooms at the PennDutch four miles beyond that, if one had a telescope that powerful; and last, but far from least, is the final resting place of Hernia's elite. This sacred plot of land is known as Settler's Cemetery. The first wave of European settlers to live in Hernia is buried up here, all with enviable views. From that generation forward, nobody but their descendants are allowed to be buried in Settler's Cemetery.

On that fine October day, after we'd consumed the delicious lunch that Freni had prepared for us, Alison and I wandered off to explore the cemetery. Being female, our noses are a bit more sensitive than Gabe's, and we'd both detected an advance whiff of soiled nappy odour escaping from Little Jacob's dungarees.

The way I see it, our son carries an equal amount of my husband's genes, ergo Gabe is equally responsible for removing waste from the little tyke's jeans.

'Mom,' Alison said as we wandered amongst the headstones, 'am I related to all these people too?'

'Just about,' I said. 'See over there, where the best views are – those were the pioneers. There are ten family names in that section, and you and I are each descended from eight of those families – the same eight families, just in different combinations.'

'What happened to the other two families?' she said.

I sighed. 'It's a tragic story, dear; history often is. The Shmatte family was wiped out by yellow fever, and it is said that the Jungfrau family turned yellow, changed their name to Jones and immigrated to Wales.'

'For real?'

I shrugged. 'That's the rumor. Personally I find that story highly offensive; good sturdy Amish stock doesn't succumb that easily to disease.'

'Yeah. Hey, Mom, that was a pretty close call we had at the Sausage Barn, wasn't it?'

'As close as they come, dear,' I said. 'You know, I'm not supposed to ask, but how do you *feel* your talk sessions are coming along with Debra?'

Alison grunted, which meant a score of two thumbs for Debra. At Gabe's insistence she was seeing a licenced psychologist to help her process post-traumatic stress.

I was raised hearing the expression: 'Talk is cheap.' Trust me; talking to Debra is anything but cheap. However, thus far it seems to have been worth every penny spent.

At any rate, not only does Alison appear to have established a rapport with the young therapist, but one of my pre-conditions of letting her go to a head-shrink in the first place was that the real 'head-case' in the family also get some counselling. And *no*, I am not referring to myself! I speak of none other than the inverted triangle with the fluctuating accent.

'Is there part of your chats with Debra that you'd be comfortable sharing with me?'

'Mom!'

For the record, Alison and I have frequently talked about our close brush with death at Wanda's hands. The subject arose dozens of times a day at first; less frequently now. To be honest, I am intensely curious about what is being said behind the closed door marked: *Debra Whittaker, PhD, Childhood Psychology.*

We wandered a bit more amongst the venerable headstones, each putting on a show of righteous indignation in order to save face. Mercifully our attention was soon captured by a small flock of crows in the treetops of a small patch of first-growth woods. Some people find Corvids to be loud – raucous, even – but their cries are never offensive to my ears.

'Ugh. Crows give me the creeps,' Alison said.

'Not, me,' I said. 'Crows, ravens, magpies – they all belong to a family of birds called Corvids. They're amongst the smartest animals that there are. Did you know that they have the ability to use tools?'

'No way! Do you mean like chimpanzees do?'

'Actually, their use of tools is even more sophisticated than that of chimpanzees. Also, sometimes they bring gifts to people who feed them.'

'Gifts?' Alison asked, suddenly more interested. 'Like what?'

'Things that the crows find, which they think people might like. For example, it could be a button or a pretty stone, or even just a scrap of brightly colored paper.'

'Wow,' she said. 'Anything else cool about Corvids?'

'Why, yes; in many cases they can be taught to speak – just like parrots can. I read somewhere that they might even understand what they are saying. Alison, you might want to read up on them.'

'Yeah, maybe,' Alison said.

Suddenly I realized that there was something especially odd about *this* flock of crows. 'Hey, Alison, count the crows – please.'

'Five. Big deal.'

'Well, dear,' I said, 'crows mate for life. This late in the year all the young crows will have found mates, so this means that one of those crows has recently lost its mate.'

'Really?'

'Really. See if you can guess which one it is.'

That is exactly what Alison did. For the next half hour we stood and watched, and then followed those birds around the top of the ridge, until Alison had sorted out who belonged to whom. Once she slipped over the edge of Lover's Leap, and might well have plunged to her death (given that she does not wear sturdy Christian underwear) had it not been for the lightning quick responses of Yours Truly.

In summation, one of the many traits that my daughter shares with me is that she is impetuous. When we came down from the mountain – er, ridge – that afternoon, we hightailed our hinnies into the town of Bedford and paid a visit to the Bedford County Library. One of the many traits that the Babester's daughter shares with him is that she is a collector. The following day she sweet-talked her father into driving her into Pittsburgh, where she was able to purchase a wide variety of bird-watching books.

We are grateful to all our many friends and family members who have assisted Alison on her road to emotional recovery. Also, we cannot emphasize enough just how important it was to have a good clinical therapist involved from the beginning. Personally, I would like to thank the Corvid family, in particular Fergie Fledging, who hopped into our lives the following spring.

As yet, that is another story.

Lightning Source UK Ltd.
Milton Keynes UK
UKOW04f1105100215

246008UK00001B/97/P